HER LONELY SOUL

BOOKS BY S.A. DUNPHY

HER LONELY SOUL

S.A. DUNPHY

bookouture

Published by Bookouture in 2024

An imprint of Storyfire Ltd.
Carmelite House
50 Victoria Embankment
London EC4Y 0DZ

www.bookouture.com

ISBN: 978-1-80314-725-3
eBook ISBN: 978-1-80314-724-6

We are such stuff as dreams are made on...

— WILLIAM SHAKESPEARE, *THE TEMPEST*

AN UNKNOWN MAN

It's happening again, and she's powerless to stop it.

A man she doesn't know sits in a room she believes is an office – it has a desk with a laptop, and papers are strewn here and there. Seeing them as if through his eyes, she notes the words 'South Coast Hotels' printed across the top. The screen of the computer, she can see, has the website of the same hotel open on it, and she thinks this man must be a manager or owner.

He looks to be in his mid-fifties and is wearing a blazingly white shirt and blue tie, which is hanging low, the shirt's top button open. His hair, which is still mostly dark, is shot through with grey. His clean-shaven jaw shows the blue shadow of a strong beard, which she can tell probably appears moments after he's shaved.

He glances up, and she can make out the rest of the room: there is a deep, plush, silver-grey carpet on the floor, and the windows, which are large and show darkness beyond, are framed by deep-blue curtains of a heavy material. There is music playing softly in the room. She doesn't know the band – something Irish and folky.

The man types rapidly on the keyboard of his computer,

clacking out numbers and making calculations. These are simple debits and credits – money in and money out – not like the complicated alphanumeric puzzles she and her dad like to do together.

She has always understood numbers on a level other people seem to find almost magical. They speak to her in ways she herself doesn't fully comprehend. It's as if the numbers themselves are a part of her.

Suddenly the man hits the 'Return' key and sits back, surveying his work. He picks up a sheet of paper from the bundle and compares the numbers on the screen to those on the page; sits forward and looks more closely, running his index finger down what looks to be a balance sheet. His finger stops – it seems he's found whatever error he's been looking for.

She follows his finger and can see that he's focusing on three large quantities of money that were paid to what seem to be accounts that have numbers instead of names.

He puts the sheet of paper down and reaches for a mobile handset, but before he dials a number, he pauses, something else catching his attention. It's the sound of a muffled movement. She heard it too – it seems to be coming from the window.

The man gets up, the mobile still in his hands, and walks to the windows, gazing out. She can see he's looking at a well-mown lawn, beyond which are the lights of a town. She immediately recognises the layout of the shops – the chemist, Leeview, in particular. The man lives in Ballincollig, a small town about 15 kilometres from her home.

He peers this way and that but can't seem to locate the source of the sound. Shrugging, he turns to go back to his desk, but as he does, he sees something reflected in the glass covering a painting on the wall behind his desk. It looks like a figure, standing in the space he's just vacated in front of the windows. He starts to turn, but there's a sudden movement, and she feels rather than sees something landing on the man's back, and then there's a wet, ripping sound and this time she feels a searing pain across her throat and a gush of wetness down her front, and the scene goes black.

She wakes screaming.

It takes her parents more than an hour to soothe her.

'I want this to stop,' she keeps repeating through her tears. 'How can we make this stop?'

'I have an idea,' her father said.

And that's how the bad times really began.

PROLOGUE

Garda Killian Rossiter was on the front desk in the Anglesea Street station in Cork city when the O'Farrells came in with their daughter.

It was 5.26 p.m. on Monday, 12 September when the little family bustled in. The wide reception area had a tiled floor, plastic seats bolted to the wall, noticeboards with information posters about Neighbourhood Watch and local homeless and drug treatment centres hanging above them. This space, where the public first made contact with the Gardai was, at that moment, empty of people, so Rossiter was able to give the new arrivals his full attention. They looked anxious and tired.

Stressed or not, they were a good-looking group. The dad was probably in his late forties, slimly built, his brown hair cut close to his head on the sides but left long enough to achieve a gelled, tousled look on top. He was wearing a rust-coloured tweed jacket and dark jeans, a paisley scarf knotted about his neck over a vintage Rolling Stones T-shirt. The mother was probably thirty-five, her slender frame draped in a vintage dress in a blue floral pattern that came to her ankles, over which she wore a faded denim jacket. Her hair was blonde and worn loose and long, reaching the middle of her back. The child, who Garda Rossiter put at about twelve, sported a red suede skirt that came to just above her knees, a bulky woollen sweater and red Converse high-tops.

'How can I help you?' Rossiter asked them, smiling his best smile in an attempt to relieve the obvious tension.

The man approached the desk. 'Guard, my name is Philip O'Farrell, and this is my wife, Cynthia.'

'I'm Killian,' Rossiter said.

'Our daughter, Ellie, would like to report a crime, Killian.'

Rossiter nodded and looked at the child.

She had auburn hair that was shaved close over her left ear but was left long, hanging below her chin, on the other side. Her blue eyes were sharp and intelligent, but the guard could see something was deeply upsetting her.

'Okay, Ellie,' he said. 'Why don't you tell me what happened?'

The girl chewed her lower lip and eyed Rossiter intently.

'It's not something that happened,' she said, her words trembling slightly. 'It something that's *going* to happen.'

'Okay.' Rossiter nodded. 'I'm listening.'

'Someone's going to be killed,' the girl said.

Rossiter blinked. 'That's a very serious thing to say,' he replied, his tone grave now, though still kind.

'I know,' the girl said. 'That's why I made Mam and Dad bring me in here this evening.'

'And who is it exactly that's going to be killed?'

'I don't know.'

'Do you know *how* they're going to die?'

'Not really – well, not exactly anyway. I'm sorry.'

'Or who's going to do the killing?'

'No. I just know that tomorrow night, in Ballincollig, a man's going to be killed. He's an important man, I think. He owns a big business – I think it might be a hotel, somewhere people come to from all over the world. And he's going to die.'

Rossiter shook his head. 'Tomorrow night, you say?'

'Around eleven o'clock.'

The guard ran his fingers through his short blonde hair. 'Ellie, how do you know this?'

'It came to me.'

'Yes, but how?'

'In a dream. I... I think I'm psychic.'

Rossiter looked at her, unsure how to proceed. He didn't want to come off as dismissive. He could see the child was genuinely upset, and while he was inclined not to take her claims seriously, he had been involved in a case two years previously where information provided by a woman who claimed to be psychic had proven useful, although he secretly suspected that was more down to good guesswork than anything else.

However, he felt sorry for the child and didn't want to make her even more uncomfortable than she already was.

'Stuff like this has come to you before?'

'Yes.'

'And when it has, has it proven to be true?'

The girl's parents glanced at each other nervously.

'Ellie told us there would be a death in Castlemartyr, that village just outside the city, three weeks ago,' Philip O'Farrell said. 'She said it would be a car accident, but it was really a murder. Two days later, I heard in the news about a bank manager who lived there who died in a car crash – hit and run.'

'Yes, we're investigating that,' Rossiter said.

'Ellie knew about it two days before it happened.'

'Hit and runs don't happen every day, but they aren't uncommon,' the guard said.

'She knew it was going to be a man who worked in a bank,' Philip said. 'And she knew the colour of the car that hit him.'

'A month before that, she told us a man who grew blueberries was going to drown in the sea off West Cork,' Cynthia said.

'You're talking about Dave Merrill,' Rossiter said, referring to the owner of a company who made fruit juices and preserves. 'Fell off his boat near Cape Clear.'

'She said it was going to happen a week before it did,' Cynthia said. 'And she insists he didn't fall.'

Rossiter looked at Ellie in puzzlement. 'But you don't know how this man is going to die?'

'I'm never certain about how,' Ellie said. 'That never comes through as clear.'

'But you've a sense of it maybe?' Rossiter pushed her. 'You've come in here to tell me, so you might as well give me everything you know and even the stuff you're not sure of. I'll make a note that you're not one hundred per cent about the cause of death.'

'I think he's going to be stabbed with a knife,' Ellie said. 'In his neck. But that's close to a guess. I have images in my head, but I'm not sure they're for this murder. I wish I could be more help. I'm... I'm tired of getting these dreams. I don't like them.'

Rossiter sighed and sat back in his chair. He could see she believed what she was telling him. It must be awful to be so young and to have all this stuff going around in your head.

'Ellie, I really appreciate your coming in. I'll make sure we have a car in Ballincollig tomorrow night in case we receive any calls. Now would you take a seat over there till I have a chat with your mam and dad?'

The girl nodded and did as she was asked, taking one of the plastic chairs by the door.

Rossiter turned to Ellie's parents. 'Mr and Mrs O'Farrell, I expect you know what I'm going to say.'

'Guard, Ellie was distraught this evening,' Cynthia said. 'She begged us to bring her here. And if those other predictions of hers hadn't been so accurate, we wouldn't have done. But... well, they *were!*'

'And that could be explained in any number of ways,' Rossiter said. 'I agree it seems remarkable, but I feel I have a responsibility to recommend you take your daughter to see a therapist, or a psychiatrist, or someone who understands these types of things.'

'Ellie is already seeing a therapist,' Cynthia said. 'She's academically advanced in some areas, and that makes her feel a bit isolated at times. So we sent her to see someone to help her deal with being a little... a little different from the other children.'

'And what does he or she have to say about these dreams?'

The couple glanced at one another again; the look suggested they were nearing a point of complete exhaustion.

'Dr Cleary suggests Ellie has a rich imaginative life and that we should encourage her creativity.'

Rossiter grinned at them both. 'There you go. You probably have a future bestselling crime writer on your hands.'

Philip gave the guard a hard look. 'Were you being truthful when you said you'd have a car on patrol in Ballincollig tomorrow night?'

'We always do.'

'That's good,' the slim man said. 'I just hope that when the call comes, they're not too late.'

And then he and his wife turned and moved towards the door, Ellie getting up to follow them.

Rossiter logged the visit, including the details of what Ellie had told him, and took note of the other deaths she'd apparently foreseen.

Then thought no more about it for a while.

Rossiter arrived at work at 8 a.m. two days later to be called into the sergeant's office.

'Sit down, Killian,' Sergeant William O'Mahoney told him.

The sarge was a block of a man who'd served the bulk of his career in Limerick, dealing with the gang situation there. He was possibly the toughest cop Rossiter had ever worked with, but his time in Ireland's most crime-afflicted city had left its mark – he carried a dour kind of cynicism that many of the Gardai who worked at the station found hard to deal with, although he was capable of occasional, surprising bursts of kindness.

Some found these even more unnerving than his usual grim demeanour.

The sarge's office was remarkably spartan, featuring only a small bookshelf containing evenly spaced folders and a small desk, upon which sat a laptop and a plastic cube that held photographs of his wife, his two adult daughters and grand-children.

'You took this call two nights ago,' the sarge said when they were both seated, pushing Rossiter's report on Ellie O'Farrell's visit across his desk.

Rossiter glimpsed at the pages and pushed them back, nodding. 'Poor kid,' he said. 'I think the whole family is under stress. As you see, I suggested a shrink, but they told me the girl already has one. I thought about recommending they get her a new one – a second opinion, y'know? But I didn't think it was my place.'

'No, probably not,' O'Mahoney said. 'I ran a check on the parents. Both have clean records. The kid is registered to an Educate Together school in Douglas. They tell me she's an exemplary student. Head of the debating team. Star of the chess club. She could go on to great things.'

Rossiter cut in. 'Boss, I didn't see any need to run those checks. If I was supposed to, I'm sorry. I must have missed the memo about procedures being changed on reports that can't be followed up.'

'No, you didn't do anything wrong, lad,' the sarge said, waving off the apology.

'Did something happen to the kid?' Rossiter asked, wondering if the stress he'd seen between the O'Farrell parents had bubbled over into violence. They hadn't seemed the type, but the fifteen years he'd served as a guard had taught him that even the most civilised people were capable of awful acts.

'Not to the girl, no. But Dominic Wilde, the hotelier, had his throat cut in his home last night. We don't have an accurate time of death yet, but it seems like it was probably in or around midnight, give or take a couple of hours.'

Rossiter felt a tingle at the base of his skull. 'Ellie was right...' he said. 'I mean, she said eleven, or close to it.'

'Pretty damned accurate.'

'So... so we're not thinking this kid is genuinely psychic, are we?'

The sarge laughed, though the humour of the situation,

such as it was, didn't reach his eyes. 'Good Lord, no. What we're thinking is that this wee girl seems to have knowledge and information regarding a series of homicides in the south of the country. The details she's aware of suggest she's in contact with some very bad people. I don't know if it's her parents or someone else, but I think we have to bring her and her folks in.'

'Yes, sir. I think you're right.'

'Can you be the point man on this one? Probably better they see a familiar face when they open the door. We want them to feel relaxed coming in here. At first anyway.'

'Of course, boss.'

'Good man. Let's tread carefully. The fact they brought her in could mean the parents aren't involved, but we can't rule it out. Let's have a chat with them and see what we can learn.'

Rossiter stood. 'I'll take Flo with me.'

'I was going to suggest as much.'

O'Mahoney watched out the window of his office as they drove out of the station car park to make the short drive to Douglas.

He had no idea about the chaos that was about to be unleashed over the next three days.

Or that it would come perilously close to killing him.

PART ONE

Tessa Burns sat at the table in her boyfriend's kitchen, watching him cook. Coastguard Captain Jim Sheils lived in a renovated cottage just outside Wexford town, about a mile on the Dublin side of what Wexfordians referred to as the 'new' bridge, though it was built in the 1950s.

It was a new relationship, and Tessa was unsure if she liked calling Jim her 'boyfriend' as he was in his forties and she would be within the next fourteen months, but there didn't seem a better term for what he was – 'partner' suggested something more long-term than she was ready to commit to just yet, and as a police detective, the word had other connotations too.

Danny Murphy, her team mate on what was known as the Burns Unit among her fellow police officers, was technically her partner, in the professional sense at least.

Tessa's phone buzzed on the table. Picking it up, she saw that it was, in fact, Danny ringing, as if the thought of his name had summoned him. She also noted there were a number of missed calls. She'd muted her phone for a couple of hours that afternoon, as she and Jim had been enjoying some personal time.

So much for taking the day off, Tessa thought.

'Hello, Danny.'

'Hey, Tessa. I'm... well, I'm parked outside.'

Tessa bristled. 'Parked outside where?'

'Jim Sheils' house.'

'Danny, I'm not going to pretend this isn't just a little bit weird!'

'No! The commissioner asked me to come and get you! We've been called to a case, and we need to leave right away.'

'Tell me.'

'There's a kid being held in the Anglesea Street station in Cork city in connection with three deaths.'

'A kid?'

'Yes. Twelve years old.'

'They think he killed these people?'

'It's a girl, and they know she didn't. But she told the guards the murders were going to happen; got her parents to bring her into the station so she could give them the information.'

'Which they dismissed.'

'Oh yeah. Told her folks to get her some therapy. But then the murders happened, exactly as she said they would.'

'So now they've no choice but to take her seriously.'

'That's it. The boss wants us down there post-haste.'

'Can I finish my dinner?'

There was a pause at the end of the line. 'What are ye eating?'

Jim, who looked as if he'd been trying not to listen in on Tessa's conversation, could restrain himself no longer. 'I'm not eavesdropping, but I heard that. Danny, would you like to come in and have a bite before you go?'

'Did you hear that, Daniel?'

'I'm on my way in!'

The three sat about the table in Jim's kitchen with its old-fashioned dressers and chequered tablecloth, chatting about everything and nothing. Tessa and Jim knew this meant they would be parting ways for a while, but with Danny there expounding on the latest Dave Baldacci thriller, they made do with smiling at one another, perhaps a little sadly. They'd known these were the demands of the job, and they accepted it. Not gladly, but with tolerance.

As Danny used a piece of bread to mop up the remaining pasta sauce from his second helping, Tessa couldn't help but grin. 'Do you think that'll hold you until we get to Cork?'

Danny popped the bread into his mouth and chewed slowly. 'If it doesn't, I have some protein bars in the car. I'll be okay.'

Jim raised an eyebrow. He was a striking man: tall and lean with a short dark beard and pale-blue eyes that twinkled with intelligence and humour. 'I can put some in a lunchbox for you,' he said. 'There's a little bit left.'

Danny's eyes lit up. 'That'd be great. Thanks!'

Tessa shook her head and pushed her chair back. 'I'll go and pack up my things. We'd best get going if we want to see this kid before it gets too late.'

'Maybe I'll just have the leftovers while Tessa gets ready, Jim,' Danny said hopefully.

Jim looked at the huge man, slightly taken aback. 'Seriously?'

'It could be all hours before we get a chance to have supper,' Danny offered plaintively.

And he wasn't wrong about that.

While Tessa threw her clothes into her travel bag and Danny finished off what was left of the large saucepan of pasta Jim had prepared, the third member of the Burns Unit, Maggie Doolan, along with her black-and-white terrier-mix dog Pavlov, were already on their way to Cork.

By 6.15 p.m., they'd just driven through the town of Dungarvan and were cruising along with Dungarvan Bay to their left, the sun starting to dip towards the blue horizon.

A lay-by opened up ahead, and, as it had been a couple of hours since Pav had been able to stretch his legs and relieve himself, Maggie decided to pull over and allow her little dog to have some fresh air and a wander. She knew the others were quite a bit behind her – Danny had texted to say they were having dinner before leaving Wexford – so she reckoned she could afford to make a short pit stop.

She guided her Ford Focus – which she'd had modified to accommodate her physical needs – into the parking area and parked beside a low stone wall, beyond which was a small area of scrub that sloped down to about five hundred yards of silt stretching out to meet the sea, which was at low tide. Oyster-catchers, redshanks and turnstones darted here and there out on the salt flats while a solitary curlew stood motionless at the waterline. A wind that had a chill note to it blew in from the south, signalling that autumn was coming.

'You go on and take some air,' Maggie said to the dog, who was standing up in the passenger seat now, his tail wagging furiously. 'I'll just stay here and watch the wildlife.'

She opened the door, and Pav jumped over her skinny legs and out onto the tarmacadam, scampering about for a few moments before coming to a sharp stop on the grass verge that separated the lay-by from the road, sniffing here and there to see what other canines had been about recently.

Maggie, who lived with cerebral palsy, a condition that meant she was dependent on an electric wheelchair, watched him for a few moments to make sure he wouldn't be tempted to dart into the road then returned her gaze to the seascape to her left. She could have got out too, but for the short amount of time they'd be stopped, it wasn't worth the effort of taking the chair from her modified vehicle. So she scanned the horizon and let her mind wander.

She wasn't really thinking about anything in particular – the new case sounded interesting, but she didn't know enough about it yet to have an opinion. Maggie was nothing if not a realist so wasn't prepared to waste time pondering what ifs. Ellie O'Farrell would have her undivided attention when she, Tessa and Danny had all the necessary details, and they would receive those when they arrived in Cork.

Another car pulled into the parking area, a red Mazda 323. Maggie noted it idly and whistled to Pavlov to finish his business and make his way back to the Ford then turned the key in the ignition.

As she did, the door to the Mazda opened and a man

climbed out. Maggie paid him no heed and whistled to Pav again.

'Come on, Pavlov. We're burning daylight.'

She reached over to her phone, which was in a cradle on the dashboard, thinking that she might listen to a podcast over the final hour of their journey – she enjoyed audio dramas, and there was a new one from the BBC, an updating of some of H.P. Lovecraft's horror stories she'd heard good things about. Lovecraft hadn't had much tolerance of people with special needs, but Maggie enjoyed the scope of his stories – no one did cosmological horror quite like good old H.P. She was punching the name of the show into Spotify's search engine when Pav emitted a shrill bark.

Maggie looked up to see that the man, whom she now noted was dressed from head to toe in black, was resting his arms on the open door of the Mazda, aiming a Glock handgun at her. As if a switch had been flipped, Maggie went into what she thought of as defensive mode.

Several things went through her mind all at once as she assessed the risk.

The angle at which the cars were parked in relation to one another offered her no protection – there was a direct line of fire, and she had no reason to believe the man in the Mazda was anything other than a decent shot. To add to this, there was little breeze, the light was good and the distance between the two vehicles was only about ten yards.

She processed all of this in a split second. She was aware her heartbeat had increased and her breathing had become shallow. Sweat broke out on her forehead, and time seemed to slow. She was scared. She knew she was scared. But Maggie had been scared before: she knew how to cope with it. Courage, she had once read, was feeling the fear but doing what had to be done anyway. And that was what she was determined to do.

Her initial physical response was more based on instinct than calculation.

Throwing herself as far back into the driver's seat as her slim frame would go, Maggie slammed the Ford into reverse, executing a rapid U-turn. The Glock boomed, but Maggie was no longer where the man had been aiming, and the sound of the detonation echoed across the salt flats like rolling thunder, the bullet disappearing harmlessly into the early autumn air.

'Pavlov!' she shouted, casting about desperately for the dog.

She glanced again at the man and saw that he'd turned so his back was to the Mazda now, holding the gun in a two-handed shooter's stance and adjusting his aim. Before he had the chance to fire, however, there was a snarl, and a black-and-white ball of fury launched itself at him, catching his wrist and sending the second shot wide.

'Get off me!' Maggie heard the man shout.

Pav, you beauty, you've bought me some time, Maggie thought. *I'd better make the most of it.*

And then she was gunning the Ford, spinning the wheels in place to build up the torque.

Please, Pav, she thought, *please know what I'm planning and get out of there in time!*

Trusting her dog would intuit her intentions, she released the brake, and the Ford surged forward on a collision course with the gunman and his vehicle.

The black-clad assailant, who was trying to prise the little dog's jaw from his right arm, looked up at the roar of the Ford's engine, and in that second Maggie saw something she hadn't noticed until that moment: the man's face looked as if it had been burned; the nose was just a slight protuberance in the middle of a flat plain of tissue, the cheeks shiny and smooth, the mouth just a gash. Her would-be killer had no eyebrows at all, and while Maggie couldn't be certain, she would have happily bet a week's wages that the tousle of jet-black hair atop his head was a wig.

A man without a face, Maggie thought, but she didn't have time to pursue the idea any further. Pav, to her delight, dropped to the ground just before the cars impacted and scuttled to the left, and the man, in a burst of speed that seemed almost superhuman, threw himself into his own vehicle, executing a forward tumble and somehow managing to open the passenger door as he did so, diving out the other side and leaping over the low stone wall as the Ford crushed the parked red Mazda into it, escaping into the salt flats.

Maggie was thrown forward, but her belt saved her. She hung there for a moment, dazed but alive, feeling the nausea that always accompanied such a rush of adrenaline.

My ribs are going to be black and blue in the morning, she thought.

She remained where she was for a moment, waiting for her breathing to regulate. Tension bubbled at the base of her skull, but the immediate danger had been quelled, and she, for now at least, had the upper hand.

It was time to consolidate that position.

Maggie didn't carry a gun, as her disability caused her to occasionally experience muscle spasms, which made firearms far too dangerous – a single involuntary clench of her right hand could result in a shot being fired at just the wrong time – but she did have a can of mace and an extendable baton in scabbards on her electric wheelchair, which was stowed right behind her, so she reached back and fumbled about until the baton was in her hand.

As she did, she heard scratching at the door of the Ford. She opened it a crack, and Pav jumped in, lapping her face frenetically.

'There's my boy,' Maggie said, almost crying with relief. 'There's my good boy.'

She hugged him tight, then pushed the door open and got out of the Ford, standing unsteadily (she could stand and walk unaided, but with difficulty) by the low wall and scanning the area.

There was very little cover on the flats. Some chunks of old masonry jutted from the silt here and there. Behind the wall was a drop of about three feet, and as she allowed her eyes to follow the base of the structure, she could see it had been constructed with breeze blocks, and every twenty feet or so, a column of these stood out from the wall – Maggie assumed these were load-bearing – and could have been used to hide behind.

'Where the hell is he, Pav?' she asked the dog, who'd jumped atop the wall and was scuttling up and down, sniffing and growling. 'If he went out towards the sea, there'd be tracks in the mud. Which means he's hiding somewhere ahead of us at the base of the wall.'

There was grass, ribwort and sea cabbage growing just below them, which meant their attacker could move without leaving a trail, so long as he hugged the structure.

'He's still close, isn't he?'

Pav executed a skittering shuffle, indicating that he was ready to give chase. Maggie considered it. As a police officer, she had a responsibility to arrest this man. However, she had to be practical too. Even if she could get her chair over the wall and onto the flats, it would get bogged down in the soft surface before it had travelled more than five feet.

And there was no way she was going to send Pav after an armed man alone.

'I am an officer with an Garda Síochána,' she called out across the marsh. 'I am offering you the opportunity to surrender yourself to me now. If you don't, it'll go worse for you.'

She waited, hearing her words echo across the empty plain,

the sound of her voice tumbling out towards the sea. There was no response.

'He's biding his time,' Maggie said to Pav. 'Come on. There's nothing more we can do.'

She climbed back into her car, Pav taking his position in the passenger seat.

They couldn't stay there, parked like sitting ducks.

Hoping the Ford wasn't too damaged, she turned the key, and in an act of mechanical mercy, the engine responded immediately. Laying the baton, still unextended, on the seat beside her, she reversed quickly and turned onto the road. For a second, she didn't know where she should go but then realised this changed nothing.

Ellie O'Farrell still needed her help in Cork.

She rang in the incident on the way, informing the police in Dungarvan that there was an armed man at large in the environs of their town. Then she called Dawn Wilson.

'Boss?'

'Maggie. You're hardly in Cork already?'

'No, boss. Me and Pav just had something of an altercation.'

'Tell me.'

She did, and Dawn listened before saying she would liaise with the police in Dungarvan. She agreed Maggie should continue for Cork so long as she was unhurt.

There was a conversation the former family liaison officer would need to have with Tessa Burns – and soon. Tessa believed her parents had been murdered by a man with no face. And in the last two cases they'd worked, they'd encountered, either anecdotally or in person, men who fitted that description.

One of them had even told Tessa they had a name: the Unattested.

Maggie wondered if their continued encounters with these faceless killers could possibly be a coincidence, or if someone was manipulating things to put the Burns Unit into the path of these strange assassins.

And she couldn't help but wonder if the attack she'd just thwarted had been brought on by their previous case or the one they were going to be working once they all got to Cork.

For now, she would just have to add it to the many things she didn't know and hope the truth would reveal itself soon.

Tessa Burns sat opposite Ellie O'Farrell in the conference room of Anglesea Street station at 7 p.m. The room was long and narrow, its walls panelled in a cheap blonde wood, the floor carpeted in sky blue, the only furniture one long table around which sat twelve chairs, all upholstered in the same blue as the carpet.

She'd specifically asked to see the child somewhere other than an interview room, which understandably held negative associations for anyone being questioned in it. She was also clear this wasn't an official interview, just a chat.

If it had been an interrogation, Ellie's parents or a social worker would have to be present under Irish law, as the child was legally a minor and couldn't be interviewed without being in the company of a guardian.

Tessa wanted to get a sense of Ellie before all that began. Which it would have to, soon enough.

'You don't look like a detective,' the girl said, peering across the table.

Tessa's dark hair was tied back in a loose, slightly untidy ponytail. She had strong features, set off by laughter lines around her mouth, and while Ellie couldn't see it because they were both seated, Tessa had a strong build: broad shoulders that tapered to a slim waist and powerfully muscled legs.

Today, the detective was dressed in her usual green parka jacket, black-and-white PLO-style scarf, blue jeans and a Rammstein T-shirt.

'Have you met many detectives, Ellie?' Tessa asked.

'No,' the girl admitted.

'Well then, you don't have much to base your opinion on. Yes, the majority of detectives in the Irish police force do wear suits, and a lot of them are middle-aged men with moustaches and beer guts. But there are more than a few women, and a lot of guys, who choose to dress more like... well... normal people. The work I do, wearing a trouser suit wouldn't really make sense.'

'What work do you do?'

Tessa could see that the girl was nervous and was trying to hide it by asking questions and appearing knowledgeable.

She's a smart one, Tessa thought, *and way over her head in whatever mess she's found herself.*

'I'm head of a team that works exclusively on cases involving children.'

'Like juvenile delinquents? Kids in gangs and stuff?'

Tessa laughed. 'Well, we haven't encountered any of those yet, although I expect we will sooner or later. No, what we mostly do is help kids who've found themselves in the system through no fault of their own. I'm talking about children who've witnessed crimes, or been abducted, or whose parents are involved in criminality and they've got dragged into it. That kind of thing.'

'So you don't arrest kids then?'

'No.' Tessa shook her head. 'Me and my people make sure kids are protected. Ellie, I'm here to help.'

The girl seemed to relax somewhat at these words and sagged a bit in her chair.

'Am I in trouble?' she asked.

There we have it, Tessa thought. *She's just a little kid, for all her bravado. She's scared. And who could blame her?*

'I wouldn't say that,' Tessa said, thinking about the question and doing her best to be honest. 'You have knowledge of a number of serious crimes that have occurred around the Cork area, and the guards would like to know how you came by it. I think that's pretty reasonable, don't you?'

'I've already reported everything I know *and* how I know it: I dreamed about those people and what happened to them.'

Tessa nodded. 'You're a smart girl, Ellie. So I know you know the investigating detectives are going to find that a little hard to believe.'

'But it's true.'

Tessa smiled. 'I can see you believe that it is. Can I ask you something?'

'Of course. I'll answer if I can.'

'Thank you. Did you have any dreams or... um... premonitions about a lady with a dog being attacked by a man with a gun?'

The girl looked confused. 'A lady and a dog?'

'That's what I said.'

'No. I haven't dreamed about anything like that.'

'The woman has a disability, though that wouldn't have been obvious. She didn't have to get out of her car to defend herself.'

Ellie shook her head. 'Is someone else dead?'

'No. She got away.'

Tessa paused. Maybe Maggie's attack didn't have anything to do with this case after all. Or maybe someone had to die for Ellie to know about it in advance – but then, how could the killers know they were going to be successful?

Tessa reckoned she wasn't going to arrive at an answer that evening, so continued: 'Can I suggest something else? Another possibility I'd really like you to consider?'

Ellie sighed. 'Yeah. Okay.'

'When bad things happen to us, our minds do their best to protect us from being hurt by building a kind of mental wall around the memory of the awful stuff that happened. So it's like we forget about it, almost as if the frightening experience never happened. Except those walls aren't always as strong as we'd like them to be, and sometimes bits and pieces of those memories leak out. And one of the ways they make themselves known to us is through our dreams.'

'How could I have hidden memories of things that haven't happened yet?'

'I – and the sergeant here and some of the other guards who've spoken to you – suspect that you overheard someone talking about plans to murder the people who died. If the people you heard were people you respect and care about, that would be very distressing. Distressing enough for you to want to hide that knowledge away.'

Ellie went very pale. 'You don't think my mam and dad could have known about this stuff! Mammy and Daddy are good people! They would never do anything bad.'

'I'm not accusing them,' Tessa said. 'I'm just putting it out there as a possibility. Can you see that it makes sense? Much more sense than your being psychic.'

Ellie seemed to consider this for a few moments, then she said: 'Do you know what my mam and dad work at?'

'No. Tell me.'

'Mam runs a bakery that sells vegan, gluten-free, low-carbon-footprint cakes, pies and breads. She won't watch crime shows on the TV because she thinks they often make the bad guys look cool. Dad works for a company that develops special kinds of social media software and also sends graduates with IT skills to countries having humanitarian crises, so they can help with rebuilding infrastructure and organise social-media campaigns to raise awareness of what's happening there. In his free time, he likes to do numeric logic puzzles, reads fantasy novels and plays *Dungeons and Dragons*.'

Tessa couldn't help but laugh. 'So what you're trying to say is that they're not the most likely candidates to have friends in the criminal underworld.'

'We don't even have any friends who are a little bit dodgy,' Ellie said. 'They're all just like my parents. I think one or two of my dad's pals smoke a bit of weed, but that's as far as it goes. And I'll bet some of *your* friends do that.'

'In fairness, Ellie, you probably don't know your parents' friends well enough to make that call,' Tessa pointed out.

'Maybe, but it's also true that I don't see their pals enough to have learned what I know. It doesn't make sense.'

'Maybe not,' Tessa said, 'but we need to explore all avenues. I bet you'd like for this to be over so you can get on with your life.'

Ellie nodded and tears welled in her eyes. 'Yes,' she said. 'I'd like that very much.'

6

While Tessa was beginning her conversation with Ellie, Detective Sergeant Danny Murphy, who'd arrived in Cork five minutes after his team leader, was being shown into Sergeant William O'Mahoney's office.

'Well you're a big fecker, aren't you?' O'Mahoney said as he stood and shook hands with Danny.

'Yes, but I'm pure of heart,' Danny said, smiling in an attempt to hide the fact he hated his size being mentioned while accepting the chair the sergeant indicated.

That evening, Danny was dressed in a black leather jacket over a red shirt and black jeans, his short black hair framing a sharp-featured, clean-shaven face, complete with piercing blue eyes.

'I'll take your word on it,' O'Mahoney said, sitting on his own side of the desk. 'I don't know why the commissioner sent you. It's not as if we aren't used to dealing with serious crimes here. Cork city isn't exactly a rural backwater.'

'I accept that, Sarge, as does the commish,' Danny said. 'We're here to lend a few extra pairs of hands because we're used to working cases involving children. We've got some expertise, and we can probably make the process a lot less stressful on the wee girl and her family.'

The sarge nodded, but his face didn't show a lot of pleasure at the thought. 'I appreciate your concern for the child, but my focus at the present time is on her parents. I think we can safely assume the O'Farrells are hiding something.'

'What makes you say that?'

'It's the only thing that adds up. I was prepared to give them some leeway, but the longer we talk to them, the more my patience is wearing thin.'

'Have they got a record?' Danny asked.

'No. But then neither did Al Capone.'

'Are they associates of any criminals?'

'Not that we know of. *Yet.* But I have some of my people looking into them closely The lawyer who represents Philip O'Farrell's firm has defended some dodgy characters in the past, but he left all that behind him some years ago and mostly works with charities now. Wants to give something back to his community, or so he says. I don't like him being involved in this, but he doesn't have a rap sheet either. Right now, the parents seem the most sensible place to look.'

'Isn't it worth considering some other lines of inquiry too?'

'Like what? The kid obviously has access to information she shouldn't,' O'Mahoney said.

'And she came to the station to share it with you. Her parents *drove her here.* That doesn't seem the actions of guilty parties to me.'

'I'm thinking it's some kind of reverse psychological move. They're both feckin' hippies. Think they're cleverer than they really are.'

'Are they here?' Danny asked.

'Yes. We've got them in separate interview rooms. The Violent Crimes Unit have been chatting with them.'

'How long have you been interviewing them?'

'Off and on for' – the sarge checked his watch – 'nine hours now.'

'Nine hours?' Danny said, whistling softly. 'And they've given you nothing in that time?'

'Not a dicky bird.'

'They're either scared out of their wits of whoever they're working with, or are extremely tough hippies.'

'Or very clever, very talented actors,' the sarge said. 'I'm going with a combination of scared witless and Oscar-winning performances.'

'Have you considered they might be telling the truth?' Danny asked.

'That doesn't leave me anything to work with.'

'The girl's parents *not* being the source of her knowledge isn't a starting point? I mean, it gives you room to look elsewhere.'

'Yeah, but where?' the sarge asked.

'Isn't it our job to work that out?'

Sergeant O'Mahoney glowered at the big detective's trite response. 'Don't tell me my job, DS Murphy,' he growled. 'I might have to put up with you and your people, but I don't have to be condescended to in my own house.'

'No offence meant, Sarge,' Danny said hurriedly.

'I'd have thought with one of your own getting attacked on the way here, you'd be more anxious to get this business sorted,' O'Mahoney growled and looked towards the door.

Danny didn't reply. He just got up and walked out.

7

Maggie had been asked to write up the details of the attempt on her life as soon as she arrived at Anglesea Street, so Danny was still chatting with Sergeant O'Mahoney, and Tessa ensconced in the meeting room with Ellie when she and Pavlov entered the squad room of the police station.

Maggie's ride was a serious piece of equipment and looked it.

She'd adapted it over the years, amping up the motor, adding a small laptop on a platform close to her right hand should she need to do some online research while in the field. Next to the laptop was a cradle containing Maggie's mobile phone. The scabbard that held her extendable baton was built into the panel at her right leg, and a smaller one on the left-hand side held her can of pepper spray. Next to it was a red button which, when pressed, activated an alarm loud enough to shock most assailants into momentarily freezing – which was just long enough to give her the upper hand, while hopefully also bringing assistance.

Maggie lived with physical challenges, but she was far from

helpless, teaching classes in wheelchair self-defence at her local community centre when work didn't take her away.

She also had qualifications in both psychology and sociology and had initially been seconded to the team as a researcher and liaison, working closely with the children their cases focused on. However, Dawn felt that this diminished her role on the team, and, before Maggie had made her trip to Cork, she'd received a call from the commissioner.

'I've got some news for you.'

'I'm listening.'

'You've just been promoted.'

'What for? In the last case we worked, my main contribution was to get taken hostage so Tessa and Sheils had to rescue me.'

'That's hardly a fair reflection.'

'I think it is.'

'Luckily, your opinion doesn't count when it comes to promotions. You've just become a detective, Maggie Doolan. I've had them run up a new ID card for you in Cork. It'll be waiting for you in the station when you arrive.'

'Seriously?'

'Am I ever not serious?' Dawn had asked.

'In my experience, frequently.'

'Well I'm being serious now. Get to work, DI Doolan. Crime doesn't solve itself.'

Maggie hadn't known what to say. She'd looked at Pavlov in surprise. 'Well isn't that something?' she'd asked him. 'I'm a detective.'

He'd panted happily, clearly pleased at her news.

A female in uniform was sitting at a desk in the bullpen when Maggie and Pavlov came in.

'Your colleagues are already here,' the guard said. 'DI Burns is with the girl, and the big fella is with the sarge.'

'I might as well meet the parents then,' Maggie said.

'Mr O'Farrell is in interview room three, and Mrs O'Farrell in room five.'

'Is there somewhere I can see them both together?'

'I can have them brought into the family room, if you like.'

'That'd be good. Thanks.'

The family room was a bright, comfortable space with a couch, a couple of soft-backed chairs and a coffee table complete with a mix of magazines (*Woman's Own*, *Ireland's Own*, *Vogue*, *Hot Press* and some old *National Geographic*s). A few framed paintings by kids who'd used the room in the past hung on the walls. A kettle and makings for tea and coffee sat in the corner, and Maggie busied herself making three cups.

Moments later, the O'Farrells were brought in by the female officer. They both looked exhausted.

'Just give me a shout when you're done,' the guard said and went back to her post.

'I've made us some tea,' Maggie said.

'I don't consume caffeine,' Mrs O'Farrell said primly.

'Would you like some hot water?' Maggie asked, unfazed.

'That would be nice, thank you.'

Maggie rolled over to the kettle and filled a cup, handing it to the woman, who was looking at her with no small amount of curiosity.

'You're a member of the Gardai?' she asked, her eyes dropping to the chair then darting back to Maggie, who that evening was dressed in a light-blue denim jacket over a white shirt, pale jeans and green Converse high-tops.

'I am indeed,' Maggie replied patiently. 'My name is Maggie Doolan, and this is Pavlov. We work for a team that answers directly to the Garda commissioner. She asked us to come to Cork to see if we can help.'

'If you want to help, tell the police we're not involved in these murders,' Mr O'Farrell said, sitting heavily onto the couch. 'They seem convinced we've been feeding Ellie the information she dreamed.'

'Have you?' Maggie asked.

'No,' Mr O'Farrell said. 'We have not.'

'Any theories on how she knows what she knows then?'

'She's a twelve-year-old girl,' Mrs O'Farrell said, perching beside her husband. 'She mixes with people other than us.'

'Who?' Maggie wanted to know.

'Her school friends. Teachers. She attends a youth club. Sees a therapist who specialises in working with young people. She might have heard things from any of those sources.'

'You haven't asked her?'

Mr O'Farrell laughed dryly. 'Stupidly, we thought the police would take the information she gave, prevent the next death she'd foreseen, and that was the last we'd hear of the whole thing.'

'Didn't work out that way, did it?'

'Not quite, no.'

'Do you both understand the seriousness of the current situation?' Maggie asked. 'Your daughter has shown foreknowledge of three deaths, one of which is undeniably a murder. Her advanced awareness of the circumstances of the other two suggest they weren't accidental. The police will now look into these deaths and try to find something to link them, and when they do, they'll try to connect whatever that is to your daughter. And to you, as you are the most likely source of Ellie's information. If investigators can prove you're guilty of knowing the details of these deaths, you'll be prosecuted as accessories after the fact. The maximum sentence for an accessory to a serious crime is ten years' imprisonment.'

'We came to this very station and informed the police of the last death!' Mr O'Farrell said. 'Doesn't that stand for anything?'

'It does,' Maggie agreed. 'But interestingly, it was the crime that couldn't be written off as an accident. A good barrister will suggest you got scared and wanted to distance yourselves.'

'So you don't believe us either?' Mrs O'Farrell said, her lower lip trembling.

Pavlov, in a small jump, moved from Maggie's lap onto the couch so he was beside the woman and put his head on her lap. She scratched his ears absently, but the action seemed to calm her.

'I used to be a family liaison officer,' Maggie said. 'I want you to clearly understand the circumstances you're in. Sugar-coating them won't help you. You have to know the risks.'

'Ms Doolan, we've done nothing wrong,' Mr O'Farrell said. 'As soon as we realised our daughter was somehow... somehow *channelling* something real, we brought her to the authorities. These dreams were clearly upsetting her, and the fact they seemed to be reflecting something genuine, well, we wanted to do the right thing, even if it were only a coincidence. We still do, despite how we've been treated.'

Maggie looked at the couple intently. If they were lying, they were seasoned professionals in the art of deception. She'd encountered people like that before many times in her career, but this beleaguered-looking man and his anxiety-stricken wife didn't strike her as being that type. At the very least, she was convinced they believed what they were saying.

'I'm going to request you be sent home,' she said. 'There's nothing to be gained by continuing to question people who don't know anything. Eventually, you'll end up admitting to stuff just to get them to leave you alone.'

'What about Ellie?' Mr O'Farrell asked.

'She's a minor. They can't keep her here if she hasn't committed a crime. And there's no suggestion that she has. Because of her age, there wasn't even a legal obligation for her to inform the police about what she knew. I'll see what I can do. Give me a few minutes to speak to my team.'

'Thank you, Ms Doolan,' Mrs O'Farrell said. 'You've been very kind.'

'You can call me Maggie. And you're welcome. Will I leave Pavlov while I go and see what I can arrange?'

Mrs O'Farrell nodded. 'He's a nice dog,' she said. 'And I'm Cynthia. This is Philip.'

'It's nice to meet you,' Maggie said, and went to find Tessa and Danny.

8

Danny and Tessa were waiting for Maggie in the reception area, and once she arrived, they went out to the car park to talk.

It was, by then, just after 8 p.m. and almost completely dark. Cars cruised past on Anglesea Street beyond the station's main gates, and the voices of people on their way to restaurants, pubs or the night shift drifted on the cool air. From where they stood, they could see the red, blue and yellow lit-up sign of a Lidl supermarket just up the road from the station.

'You had an eventful trip,' Tessa said, leaning over and hugging Maggie.

'Just a bit, yeah. Sergeant O'Mahoney has some guy in the motor pool replacing the front grille of my Focus. Those cars are built like jeeps, so he says he can have it sorted before we leave. I'm lucky I didn't crack the radiator, or I wouldn't have been able to get away, and Pav and me would have been fish waiting to be shot in a barrel.'

'Any word on the guy who opened fire on you?'

'Not as yet. His car has been impounded, but I'm not hopeful they'll find anything on it.'

'Did you recognise him at all? Maybe one of the crew who held you in Wexford out for revenge?'

During their last case, Maggie had been abducted and held for twelve hours by a local gang – Tessa, Jim, Pav and a fixer from the shipping company who owned the vessel that had trafficked the children involved had rescued her, and in so doing had been forced to shoot and kill several of Maggie's captors.

'No, it wasn't one of them. The guy did look kind of familiar though.'

'Yeah?'

'He looked as if he'd had a lot of cosmetic surgery, Tess.'

Tessa froze. 'You're sure?'

'I am. It was as if he... well, as if he had no face. None to speak of anyway. His features were blurred. Indistinct.'

Danny watched both women. He was aware a man who fit that description had murdered Tessa's parents, but he and Tessa had almost been killed by a Faceless Man on a previous case too. And Maggie had been forced to kill one when he'd attempted to murder a child she was watching over. The Burns Unit had all become familiar with Faceless Men.

'Could this be about the case in Monaghan?' he asked. 'We pretty much wiped out a cluster of these guys during that investigation. It might be a vengeance thing.'

'Could be,' Tessa agreed. 'But the Merrow said her parents were killed by one too.'

The Merrow was a woman they'd met in Wexford. She'd been employed by the gang to escort the children during their boat voyage to Ireland and had become enraged when she'd discovered the safe, loving adoption she'd been assured they were destined for wasn't going to happen. She'd gone on a rampage, wiping out all those involved in an attempt to protect the kids.

'How could that be connected though?' Maggie asked.

'We seem to be coming in contact with these faceless killers, these Unattested, everywhere we go,' Tessa said, using the name of their guild. 'It can't be a coincidence.'

'You're saying someone is choosing cases for us to bring us into the path of a gang of faceless assassins?' Danny asked, incredulous.

'That's what I've been starting to wonder,' Maggie said.

'What the hell for?'

'I don't know,' Tessa admitted. 'But something weird is going on. We'd all best be careful is all I'm saying.'

This received nods and murmurs of agreement.

'So what do we think about Ellie O'Farrell?' Tessa continued.

'Sergeant O'Mahoney – and I'm assuming he's speaking for the rest of the team involved – is convinced the parents are mixed up in something serious, and the kid is picking up on it,' Danny said. 'Whether it's some kind of unconscious cry for help, or if she's doing it on purpose out of guilt, O'Mahoney thinks it's the O'Farrells who are the source of what she knows.'

'Yet she is absolutely adamant they're not,' Tessa said. 'If she wanted to have them caught, wouldn't it be easier just to get a bus into town on her own and go to the police directly? Or just ring it in?'

'I don't think it's the parents,' Maggie said. 'I've just spoken to them, and if they're guilty, then I know nothing about how families behave under pressure. I won't rule out that both they and their daughter have experienced something traumatic and they're all repressing it though.'

'How was Pav with them?' Tessa asked.

'When Mrs O'Farrell – Cynthia – got upset, he went right to her.'

Tessa nodded. 'That weighs considerably in their favour.'

'It does,' Maggie agreed.

'Add to that the guards here have been grilling them both

for hours,' Danny said. 'If they're as green as the sarge thinks they are, they'd have broken if they did know anything.'

'We don't know how tough they went on them,' Tessa pointed out.

'The sarge didn't seem like he would have favoured the gentle approach,' Danny said.

'I can vouch that they're exhausted,' Maggie offered. 'They've had a tough day.'

'You saw Ellie, the wee girl?' Danny asked Tessa.

'I did,' Tessa agreed. 'She's very smart, very scared and determined to do the right thing if she can. And I concur with Maggie – I don't think she's spoofing. She doesn't know how she knows this stuff.'

'So what do we do now?' Danny asked.

'I don't think there's any point in holding the family here,' Maggie said. 'I'm going to ask for them to be sent home.'

'Agreed,' Tessa said. 'They're being punished for being civically minded. Let them get some rest before the investigation really gets into its stride.'

'The sensible thing to do would be to look at the three murders she says she dreamed about and see what we can learn about them,' Danny said. 'There's three deaths, so we can each take one, cover the ground faster.'

'Sounds like a plan,' Tessa said. 'Maggie, any thoughts on how we can help Ellie access where these memories or precognitive dreams or whatever they are came from?'

'The obvious thing would be to use hypnotic regression,' Maggie said. 'But to be honest, it's not reliable – it's dangerously easy to accidentally implant memories even while the regression is being carried out. Her parents say she's seeing a therapist. I'd say a conversation with him might prove useful.'

'I'll let you do that,' Tessa said.

'He might not tell us much. Client confidentiality and all that.'

'I'd have thought this was a slightly unusual circumstance, wouldn't you?'

'Still,' Maggie said, 'shrinks tend to take that stuff pretty seriously. And rightly so.'

'See what you can learn,' Tessa replied. 'If we have no luck, we can always get her checked out by someone ourselves.'

'I'll get the name from the O'Farrells.'

'Okay,' Tessa said, 'let's go back inside and see if we can get these people released, for a while at least.'

And they did.

Though things didn't go according to plan.

9

They found Sergeant O'Mahoney sitting at one of the five tables in the station's small canteen, drinking tea and reading a report.

'Well, have ye satisfied yourselves there's nothing to be done that we humble Cork people can't do ourselves?' he asked as they approached.

'We have of course,' Tessa said. 'But I think we might stick around for a while anyway.'

The sergeant snorted. 'I don't see what the fuss is about,' he said dourly. 'That child either heard murderous intentions towards three separate individuals from her parents or someone else close to her. That's all there is to it. All we need to do is work out who that person or persons is, and the rest will follow.'

'Maybe,' Tessa said. 'I'm sure you won't say no to three extra pairs of hands and four paws to help you find that out though. And some fresh perspectives can't hurt.'

O'Mahoney made a sound that might have been a laugh and might have been a grunt.

Tessa smiled. 'I'll take that as a yes. Now, we were

wondering if it might not be a good idea to send the O'Farrells home? You're not going to get a confession from Ellie's parents, and the child has told you everything she knows. There doesn't seem a lot to be gained from holding them.'

The sarge took a drink of his tea and turned back to the report. 'Mr and Mrs O'Farrell can go home for the moment. I've arranged with the Child and Family Agency to have Ellie moved to a juvenile detention centre just outside the city. She can stay there until we get this mess cleared up.'

Maggie rolled forward. 'Sergeant O'Mahoney, the usual practice when we become involved in a case is that the child is deemed to be in *our* care while the investigation is taking place. No one discussed any such move with us.'

The sarge grinned, and it wasn't a particularly pleasant sight. 'I had no idea I had to share my plans with you,' he said. 'I received no document declaring Ellie O'Farrell is your responsibility. As I understand it, we're looking at a young girl who's crying out for help. She may well be living with parents who are involved in violent crime, and therefore it's my duty as a guardian of the peace to ensure she's placed somewhere safe.'

'Sergeant, Ellie has been very clear her parents are *not* involved in criminal activity, as far as she's aware anyway!' Tessa said sharply. 'In fact, she's explicitly told me they're both pacifists!'

'And yet, here we are,' the sergeant said. 'Whether we're dealing with a pair of tree-huggers or not, that girl has been privy to information that could have saved lives, had it been brought to us sooner. I'm wondering what else is locked up in her head, and I want to make sure she's somewhere they'll be watching her twenty-four hours a day so we can act immediately the next time something important pops out.'

'We could have ensured that!' Tessa said.

'Well now you don't have to,' O'Mahoney said. 'If you really want to help, there's plenty of other work that needs to be done – interviews, door-to-door canvassing of the areas where the deaths occurred, going over CCTV footage from some of the crime scenes – you don't need me to tell you what we have ahead of us. Apply yourselves to that.'

And he returned his gaze to his report, saying, 'I'll bid you goodnight. You can tell Mr and Mrs O'Farrell they can go home. A car is coming for Ellie within the hour. I'll see to that.'

'Can I at least say goodbye to her?' Tessa asked.

'I don't think that would be useful,' the sergeant said.

'I disagree,' Tessa said.

Sergeant O'Mahoney looked up at her, and there was something hard and immutable in his gaze. Tessa had seen the look many times before, on the faces of people on both sides of the law. It didn't scare her, but she didn't think fighting the aggression behind it would benefit either her or Ellie just at that moment.

'You're in my house now, Detective Burns,' O'Mahoney said. 'It'd serve you and your people well to remember that.'

Tessa sighed, looked at Danny and Maggie, and motioned with her head that they should follow her.

'Are we just going to back down and let him send Ellie to a juvenile detention centre?' Maggie hissed as they moved towards the door leading to the family room, where they would collect Pavlov and break the news to the O'Farrells.

'Sometimes you have to pick your battles,' Tessa whispered back.

'I would have thought this was a battle to pick!' Maggie shot back in annoyance.

'If Ellie is brought to the new unit this evening, she'll more than likely be sent right to bed. It'll be much the same as her being kept here. In the meantime, we'll pull rank and call Dawn and get her to bring some pressure to bear on our dear sergeant. And then we'll see how things look in the morning.'

Danny grinned. 'So you're not backing down from the bully at all.'

'Nope,' Tessa said. 'I'm telling the teacher on him.'

THE WATCHER IN THE SHADOWS

He watched the van from the youth detention centre turn into the Garda station from his position in the doorway of the Lidl store a hundred yards away, up Anglesea Street. Slowly, looking as if he was taking an evening ramble, he strolled up the footpath so he was directly opposite the station and watched as the girl was led out into the car park.

She was crying, as was her mother. Her father's face remained blank, as if he was trying not to allow how he was really feeling to show, and the only way he could do that was to shut down his feelings completely.

Two big men, whom the Watcher took to be staff from the detention centre, stood to one side, talking to O'Mahoney, the station's sergeant, who'd brought the girl out. The senior Garda kept a close eye on the family's exchange but permitted them to say their goodbyes. After a few minutes of observing the weeping and wailing, however, he seemed to lose patience and stepped forward, taking the girl by the arm and steering her towards the back of the van. She pulled against him for a moment, but he wasn't to be dissuaded, and despite an even louder cry from her mother, the girl, cheeks glistening with tears, climbed into the dark interior of the vehicle.

The Watcher crossed the road and came to a stop at the pillar to the right of the main gate of the station, so he could hear what the small group said to one another.

He didn't exactly have to strain to listen in.

'How could you do this?' the girl's mother was screaming at O'Mahoney. 'We came to you in good faith! We wanted Ellie to see that doing the right thing is always best, and instead of showing her that, you've treated her like a criminal!'

'I'm going to be kind to you, Mrs O'Farrell, and advise you to carefully consider anything you say to me,' O'Mahoney said, his voice a low growl, though still clearly audible to the Watcher. 'You haven't been formally arrested, but your words can still be used as part of a trial. It's not too late to come clean and let me know how your daughter is in possession of the facts and details she possesses. Unburden yourself now and it'll go easier for you.'

'We've told you everything we know – everything!' the girl's father said, his voice less shrill than his wife's, but the emotion he'd suppressed for his daughter's benefit was back in his voice and writ large on his face. 'What do you want us to say? If it means my daughter can go home tonight, I'll tell you whatever you'd like to hear!'

The Watcher saw Sergeant O'Mahoney considering this offer. He and the bearded younger man gazed at each other for a long moment, but then the sergeant smiled a dark smile and said, 'You're a smart one, Mr O'Farrell. I'll give you that much. You've the rest of them fooled, but you can't pull the wool over my eyes. I thank you for your offer, but I won't take a confession from you under these conditions. Why don't you sleep on things, and we can chat again tomorrow? Maybe you'll be more accommodating after a good night's rest and some distance from all the fuss of today.'

Ellie's father looked as if he was about to collapse from misery and exhaustion.

'You won't get away with this,' his wife hissed, and even from his position at the gate, the Watcher could hear the hysteria in her voice and see the mania evident in her body language as she began to stalk towards the policeman. 'I'll see to it that you lose your rank and are disgraced for what you've done to us. I have friends, Sergeant O'Mahoney, and I'll drag you through every court in this country until I get satisfaction.'

O'Mahoney laughed. 'You go right ahead, Mrs O'Farrell,' he said. 'I've done nothing that exceeds the remit of my office nor contradicts the oath I took as a member of an Garda Síochána.'

'If so much as a hair on my daughter's head is harmed in the awful place you're sending her, I'll be coming to see you about it,' the woman said, and now the hysteria was replaced by something else. Something predatory. Something savage.

The Watcher viewed it with interest.

'Is that a threat, Mrs O'Farrell?'

'Oh no,' the woman said. 'That's a guarantee.'

'Come on, Cynthia.' Her husband took her by the shoulders and gently pulled her towards the street. At first she shook him off, but he didn't relent, and finally she allowed herself to be led away. 'There's nothing more we can do here,' the man said. 'We have to hope Detective Burns and her team can help us.'

'Don't say I didn't warn you,' Cynthia O'Farrell shouted back at O'Mahoney. 'I gave you a chance to fix this.'

The Garda gazed after the woman with what the Watcher believed was a kind of fascination, and the unnoticed observer saw that as the couple left the grounds of the station, moving past him close enough that he could have reached out and touched them, the woman's eyes never left the sergeant.

And in that moment, he pondered that he might be seeing nothing more than a woman vowing to protect her child.

Or could it be a stone-cold killer warning her next victim that she was coming for him?

10

Originally a separate village, Douglas was now a suburb of Cork city, with two large shopping malls and a number of good restaurants, plus some decent pubs. It was surrounded by housing complexes and estates, many of which housed upper-middle-class families who didn't want to raise their children amid the hubbub of the city.

The village core was pretty, with whitewashed houses and shopfronts, the malls tastefully set apart so they didn't take away from the overall look of the area.

The O'Farrells lived in a three-storey house in a small, gated community on the Rochestown Road, a three-minute drive from Douglas village proper. The house had a large garden, most of which looked overgrown to Tessa, but which Cynthia assured her had been 'wilded' for the benefit of the local fauna.

They all sat in the big house's front room, which was far untidier and more cluttered than the detectives would have expected, and drank herbal teas (Maggie opted for a decaf coffee).

'I can't understand what's happened here,' Philip kept

repeating. 'How is my daughter being punished for crimes she absolutely couldn't have committed?'

'I promise you, we'll do our best to get her out as soon as we possibly can,' Tessa said.

'I'm going to sue,' Philip said. 'My lawyer is on his way.'

'That's your prerogative,' Tessa said. 'I can give you the details of the Garda Ombudsman. It is absolutely within your rights to take a case, and to be frank, I don't blame you.'

'Will you speak on our behalf?' Cynthia asked, her tone betraying more than a hint of derision – she clearly didn't expect Tessa or either of her colleagues to say they would.

The woman had a worn-looking blue teddy bear pressed to her chest. Tessa thought it a bit odd but kept the opinion to herself.

'I'd be very happy to state that I don't agree with taking Ellie into custody,' she said.

'Same here,' Maggie agreed. 'I can see why the sarge has done it, but I believe it's ill-advised.'

'You can count me in on that too,' Danny said. 'I don't see the point in it. I think he's trying to scare her, and I don't like scaring children. It's abusive.'

'Thank you,' Cynthia said, her voice betraying her surprise at the team's response. 'We both appreciate that.'

There was a ring on the doorbell, and the woman excused herself, leaving the room still holding the stuffed animal.

'That'll be Conor, my lawyer,' Philip said. 'He works for my employers. I'm hoping a bit of pressure from him will help with getting Ellie out.'

Tessa, Danny and Maggie exchanged dubious glances – units like the one Ellie had been sent to were used to lawyers bringing injunctions to have children released. The Irish judicial system had ring-fenced its ability to prevent such things from being effectual. If this Conor was worth his salt, he'd know that.

'Do you mind my asking about your wife's... comfort object?' Danny asked, broaching the stuffed elephant in the room.

'That's Ojo. Ellie always sleeps with him. I suppose it's giving Cynthia some comfort.'

There was nothing to say to that, so no one did.

They heard voices in the hallway, and Cynthia returned with a tall man in a grey silk suit and open-necked pale-blue shirt. He had dark hair, a sharp, pointed nose and very dark-blue eyes. The feature that immediately made him stand out, however, was that one side of his face was heavily scarred. It looked as if he might have had acid thrown at him at some point or he'd been dragged across a rough surface for a long time.

Whatever happened, it must have been painful, Tessa thought.

'This is our solicitor, Conor Stokes,' Cynthia said. 'Conor, these are the detectives I told you about: Tessa Burns, Daniel Murphy and Maggie Doolan. Oh, and Pavlov.'

The man didn't extend a hand, but he nodded in the direction of the team. Tessa noted that Pavlov didn't growl, but his hackles did rise slightly, and he seemed to sit up a bit straighter on Maggie's knees.

'Might I advise that we not speak about this matter in front of representatives of the organisation we're preparing to bring a case against?' Stokes said, his voice a dry rasp.

'They've all said they'll speak up on our behalf,' Philip replied.

'Until I have signed statements to that effect, I'd still be very wary of saying too much.'

'That's quite alright,' Tessa said, standing. 'We'll go and check in to our hotel. We just wanted to make sure you're okay before we clock off for the night.'

'My clients are very far from okay,' Stokes said. 'Your people have seen to that.'

Tessa smiled sweetly at the lawyer. 'It's been nice to meet you, Mr Stokes. I daresay we'll cross paths again.'

The team said their goodnights to the O'Farrells and headed out to the vehicles.

'He's a piece of work, isn't he?' Maggie said to Tessa.

'O'Mahoney mentioned to me that he used to defend some unsavoury sorts,' Danny said. 'Though he did add that he's moved to only representing charitable groups these past few years.'

'Even so, we'll have to check into Mr Stokes,' Tessa said. 'I'll bet there's a story there.'

11

Cork was a small city in the very southern end of Ireland, all narrow streets and small shops, quaint bistros and second-hand bookstores. The River Lee cut through its centre, and at night, the light of the stars, the beams of the headlights of the ever-present waterside traffic and the glow from shop windows were reflected in its glassy surface as it made its steady way towards the Celtic Sea.

Garda administration had booked Tessa and her team into rooms in the Hotel Isaacs on MacCurtain Street in Cork's bustling centre, and they went there after they left the O'Far-rells, taking up seats in the bar, which was long and narrow, furnished in dark wood with warm lighting. It was busy for a Wednesday night, the room alive with chatter and the clink of glasses.

They found a corner table, and while Danny went to get them drinks, Tessa picked up her phone and dialled the commissioner.

'How's it all going down there?' Dawn asked in her characteristically booming phone voice – the commissioner was from Antrim and brought the no-nonsense, down-to-earth attitude of the six counties of Northern Ireland into her police work.

'Hard to tell as yet,' Tessa admitted. 'The reason I'm calling is that Ellie, the wee girl who's allegedly dreaming about murders before they happen, is being transferred to juvie as we speak. The sergeant, O'Mahoney, wouldn't budge on it. I thought discretion was the better part of valour and let it slide, but we hoped you might be able to pull some strings and have her discharged into the team's care tomorrow. The O'Farrell parents have contacted their lawyer, but we both know how that'll go.'

'I'll see what I can do,' Dawn said. 'Did you see a care order? There would have to be one.' A care order was a legal document placing her in the care of the state.

'No, nor did I think asking to see one was a good idea based on the mood of the sarge,' Tessa admitted. 'He's not happy we're here, and our even suggesting his actions might not be for the best seemed to nark him considerably.'

'Willie O'Mahoney is a tough nut, that's for sure,' Dawn agreed. 'He cleaned up the gang problem in Limerick almost single-handedly. I don't think there's another individual on the force could have done it, myself included. He was facing threats to his own life and his family, witness intimidation on a colossal scale, leaks within his department... It was a horrendous position to be in, but he stuck with it until the job was done. Do you know he was kidnapped at one stage?'

'I never heard about that,' Tessa admitted.

'Might have been before your time,' Dawn mused. 'He was taken at gunpoint from outside his home; forced to get into a car with three gangsters. I think their intention was to take him to the countryside and shoot him, but it didn't quite work out that way.'

'What happened?'

'They were on the outskirts of the city when Willie elbowed

the man in the back with him in the throat, grabbed his gun and shot the two boys in the front of the car through the back of their seats. The car crashed, and he climbed out of it with a fractured collarbone and a concussion, but he was the only one who walked away.'

'You're telling me he's a hard man,' Tessa said.

'One of the hardest,' Dawn agreed. 'He was appointed to the Anglesea Street gig before I became commissioner, but I met him a few times when he was based in Limerick. He took no bullshit, but he gave none either. Willie places a great deal of weight on courtesy and honour. Good manners. If you can make him feel you're respecting his authority, you'll get a lot of good from him. If he sees you as an upstart who's come down from the big smoke to walk all over him, he's liable to take umbrage.'

'That ship might already have sailed,' Tessa said ruefully as Danny returned to the table, placing a large Bushmills Irish whiskey in front of her.

'Then get it back to port and play nice,' Dawn said and hung up.

'What'd she say?' Maggie asked.

'That we might be in trouble with Sergeant O'Mahoney,' Tessa said and downed her whiskey in one.

ELLIE O'FARRELL

She tried to be brave, but it was hard and getting harder.

When they brought her into the place for bad kids (she couldn't think of it any other way), she was taken to an office and one of the staff, a woman named Talulah, who was big and smiling and dark-skinned, told Ellie she'd been placed in care and that it was the job of St Killian's to work out what she needed while she was a ward of the state.

'I need to go home,' Ellie told her earnestly.

'And if that's so, the psychologists and social workers will know,' Talulah said gently. 'Now, are you currently taking any medication?'

Ellie was weighed, her height measured, her coat pockets turned out and her phone confiscated.

'A doctor will see you tomorrow just to give you a quick examination,' Talulah told her as they walked towards an elevator, 'but you seem healthy enough to me.'

They travelled to the fifth floor and walked along another long corridor, lined with doors, each of them numbered. As she moved past them, Ellie could see that each had a glass panel set at eye level, and many of these panels revealed sets of eyes, all peering at her.

'Don't be freaked out,' the big woman told her. 'They're always interested in new arrivals.'

Her room was number 545. It consisted of a bed, a dressing table and a small bedside locker. A plain blue nightdress was folded on top of the locker, and there was a toothbrush, toothpaste, a bar of soap and some roll-on deodorant sitting on a shelf above a small sink.

'If you'd like to call your parents and ask them to send you in some clothes, we can arrange that,' Talulah told her, 'but if you'd prefer not to, or you don't have any more, that's okay. We can get some for you.'

'I have lots more clothes,' Ellie said.

'That's nice. We'll talk about it again tomorrow.'

Ellie looked around the room. There was no radio, no television, and, more worryingly, no books.

'I need my Ojo,' she said.

'Your what?'

'My teddy. I can't sleep without him.'

'I told you, you can call your parents tomorrow and have your toy brought in. It'll have to be held for twenty-four hours though, while it's checked.'

Ellie was puzzled by this. 'Checked for what?'

'Drugs. Weapons. Phones. Other contraband.'

'My parents wouldn't try to smuggle in stuff like that,' the girl said, her voice breaking with unhappiness.

'You won't mind us looking then.'

'Can I have something to read then please?' Ellie asked. 'I like detective novels or true crime. Either will do.'

'It's time for lights out now, love,' the big woman told her. 'I'll schedule a stop at the library for you tomorrow, and you can find something nice to read.'

'I need something to read as I fall asleep,' Ellie sobbed. 'Even just a pen and paper. I like to do mathematical puzzles.'

Talulah's face took on a sterner cast. 'Missy, you're not at home now. There are rules we all have to follow. The library is closed. You can go tomorrow. For now, get washed, get into bed and go to sleep.'

'But I need a book! Please! That's not too much to ask, is it? A newspaper even...'

Talulah took a step towards her, and Ellie found herself retreating so the back of her legs were touching the edge of the narrow single bed.

'If you give me any trouble, we can talk about the sanctions we have here,' the big woman said, enunciating each word carefully. 'I don't think you want one of those before you've even spent five minutes in your room.'

Ellie closed her mouth quickly and just gazed at the woman, tears streaming down her face.

'I didn't think so. I'll leave you to get settled in. Breakfast is at 7.30 a.m. A bell will go off at 6.45 a.m. to give you time to get up, washed and dressed. I'll bring you and the others on this floor to the breakfast room, and you'll be taken to your assessment from there by Mildred, who's on the dayshift tomorrow.'

'Okay,' Ellie said.

'Goodnight then. I'll see you tomorrow evening.'

'I... I might have gone home by then,' Ellie said hopefully.

'You won't.'

And the woman walked out, locking the door behind her.

Ellie curled up on the narrow bed and wept.

12

The team sat quietly for a while, each in their private thoughts about this strange new case they'd been parachuted into.

Finally, Tessa, who'd been scratching Pavlov's back – the dog had lain his head on her leg – said, 'I heard on the grapevine you've had some good news, Maggie.'

Danny raised an eyebrow and looked at his friend. 'What's that then, Maggie?'

The newly officially appointed inspector flushed and shook her head. 'I don't know what to think about it,' she said. 'It doesn't feel right.'

'What doesn't?' Danny asked again, puzzled.

'Say hello to Detective Inspector Doolan.' Tessa grinned, reaching over and squeezing Maggie's arm.

'That's brilliant!' Danny said, throwing his arms around her.

'Is it?' Maggie asked. 'I mean, yeah, it's something I used to dream about, but I'd resigned myself to the fact it was never going to happen. I mean, I was lucky to be given the job of family liaison officer, and there was a hell of a lot of opposition when I was given *that* post.'

'That was all bullshit,' Tessa said. 'The guards are as prejudiced as any other organisation, and there was a small, vocal minority who couldn't believe someone who was a little bit outside of the norm could be effective in any role. Which is complete crap. Anyone who knows you and who's worked with you knows you're a huge support to any family lucky enough to get you. You and Pav of course.'

'Maggie, I've never known anyone who can do everything you do,' Danny said. 'You might be one of the smartest people I've ever met, you can kick ass with the best of them, and kids just open up to you. Back in Wexford, when that child was abducted right from under our noses, it was you who worked out where he was. Yeah, I climbed down to the cave and got him out, but *you* worked out he was there, which was as fine a piece of detective work as I've seen. You deserve this, Maggie.'

'Why don't I feel like I do then?'

'I got promoted too when I joined this team,' Danny said. 'And I had this exact same conversation with Tessa.'

Tessa laughed. 'And I told him to cop on and just be thankful too. Maggie, you're as deserving of the rank of detective inspector as anyone, and probably more deserving than many.'

'There'll be uproar when word gets out the crippled family liaison officer is now an inspector,' Maggie sighed. 'You know that as well as I do.'

'If anyone says so much as a word to me about it that isn't positive and supportive, they'll be getting a kick up the arse and a piece of my mind,' Tessa said.

'I'd like to echo that sentiment,' Danny agreed.

Maggie laughed and shook her head in resignation. 'You are two pig-headed, stubborn and wonderful friends,' she said.

'Agreed,' Tessa said. 'Now, can we talk about Ellie O'Farrell for a bit?'

'What are you thinking?' Maggie asked.

'How about we try to look at her case from a slightly different angle?'

'How do you mean?' Danny wanted to know.

'Well,' Tessa said, choosing her words carefully, 'Maggie, you've got a degree in criminology, don't you?'

'At undergraduate level, yes.'

'And, Danny, you read a lot of crime, both true and fiction.'

'I do.'

'Let's take Ellie at her word: assume she really has had these dreams and that she really hasn't heard anything about the murders from anywhere else.'

'That's a pretty big leap of faith,' Maggie said.

'Just roll with me for a bit,' Tessa said. 'Is there a precedent in anything either of you have read to suggest psychics have genuinely helped in criminal investigations? I mean, given evidence that helped crack cases in a practical sense with information that couldn't have come from anywhere else?'

Maggie took a sip of her beer and thought for a moment.

'I believe a psychic played a part in the Soham murders, in the UK,' she said. 'You know, the case where those two little girls were abducted and killed? A man named Dennis McKenzie gave the police an accurate description of Ian Huntley, the bloke who killed the girls, and Maxine Carr, his girlfriend, who gave him a false alibi. I read an article where the girls' parents praised him and said they were convinced he was the real deal.'

'Didn't he help out on a case here in Ireland too?' Danny interjected. 'The Richard Kelly case, in Limerick? Kelly's parents reached out to him, and McKenzie did a reading or whatever it is he does and from that provided the Gardai with the words "Brigid" and "Bodyke", and said a concrete slab was the murder weapon. As it turned out, the lad's body was found in Loch Brigid, near the townland of Bodyke, in County Clare, and his body was tied to a concrete slab to keep it weighted down.'

'That's pretty accurate,' Tessa said. 'And with him being English and not knowing the area, it adds some credence to his abilities.'

'He could also have just looked at a map, seen a good-sized lake within easy driving distance and had a guess,' Maggie added. 'Sorry, Tessa, but I just don't buy it.'

Tessa nodded – it was hard to argue with that logic.

'The CIA conducted a study about five years ago,' Danny said, 'looking at the reliability of psychics and how law enforcement felt about them. According to their findings, something like eighty per cent of the police officers interviewed said they'd obtained information they would otherwise not have acquired from psychic sources, and thirty per cent said they'd solved cases they would never have closed but for the help of a psychic.'

Tessa mulled that over. 'Thirty per cent isn't exactly high, but it's not exactly low either,' she said. 'Do we have any instances, though, of a psychic calling the police to say a murder is *going to be* committed? In most cases I've read about where psychics are involved, they're giving information about crimes that have *already been* perpetrated.'

'I've never come across it either,' Danny admitted.

Maggie shook her head too.

'So we're dealing with something unusual here, even within the realm of... of psychic phenomena,' Tessa mused. 'Which is already unusual to begin with!'

'I think the safest way to proceed is to assume Ellie believes what she's saying but that she's masking something traumatic,' Maggie said. 'The information she's providing is too detailed, even by the standards of successful psychics.'

'That bloke Danny just mentioned gave the name of the lake and the townland it was in!'

'Ellie knows times and methods of death,' Maggie said. 'She knows the locations of the murders and the occupations of the people who are killed. That's a lot. We're going far beyond just general geographical areas and vague physical descriptions.'

'If we take that as our working hypothesis,' Tessa said, continuing with her train of thought, 'it means that someone is planning these deaths *way* in advance. For Ellie to have heard about them, repressed that experience and then dreamed about it, she must have been aware of the details for, at a minimum, several days, but more likely we're talking weeks.'

'Maybe even longer,' Maggie said. 'Trauma dreams most often deal with stuff that's festered in the unconscious for quite a while.'

'So someone – or perhaps a group of someones – is plotting a cluster of murders and slowly implementing their schemes,' Tessa said. 'I know we've already decided our initial course of action will be to look at the three deaths, but what connects the deceased? We've got a hotelier, a fruit grower, a banker... other than being in business, I can't see a clear link.'

'It has to come down to money,' Maggie said. 'These things usually do.'

'So we follow the money trail?' Tessa said.

'I don't see another trail to follow just now,' Danny agreed. 'It's a place to start.'

'Let's hope the commish can get Ellie out of lock-up,' Maggie said. 'I'd like a chance to have a chat with her. If I can hear some more about these dreams, I might have a better sense of what we're dealing with.'

'Dawn can be pretty persuasive,' Tessa said. 'I reckon she'll win O'Mahoney over.'

'Here's hoping,' Maggie said, raising her glass.

They drank a toast to Dawn Wilson's success.

Little did they know how much she was going to need it.

THE WATCHER IN THE SHADOWS

He called the boss from an alleyway a hundred yards from the Hotel Isaacs. The boss had told him that's where the detectives would be booked in, and after Ellie O'Farrell had been driven away in the unit's van, he'd walked across town and positioned himself outside the hotel.

'They're in the bar.'

'You're sure?'

'Yeah. They went in and haven't come out. I watched the entryway – the one with the waterfall inside it – for two hours. They'll go to bed once the bar closes – they've all been drinking, so they aren't going to drive anywhere. I can come back tomorrow.'

'Be there early. I want to know where they go.'

'There's three of them. I can't watch them all.'

'I'll send more people. You can decide how you want to divide the work.'

'They've all got cars.'

'I know. I'll make sure you're equipped.'

'We'll need drivers.'

'You'll have them.'

'Boss, I'm scared. This doesn't seem like something we can handle. We're dealing with the police. This is... this is a whole other level.'

There was silence on the end of the phone. The Watcher stood flat against the wall of the alleyway, smelling stale urine and rubbish from some bins to his left.

'Boss, are you still there?'

'Have I ever steered you wrong before?'

'No, boss.'

'Have I always repaid your faith in me with success?'

'Yes, boss.'

'Have I ever broken a promise to you, or let you down?'

'No, boss.'

'Then don't let me hear you talk of fear. I know what I'm doing, and I'm telling you, return tomorrow, and you'll have support and vehicles and people to drive them. Just report back to me what you learn and that's all I need you to do. Am I clear?'

'Yes, boss. Completely clear.'

'Good. Now go home and sleep. Be there at six tomorrow. I'll compensate you for the unsociable hours.'

'Thanks, boss.'

And the call ended.

He walked back home slowly, keeping to the laneways and alleys to avoid drawing attention to himself.

No one heard him sneaking in through the bathroom window he'd left open for the express purpose of facilitating his ingress – not that he thought for a moment anyone in the house would be checking on him during his absence.

He left a note on the kitchen table to explain why he would be gone early.

He didn't think that would cause anyone concern either.

13

Tessa was woken from a dream by the sound of movement.

The detective wasn't like other people. Most folks took time to come fully awake, spending a minute or two in a state of grogginess, half in and half out of slumber, dreams still blending with reality in their heads. Even when they did come fully into wakefulness, if they were somewhere strange, it could take them a few seconds to recall where they were, their memories racing to catch up with their reality.

Tessa didn't experience any of that.

On the day of her eighteenth birthday, she'd joined the military, and her time in the army had conditioned her to be a light sleeper: the most delicate of sounds roused her into full, sharp awareness immediately. When her eyes snapped open, she was completely conscious of where she was and could summon a schematic of wherever she was sleeping to mind with little effort.

Just then, she knew she was in a single room, with the bed in the middle of the space. A window that looked down onto the street was to her right, in front of which was a small table and two chairs. To her left was a wall, beyond which was the room's small en-suite bathroom. There was a gap of about three feet between the foot of the bed and the wall, upon which hung a flat-screen television.

The room had blackout blinds so was currently in pitch darkness, save for a small sliver of light that spilled under the door.

She lay on the flat of her back, gazing at the ceiling, wondering what had snapped her into consciousness. Listening intently, she could hear the ambient sounds of the hotel – distant voices, footfalls, pipes hissing gently, lift bells pinging – and there was also the sound of the street: traffic, shouted voices in several languages, the wind blowing between tall buildings.

She waited for several seconds but heard nothing out of the ordinary, and was about to go back to sleep when it came again: a slight shuffling sound, as if someone was trying very hard to stand still but was having difficulty doing so. Tessa didn't stir. Every muscle in her body tensed, and she focused every fibre of her being on the intrusion, a sound that didn't belong in her room as she was supposed to be the only person in it.

Seconds ticked by. She felt a bead of sweat form at the hairline in the centre of her forehead. It hung there for a second before rolling down, coming to rest on her eyebrow. She wanted to reach up and brush it away, but that might warn the intruder – for she was now certain there was one – that she wasn't fully asleep, and she was going to need the element of surprise. The only way she was going to come out of this in one piece was to turn the tables on the interloper.

Tessa counted out a full minute in her head, and no further sound came. She was beginning to believe she'd imagined it, but then, almost imperceptibly, there was another slight shuffle, followed by a gentle intake of breath.

That was what she needed.

Her spatial awareness told her the person was standing in the far-right-hand corner of the room, placing them more or less opposite her right ear. Not an ideal position for her to launch an attack at, but good enough so she could put some distance between her and the individual.

Also, her gun and phone were on the bedside locker on the left-hand side of the bed, which gave her an advantage – if they were still there of course. The person had somehow got into her room without waking her, and if they were halfway trained, they'd have taken the weapon or at the very least its load.

Of course, they would also know Tessa Burns wasn't someone who was going to be an easy target and might have simply devoted their attention to getting into the room and secreting themselves. So perhaps, in the pitch darkness, they'd overlooked her Sig Sauer P226. She had to hope they had.

Preparing herself, she took in as much oxygen as she could and gathered a bunch of the duvet into her fist. After counting to three in her head, she threw the duvet off her and rolled to her left, relief washing over her as she felt the familiar weight of the Sig. Then she was on the floor, on her knees, using the bed as cover.

'I'm aiming a gun at you,' she said, her voice seeming too loud in the darkened room. 'I'm going to turn the light on, and you are not going to move. Am I clear?'

There wasn't so much as a sound in response.

'Okay. You can play the strong silent type if you wish. I'm an officer of an Garda Síochána, and unless you're a member of the hotel staff who's wandered in here by accident, I'd say you're in a shitload of trouble.'

She hit the light switch, and as she did so, the person who'd been standing in the corner of her room fired at her. The detonation of the gun sounded cataclysmic in the small room, and a chunk of wall a foot above Tessa's head exploded, blowing plaster dust and wood splinters onto the rumpled bedclothes.

Either he's a terrible shot or that wasn't meant to hit me,

Tessa thought as she threw herself to the floor, momentarily blinded by the sudden illumination of the room.

Footsteps thudded across the floor. Tessa had her gun trained on the corner of the bed and watched black-clad legs come around it at rapid speed. It would have been so easy to fire, hitting the person in the ankle and bringing them down, but this was a busy city hotel, and if one of her bullets went awry, it could injure or kill an innocent guest, next door or in the hallway or in the room above – the shot that had already been fired could have hurt someone. She was going to have to try and resolve this without any more shooting. Which wasn't going to be easy. She called (untruthfully), 'Freeze or I'll shoot!'

The figure stopped, levelling a Glock 17 at her. The person was of average height, possibly five feet eight or nine, and dressed in black boots, jeans and jacket, with a black woollen ski mask covering their face. Tessa was lying on her back, her Sig trained on the intruder's centre mass. They, in turn, had their Glock aimed at her.

'I will shoot you,' Tessa lied again through gritted teeth. 'Put the gun down and give yourself the chance to fight another day.'

The black-clad man, seemingly unconcerned with his situation, eyed her through the holes in the mask. She could see his eyes were brown.

'I don't believe you,' he said in a dry, accent-less voice.

They stared at each other wordlessly for what felt like forever.

'What do you want?' Tessa finally asked, breaking the stalemate. 'Why the hell are you here?'

'To deliver a message.'

'I'm all ears.'

'Very well. If you and your colleagues continue to investigate your current assignment, people will die. Your people. A solution will be delivered to you tomorrow that explains everything while exonerating the child and her family. Accept it as valid and take your team away.'

The man spoke without emotion or inflection. It seemed to Tessa as if everything he recited had been learned by rote. There was neither compassion nor interest in his words. He could have been talking to a wall.

'Who do you work for?' Tessa asked.

The man remained motionless. 'No one you know.'

'Try me,' Tessa growled.

'I'll give you something instead,' the man offered. 'Something you'll find most interesting. I'm going to raise my left hand but not to reach for a weapon. Don't shoot me.'

He reached up and pulled the mask off slowly, revealing first a smooth, red chin, then an unblemished cheek, its texture like modelling clay. A shapeless nose, a heavy brow devoid of any hair. A similarly bald head.

'We haven't met before, Detective Burns,' the Faceless Man said, 'but I know you've met several of my comrades.'

'Me and my friends have *killed* or *arrested* several of your comrades,' Tessa corrected him.

'We underestimated your abilities,' the Faceless Man said. 'We will not again. I didn't come here tonight to kill you, however. The shot was simply a warning. I could have taken your weapon when I entered the room. I left it with you as a mark of respect. One professional to another.'

'That was stupid.'

'No. It was courteous – I knew you wouldn't risk a gunfight in a room in a busy hotel. Heed my message, Detective Burns. There are matters afoot of which you have no comprehension. Tomorrow, a perfectly plausible solution to the mystery will be presented to you. Do not question it. The child will not be harmed, her family will not be interfered with, your people will not be hampered while you retreat.'

'Are you the one who tried to shoot Maggie?' Tessa asked grimly.

'That was also meant as a warning. My employers hoped it would stop you in your tracks, take your attention away from Ellie O'Farrell and her visions of murder.'

'Didn't work out too well, did it?' Tessa asked.

'Which is why we're currently having this conversation. It seemed more sensible to cut out the posturing and simply get to the point.'

'The answers you say we're going to get tomorrow – will they be genuine? If they put the O'Farrells in the clear, do they point the finger at someone else?'

'I don't know. I've simply been informed to tell you to accept them and leave Cork. To not look this gift horse in the mouth, so to speak.'

'I've never been very good at receiving gifts,' Tessa said. 'I always feel I don't deserve them.'

'Take this one in the spirit in which it is intended,' the man said. 'And now, I must take my leave.'

He reached for the door.

'Don't move another inch!' Tessa said, raising the Sig so it was pointed at the man's featureless visage.

'Please, Detective. Enough. We've had a pleasant conversation, but you need your sleep, and I must away. Goodnight.'

'I said don't move! I'll shoot you – just try me!'

The man made an expression that could have been a smile. Whether it was one or not, it was utterly terrifying.

'I'm going to call your bluff,' he said, and with uncanny speed opened the door and slipped out.

It took Tessa less than ten seconds to gain her feet and reach the door, but when she did, the intruder was already gone.

14

Two hours later, at 4 a.m., Tessa sat sipping tea with the head of the Isaacs' security team, a rat-like man with a droopy moustache named McCoy. They were in his office, peering at his laptop.

'This is the image array for our security cameras,' he told her, showing her a grid of black-and-white thumbnails. 'As you can see from these blacked-out squares, CCTV was down all across your floor. So I can't say for certain, but I'm fairly sure your intruder climbed a fire escape on the west wall of the hotel and entered through a security door, getting him onto your floor about ten yards from your room. We found that security door had been broken in, probably using a crowbar.'

'Alarm disabled, I take it?' Tessa asked.

'It was,' McCoy said. 'My boys caught it, but we thought there was an electrical fault and were trying to resolve it. No one assumed a killer was storming the castle.'

'I don't suppose it would have been anyone's first thought,' Tessa sighed. 'And how did he get into my room?'

'It looks like he cloned the key card for your door.'

'How would he do that?'

'My best guess is he or one of his associates hacked into the hotel computer system, identified which room you were in and had a card generated. It's not easy, but it can be done with the right know-how. I mean, it looks like this was a very professional operation.'

'You don't say. Did he get out the same way he came in?'

'Seems likely. There's a camera across the street from the hotel that we monitor, and we have someone dressed in black being picked up by a grey Transit van at 2.14 a.m.'

'You'll send those images to the boys at Anglesea Street?'

'Already done.'

'Thank you.'

'I've had another room organised for you,' McCoy said. 'Seeing as there's a bloody great hole in the wall of your old one.'

'I appreciate that.'

She said her goodnights to McCoy and went to find Danny, Maggie and Pav, who were in what had been her room. When she went in, she saw that Sergeant O'Mahoney had joined them.

'What the fucking hell is going on, Burns?' he asked as soon as he saw her.

'Thanks for coming to check on me, Sarge,' Tessa said, her expression neutral. 'I'm doing fine, thanks.'

'You've brought a war to my city, DI Burns. We do not have gangsters shooting out hotel-room walls in Cork! I had enough of that in Limerick, and now here you come with your inner-city problems, bringing maniacs travelling in your wake!'

'It's funny you should say that, Sarge, as the man who paid me a visit was only interested in talking about the O'Farrell case. Which is, I believe, very much a Cork problem.'

O'Mahoney gaped at her but lowered his eyes and said,

'Oh. Right, well, we'll have to see about that. Forensics are on their way. We'd best clear out so they can do their thing.'

'Sounds like a plan,' Tessa agreed.

15

Three hours later, all looking a bit worn and tired, they gathered in the Isaacs' breakfast room, which achieved the sense of a traditional, old-school hotel dining room with muted lighting and a lot of crystal. Tessa was just finishing her eggs Benedict when the commissioner rang.

'Fill me in on last night,' she said without preamble.

Tessa did.

'Boss, what's going on?' Tessa asked when she'd finished recounting what had happened. 'Why do we keep tripping over these Faceless Men? Is there something you're not telling me?'

'I should be offended at the question,' Dawn said.

'I have to ask,' Tessa said. 'It's becoming too frequent. Everywhere we go, these guys seem to either have been there before us, or they show up when we're there. It's starting to feel like we're being sent to specific locations so we'll have to butt heads with them.'

'I promise you, Tessa, the cases you're being given are chosen purely because they involve kids. That's the only criteria I'm using.'

'And no one else is involved in the selection process?'

'No one. The files come across my desk, and I make the decisions based on greatest need.' Dawn paused for a moment. 'You're aware, I presume, that there's no onus on me to enlighten you on how I assign your team's cases, DI Burns? You're overstepping, and then some.'

'I know, boss. But Maggie's been attacked, and now me. I have to consider the welfare of my team.'

'Granted. Consider it forgotten.'

'Thanks, boss. Any word on getting Ellie out of the pokey?'

'I'm afraid I've drawn a blank on getting the wee girl out of that remand unit,' Dawn said, sounding as tired as Tessa felt. 'O'Mahoney is convinced she knows more than she's saying and that some time in a juvenile detention centre will give her a chance to consider coming clean.'

'He's wrong,' Tessa said, horrified. 'This is a middle-class kid who's never been in trouble a day in her life. She'll be brutalised by the experience and will clam up even more.'

'The sarge doesn't see it that way,' Dawn said. 'Ellie has been placed under a full care order as per the Child Care Act.'

Tessa sighed. To have the Care Order overturned, an emergency case review would need to be called, and the findings of that review would have to be agreed by a majority or Ellie would remain in care.

'Can you get a review called within the next few days?' Tessa asked.

'I can try.'

'Do, please. If we can have the case looked at by the professionals involved, I'm sure they'll see how pointless Ellie being locked up is.'

'Don't be too sure,' Dawn cautioned. 'Willie O'Mahoney can be a persuasive man.'

'By which you mean a bully and a thug?' Tessa asked innocently.

'Something like that,' Dawn replied and hung up.

'That sounded like bad news,' Danny said, putting a piece of bacon into his mouth – he was three-quarters of the way through consuming the largest full Irish breakfast Tessa had ever seen.

'That's because it *was* bad news,' she said, setting her phone aside and picking up her mug of tea. 'Ellie is in the juvenile detention centre under a full care order, which means we can't just ask for her to be released. We have to go the official, legal route.'

Under Irish law, children could be taken into care through a number of different orders. The most common was a voluntary care order, by which a parent or guardian signed their child over into the care of the state. Voluntary care orders were designed to be reviewed at any time with a view to reunifying the family with as little trouble as possible. A full care order, which was usually a last resort, was far less common and much more difficult to have overturned as it was based on the premise that the child's parents were unfit, and a high threshold of proof was required to establish that was no longer the case.

'The legal route could take months,' Maggie said darkly.

'How the hell did O'Mahoney get her placed under an order like that so quickly?' Danny wondered. 'You need a lot of evidence to persuade a judge to grant a full care order.'

'He must have one who's a golfing buddy or a drinking pal,' Tessa said. 'And I'd guess he was planning this move from the moment the case came across his desk.'

'So what do we do now?' Maggie asked.

'Dawn is going to work on the judicial process, so we'll deal with the rest. Let's go out and let Ellie know we haven't forgotten about her, then each take one of the deaths she dreamed about, as planned, and see if we can learn anything new.'

'Shouldn't we check in with Sergeant O'Mahoney first?'

Danny suggested. 'Clarify what we're proposing to tackle so we're not stepping on his toes more than we already have?'

Tessa grimaced at the suggestion. 'We're not here to do busywork that doesn't impact directly on Ellie, and that's exactly what O'Mahoney will want us to do. I think we need to be clear: our task is to prove Ellie isn't guilty of anything more than wanting to be a good kid and save some lives. To do that, we're obviously going to need to find out who *has* been transmitting the information to her and how, but that's secondary. So no, I'm not going to be pushed around by O'Mahoney any further. We answer to the commissioner and no one else. Also, what with two of us having been attacked, I think it might be a good thing no one except we three know where we're going. We'll do what we usually do and file our reports to Dawn after the fact, but we won't be seeking permission from Willie O'Mahoney to do the job we've been sent to accomplish.'

'He'll be pissed,' Maggie said.

'Let him be,' Tessa replied. 'It'd be easier if he was prepared to cooperate, but his being oppositional won't stop us. It's not like people haven't been annoyed at us before, is it?'

'True dat,' Danny said, wiping egg yolk off his plate with some toast. 'I have a feeling there's some politics at play here. O'Mahoney is considered quite a big deal, isn't he? I mean, if he was responsible for clearing up the gangs in Limerick, he must have been tipped for moving up the ladder.'

Tessa thought about that for a moment. 'I suppose he was, yes. If you compare his situation to my own, I got this gig because I saved a kid from a well-known family who'd been kidnapped. In the grander scheme of things, O'Mahoney did something a lot more important than that.'

'So why is he still stuck in a police station in Cork, and at the rank of Sergeant?' Danny asked, taking another slice of toast and spreading butter thickly over its surface.

'Maybe he wants to be,' Maggie offered. 'Some cops love the nitty-gritty side of the job. Don't want to leave the streets.'

'You can still have the thrill of busting villains and move up the ladder,' Tessa said, following Danny's train of thought. 'He would have been an ideal appointment to the Organised Crime Unit in Harcourt Street.'

And being promoted to Ireland's equivalent of the FBI would surely have been something an egotistical man like Willie O'Mahoney would have relished.

'I wonder what stopped his progress,' Maggie said. 'And if that, whatever it is, might be what's behind his irritation at Dawn sending us to meddle in his affairs.'

'It's an interesting thought,' Tessa agreed, 'and we can return to it when the case is closed. For now, we're wasting time. Let's go and see Ellie. We can divvy up the jobs after that.'

'Right you be,' Danny said, consuming his slice of toast in two bites.

Tessa grinned. 'You sure you're quite full?'

'I was considering getting a bacon sandwich for the road,' Danny said, winking at Maggie, who giggled at his taking Tessa's bait.

Tessa laughed. 'Well, you wouldn't want your blood sugar dropping due to not having eaten in a full quarter of an hour,' she replied before leading them towards the car park.

ELLIE O'FARRELL

The breakfast room of the female wing of St Killian's was long, wide, high ceilinged, and smelled of semolina and bleach. A line of chafing dishes filled with various breakfast foods was at one end, and three women in hairnets and plastic aprons spooned out whichever items were requested. The rest of the room was taken up with tables and chairs.

Ellie had assumed staff would patrol to make sure everything remained peaceful, but instead Talulah and four other female workers sat at a table near the door and chatted animatedly while they had their own breakfasts.

I've seen too many prison movies, *Ellie thought.* Maybe this place isn't going to be as scary as I thought.

She got some porridge, a strawberry yoghurt and an apple juice and sat at a table on her own, watching the other girls and wishing she was somewhere – anywhere – else. She always loved breakfast at home: her mammy always made something different – today it might be blueberry pancakes, tomorrow banana muffins with chocolate sauce, the next day French toast with vegan bacon slices. There would be nice music on the stereo, the kitchen always smelled wonderful and Ellie would sit, Ojo propped up on the table beside her, munching contentedly and sipping the orange juice her mammy had just squeezed for her.

Her current situation was very different.

The room looked like it could hold about two hundred hungry breakfasters, but it was half empty that morning, which suited Ellie down to the ground, as it meant she wasn't forced to mix. All the other girls seemed to know one another, or at least be on speaking terms. There was a buzz of chatter and the sound of plastic spoons scraping plastic bowls, the occasional cackle of laughter, a shouted hello or holler of insult.

No one paid her any attention until the bell for the end of the meal went off and the girls were lining up to return their plastic crockery. Ellie was at the end of the line, having waited for everyone else to move first, not wanting to get caught in the throng. As she placed her meal things on a high, tiered trolley, a big-boned girl who was in front of her, a splash of freckles across her broad face, her hair cut almost in a crew cut, said, 'What's your name?'

'Um... Ellie. I'm Ellie.'

'Ellie, I'm Bridie.'

'It's nice to meet you, Bridie.'

The bigger girl smiled, and it wasn't an altogether pleasant sight.

'You're the new rich kid, aren't you?' Bridie asked.

'I'm not rich,' Ellie said.

'I heard you were.'

'I'm really not.'

Bridie sighed impatiently. 'I think you're full of shit. If you want to get out of here with all your fingers and toes, ask your folks to leave you money for concessions. I'll give you a list at lunch of the stuff I want.'

Ellie blinked. 'I don't know what you're talking about,' she said. 'I'm not going to be in here for long anyway.'

The girl scowled and caught her by the arm so tightly, Ellie squealed, in spite of herself.

'Shut up and listen! You're not going home. Everyone thinks they are, but they aren't. You're no different. Whatever shit you pulled to get you in here, you'll be here until they shift you on to somewhere else. Now, I can make it so you have an easy time and everyone leaves you alone. Or I can make it very fucking hard for you. You can decide which you want; suits me either way. If you want things easy, make sure I get a steady supply of chocolate and smokes. If you want it hard, I'll have the fun of messing up that cute face of yours.'

And with that the bigger girl gave her arm one more squeeze and hurried off to catch up with her friends.

Ellie thought she was going to be sick.

THE WATCHER IN THE SHADOWS

The boss had been as good as his word.

The Watcher arrived outside the Hotel Isaacs at ten minutes before six to find two others already there: a male, slightly younger than himself, making him probably twenty-one or twenty-two years old, who was huddled in a sleeping bag in a doorway on the same side of the street as the hotel; and a similarly aged female, bundled up in a heavy bubble coat across the street adjacent to the hotel's entrance. She had an eco-scooter with her, one of the ones that could be folded up and stowed on your back.

The two spotted him as he arrived, but none of them acknowledged any of the others. Plausible deniability was the order of the day, and they all knew it.

He took up position in the mouth of the alley where he'd called his boss the night before, leaned against the wall and waited. He'd long ago learned the art of remaining totally still and letting his mind go blank. He'd spent most of his childhood in situations where not being noticed was highly desirable, and the experience had forced him to become an expert at blending in. He saw it as being like a computer going into sleep mode; he simply let his consciousness wind down, and then it was just his body doing what it needed to do to remain alive.

He lungs inflated, his heart beat, his skin was aware of the coldness of the early morning, but those were just observations. If thoughts flitted across his mind, he let them do just that – drift into his mind's eye then float away again. They were never anything he needed to devote attention to anyway.

And that was, in itself, a joy. It was freeing. Ever since the boss had come into his life, he'd learned that the things that had preoccupied him for so long – had made him anxious or miserable or brought nightmarish dreams to disturb his sleep – need not hold power over him anymore.

'Release yourself,' the boss had told him during one of their talks. 'I can't do it for you; you need to give yourself permission to do it. But I think you deserve it. You are entitled to be at peace.'

Those words resonated with him. They broke his heart actually: You are entitled to be at peace. It was so simple, but it had never occurred to him before. He had, in fact, resigned himself to the fact that he was never going to know what it was like to relax.

Now, he could access that peace any time he wanted. All he had to do was switch off and let it come.

The morning wore on, and then there were the three detectives and their mutt, coming out of the entrance to the hotel. He lowered his eyes and stepped backwards so he was inside the alley. Moments ticked by, and then he saw them go past on their way to the yard the Isaacs used as a guest car park, a five-minute walk from the hotel proper up a steep hill. He gave them ninety seconds then ducked out of the alley as the other two drew level with him.

'I'll take the woman in the chair,' the female said.

'I'll take the big bastard,' the male said.

The Watcher nodded. That left him the tough-looking woman in the parka.

They got to the car park just as that same woman – she

seemed to be the leader of the group – was pulling out in her old car. As she turned onto the street, a black Lexus that was parked across the road flashed its lights. The Watcher ran to it and got into the back.

A thin woman, probably in her early thirties, was behind the wheel.

'The boss says hello,' she said.

The Watcher grinned, sat back and prepared to enjoy the drive.

16

St Killian's Juvenile Detention Centre was situated on the N40, just off the Dunkettle Interchange, a major road junction that facilitated traffic travelling east to west (or vice versa) across Cork city to avoid congestion on the notorious Dunkettle roundabout.

A large complex that catered for young offenders of both genders across two separate units, St Killian's was an assessment centre, meaning residents were placed there while they were given various psychological tests to establish how best to reha-bilitate them and hopefully to ascertain where they should be placed for said rehabilitation.

The team parked their vehicles out front of the main recep-tion building, which was long and single-storeyed. All guests had to sign in here on arrival, and it was also where the facility's administration was done. The rest of St Killian's infrastructure was made up of two tall buildings that looked very like apart-ment blocks. The residents slept in these, received therapy and were interviewed for their assessments. Out front was a wide lawn, to the rear a sports fields and an outdoor gym, and the whole complex was enclosed by a high metal fence.

'This place doesn't look so bad,' Danny said as they approached the front door.

'Don't let the polished surface fool you,' Tessa said. 'I've been in units like this, and they're little more than prisons for kids. The staff generally have good intentions, but none of the youngsters who are here right now will still be here in five weeks' time. They'll all have been moved to other places that are far, far worse. This is a processing plant, and the kids know it. Abandon hope all ye who enter here.'

'Well at least Ellie won't stand out by being new,' Maggie said.

'She'll still stand out,' Tessa said. 'She'll stick out like a sore thumb. The other kids will all be from local authority neighbourhoods, many will have gang affiliations and the majority will have been here before. They'll peg her right away as a fish out of water. She's going to need her wits about her if she's not going to have a very hard time.'

'I know what that's like,' Maggie said.

During her childhood Maggie had experienced a lot of bullying due to having a disability, and it was in a unit just like St Killian's that Maggie had first met Tessa, who'd come to her aid when bullying from a group of much older girls had turned physical.

Tessa had made sure the girls never bothered Maggie again.

'We need to get her out of here as quickly as possible then,' Danny observed.

'It's going to take a few days at best,' Tessa said. 'Ellie's going to have to tough it out until then.'

The reception area was bright and airy. A slim woman sporting purple hair and a figure-hugging black dress sat behind a desk wearing a headset complete with microphone. Three couches, upholstered in leather, were arranged in front of the desk, and the walls behind it were decorated with abstract paintings, all red and green squares and triangles, to match the colours of the chequered carpet.

Tessa held out her identification. 'I'm DI Tessa Burns. This is DS Danny Murphy and DI Maggie Doolan. And that's Pavlov.'

The woman stood and peered over the counter to look at the terrier mix, who wagged his tail in hello.

'I don't think we allow dogs in here,' she said in a dense Cork accent.

'He's a service animal,' Maggie said, which was her routine response when people tried to deny Pav access.

'What services does he provide?' the woman asked, raising an eyebrow.

'Oh, too many to list,' Maggie said, smiling beatifically, although Tessa knew her friend was far from pleased by the exchange and the lack of tolerance behind it.

'Fair enough. What do you want?'

'We'd like to see Ellie O'Farrell. She was brought in last night.'

'Residents aren't permitted visitors within their first twenty-four hours,' the purple-haired gatekeeper intoned, her eyes on the screen of her laptop. 'Ms O'Farrell will be underdoing assessment today, and that doesn't allow any time for chatting.'

It was Tessa's turn to smile now. 'We haven't come to chat, Ms...?'

'Cassidy,' the woman said. 'Marla Cassidy.'

'We are a special task force assembled by the police commissioner to investigate crimes involving children. Ellie is involved in one of those cases. We would like to see her please.'

'That won't be possible today.'

'You're refusing the request of a police detective in the execution of her duty?'

'I am. I don't answer to you. Once the kids come here, your duty is temporarily curtailed. They're in the system, and it's up to us to work out what happens next. If you come back tomorrow, you can see Ellie O'Farrell. In the meantime, I'm sure you have other things to do.'

Tessa looked at Danny, who looked at Maggie.

'This is a murder investigation,' Tessa said, a bit nonplussed, despite herself. 'Ellie is a key witness.'

'That's above my pay grade,' Marla Cassidy said. 'All I know is that she's here. And that means we have a job to do, and no one, not even our courageous guardians of the peace, are going to stop us doing it.'

Tessa felt anger beginning to rise and fought to hold it in check. 'I could just go ahead in and see her.'

Marla grinned from ear to ear at that. 'Detective, you go right ahead. I'll call security, and we can see how that goes. You look like you can handle yourself, and your associate here is a sizable lad.' Her gaze lingered on Maggie. 'I'd say there's more to you than meets the eye too. But this is a big compound, and even unimpeded, it'd take you some time to track your girl down, particularly seeing as we keep all the doors locked. Our team are used to restraining rough cases, and while I don't doubt you'd hold your own for a while, I can promise, we've got you on numbers. D'you think you're the first person to threaten to storm the place?' She laughed. 'Take a number and get in line.'

Tessa's frustration was building, and to her surprise, as if mirroring her inner turmoil, Pavlov stood up in Maggie's lap and began to growl. The little dog looked at his owner and barked once, a high-pitched yip, then gazed towards the front door before looking back at Maggie.

'Your service dog is losing the run of himself,' Marla said. 'I thought they were much better trained than that.'

'Ssshh, Pav,' Maggie said, looking perplexed at his unusual behaviour.

The dog sat back down on her knee, but his hackles were

still up. He kept casting an eye at the door then looking up at Maggie as if he wanted her to do something.

'Could you do me one favour?' Tessa asked, ignoring Pav's uncharacteristic conduct and focusing instead on the smirking woman in front of her.

'You can ask.'

'Could you get one of the staff dealing with Ellie to give me a call?' She reached into the pocket of her parka jacket and passed a card with her name, rank and contact details on it over to Marla.

'I'll pass your request on,' the receptionist said.

'Thank you.'

'You're very welcome. Have a nice day now.'

And the purple-haired woman returned to her computer screen.

Their visit, it seemed, was over.

THE WATCHER IN THE SHADOWS

The Lexus idled outside St Killian's, and the Watcher felt a surge of nausea, regret and fear, which almost overwhelmed him. It took every ounce of resolve he had to perform his mental trick and force the negative emotions away.

He knew this place all too well. Had spent time here at various points in his younger days. His experiences had been... less than pleasant, and he'd come to dread the sight of the unit. Even after completing the meditation, he had to fight the urge to tell the thin woman to keep driving.

'Are you just going to sit there?' she asked him after they'd been parked for four full minutes.

'Sorry?' he said, unsure what she meant.

'Hadn't you better go and see what they're up to in there?'

He considered the suggestion. 'Yeah. Yeah, I suppose I should.'

'Go on then. If I'm not here when you get out, don't panic. I'm parked on a double yellow, and I might have to circle the block if a copper shows up.'

'Okay. I'll wait for you.'

He got out and passed through the gates without looking

back. Once inside, he cut to the left across the lawn, keeping low, the small bushes and shrubs perfect cover for someone with his slim build and diminutive height.

It took him a couple of minutes to get as far as the car park in front of the reception building, and he spied the detectives' three vehicles immediately. He sidled up behind the big dark-haired copper's Golf GTI and made a low run towards the door, coming to a stop just beside it. Luckily it was open, so he could hear the conversation going on inside. It was clear the subjects of his surveillance weren't going to be allowed to see the girl.

He peered around the door frame for a second, just to get a sense of the group from their body language, as the boss often asked about stuff like that, and to his horror saw the little dog was gazing right at him over the disabled copper's shoulder. He pulled back in immediately, but as he did so, he heard the animal give a high-pitched bark, and with that he threw caution to the wind and sprinted back across the car park, not bothering with the cover of the scrawny bushes this time.

Luckily, the woman in the Lexus was there when he tore out the gate.

'Go up the road and park among those cars,' he said.

'Did they make you?'

'I don't know. That fucking dog smelled me, and I didn't wait to see if the rest of them caught on.'

'They have a dog?'

'A terrier kind of thing.'

The woman signalled and pulled into the road.

'That's no good for close-up work,' she said. 'I'd advise the boss to change his tactics, if I was you.'

'Well, you're not me,' the Watcher said.

'Stay downwind then.'

The Watcher knew this was good advice but was too proud to acknowledge the driver was right.

'Just move up the road a bit,' he said. 'I fuckin' hate bein' so close to this place.'

The driver complied without further comment.

17

The Burns Unit walked back out to their cars in silence.

When they reached Tessa's ancient Ford Capri, she leaned against it, her head lowered. 'Fuck!' she said, almost to herself. 'Fuck, fuck, fuck!'

Danny and Maggie remained behind her, knowing there was no point in saying anything until their friend's annoyance had passed.

Tessa remained as she was, her back to her friends as she battled her frustration, then spun to face Danny, Maggie and Pav.

'Why are we hitting brick walls everywhere we turn in this case? Can either of you tell me that?'

'We've dealt with worse,' Maggie said. 'It's tedious, but what I'm most concerned about right now is getting word to Ellie that she hasn't been abandoned.'

'Any ideas as to how we can do that?'

'Hopefully our purple-haired St Peter will pass your card along and we can appeal to the better nature of whoever deigns to call you.'

'Or one of us could hang about in the hope Ellie comes out,'

Danny said. 'We could probably have a quick talk with her before we get evicted.'

'She most likely won't be coming out if she's booked into assessment stuff all day,' Tessa said.

'Still, we can't be sure of that. Might be worth a go.'

'Danny Murphy, you're not exactly difficult to spot,' Tessa said, unable to hide a smile at the thought of her friend valiantly trying to hide about St Killian's lawns. 'Where are you going to secret all six feet four inches of yourself while you wait for our girl to emerge?'

Danny cast about, looking for an alcove or a bush in which he might hide.

'I dunno,' he said after a few moments of fruitless searching. 'Unfortunately, I left my invisibility cloak back in Dublin.'

That broke the tension, and they all laughed.

'Right, let's stop weeping and wailing and see what we actually *can* do,' Tessa said.

'I've got the details of the three murders here,' Maggie said, tapping some keys on her laptop.

'Excellent. One was on a boat, wasn't it?' Tessa asked. 'I could get Jim to make the introductions I need so I can get a look at the vessel and access the witnesses.'

'Sounds like a plan,' Maggie said. 'The deceased person you're referring to was one Dave Merrill, who ran a fruit company that produces and sells preserves, juices, smoothies and the like. He allegedly fell off his boat in the waters near Cape Clear, just off Schull, in West Cork.'

'I'll call Jim and see if he can help us out,' Tessa said.

'So that leaves us the car accident and the knife death,' Maggie said.

'Tell me about the motor collision,' Danny said.

'Miles McGuinness, a bank manager,' Maggie read from her screen. 'He'd just picked up an Indian takeaway and was crossing the road on the way back to his car when a vehicle hit him. Eyewitnesses say it was a grey saloon, possibly a BMW. At any rate, it kept going.'

'Where did this happen?' Danny asked.

'The village of Castlemartyr, about half an hour on the Waterford side of Cork.'

Danny nodded. 'I'll cover that one. Have a chat to the witnesses. See if anything has been missed.'

'Me and Pav'll take the murder of Dominic Wilde the hotelier then,' Maggie said. 'Had his throat cut while working late in his home office. No one saw anything that might help us, apparently.'

'Were there other people in the house?' Tessa asked.

'No, just him. He was discovered by his wife, who was out visiting a friend. He has a son who's away at college in Dublin.'

'And can we be sure his wife didn't do it?'

'Times don't match up. She was out until late – the friend confirms it. Police were on the scene within minutes of her calling it in, and the blood was already well dried up when they arrived.'

Tessa nodded. 'Fair enough. Okay, we've all got our jobs. Let's meet back up at the station this afternoon and compare notes.'

They were moving towards their respective cars when someone called from the direction of the reception building. 'Detective Inspector Burns?'

A tall, slim man was walking briskly towards them across the parking area. He was dressed in a blue suit which, Tessa saw as he got closer, had thin red pinstripes, and he was carrying a leather briefcase. His hair was dark and slicked back on his domed head, and he sported a neatly cropped beard which was greying about the chin.

'DI Burns, my name is Dr Laurence Cleary. I'm Ellie O'Farrell's therapist. I was given your card by one of the staff, and she intimated you'd just left, so I hoped I might catch you and your colleagues before you drove away.'

Tessa shook the man's hand, and introduced Danny, Maggie and Pavlov.

'Are you part of Sergeant O'Mahoney's team,' the therapist asked, 'because if you are, I wish to express my dissatisfaction with how Ellie's reporting of her premonitions has been handled.'

'Dr Cleary, we work directly for the police commissioner,' Tessa said, 'and we're also very concerned about Ellie's welfare. She doesn't belong in a place like this. Is there any way you can speed things towards having her released under the recognisance of her family?'

'I've already made that recommendation,' Cleary said. 'Ellie is in a very delicate frame of mind. These... dreams she's been having have drained her on a psychic level, and I fear that being here, where she understandably feels very unsafe, is only exacerbating her condition.'

'Can you fix it so we can see her today?' Maggie asked.

'I'm afraid not. The procedures here are very strict – St Killian's runs along the same procedural lines as an adult prison, except with young offenders. They won't budge from their schedules or routines, and the law protects that right.'

Tessa nodded. She was aware of the separation of authority between the police and the prison system in Ireland, but this was the first time she'd encountered such resistance. Prison staff usually saw themselves as part of the same justice family as the Gardai and were happy to cooperate, despite their technically being employed by different departments.

'Have you seen Ellie today?' she asked the therapist.

'I work here on a pro bono basis, overseeing some of the assessments,' Cleary said, 'so yes, I spoke with her only a few moments ago.'

'How's she holding up?'

'As well as can be expected. She was tearful and shared with me that she's very frightened.'

'Poor kid,' Tessa said, feeling genuinely upset herself. 'Doctor, can you give us your sense of what's happening with Ellie and these dreams? Where do you believe she's picking up the details of the deaths she's dreaming about?'

'That's not as simple a question as you'd think,' Cleary said.

'Isn't it?' Tessa asked. 'I would have thought—'

'Ellie is at a very complex stage developmentally,' the psychiatrist said, leaning against Tessa's Capri. 'She's opening up physically, intellectually, emotionally, spiritually. Her mind is like an antenna taking in and processing signals from every direction. And she isn't even aware she's receiving many of these transmissions.'

'You're losing me, Doctor,' Tessa said.

'Okay, let me give you an example. Have you ever heard of a man named Kim Peek?'

Tessa shook her head before looking at Danny and Maggie.

'The name rings a bell,' Maggie said. 'Isn't that the person the movie *Rain Man* is based on?'

'Precisely,' Cleary said. 'Kim Peek was born with severe neurological damage. I don't believe he was autistic, as the film portrayed, but he's generally classified as an "autistic savant", someone who tests as having a very low average IQ in many areas – Mr Peek couldn't dress himself without assistance, for example – yet he could do all sorts of things most of us could never accomplish.'

'What kinds of things?' Danny wanted to know.

'He'd read and memorised the entire Bible and the complete works of Shakespeare by the time he was seven years old. He could do mind-boggling feats of mental arithmetic, adding or multiplying huge numbers accurately. His parents had to stop taking him to musical concerts, because he knew the majority of classical symphonies by heart and could differentiate what parts each instrument in the orchestra was playing. He would become loudly, vocally upset if any of the musicians made a mistake.'

Tessa shrugged. 'That's very interesting, Doctor, but what does it have to do with Ellie?'

'One of the lesser-commented-upon skills that Kim Peek had was his ability to forecast the weather with pinpoint accuracy. He could tell you what the weather in his hometown in Utah would be like weeks in advance. His forecasts were considerably better than those of the local news stations, and his neighbours came to rely on his predictions rather than what they heard on the TV or radio.'

'You're saying he was psychic, but in a meteorological sense?' Danny asked, looking confused.

'Not at all. Kim Peek made his predictions based on what he saw around him. Many people on the autistic spectrum have what's called "weather salience", an exaggerated interest and fascination with weather and atmospheric conditions, a heightened awareness of everything from humidity, to temperature fluctuations, to an obsession with cloud formations. Kim Peek was sensitive to all these things, but unlike most autistic individuals, he had also read multiple advanced texts on meteorology and combined his weather salience with an understanding of how weather is predicted. Of course, meteorological services use satellites, rain gauges, windspeed detectors, scientific barometers, all sorts of technological equipment to aid them – Kim Peek had none of these things, yet just by using his physical senses and that amazing mind of his, his predictions turned out to be vastly more accurate than those of the professionals.'

'Are you suggesting Ellie may be doing something like this, but instead of the weather, she's predicting murders?' Tessa asked.

'I am. The three men who were killed were all featured in the news before their deaths. The stories had nothing to do with crime; they were all about these men's professional accomplishments. But there have also, of late, been a number of investigative pieces published in the local papers linking a number of unnamed businesses in the area *to* criminality. Ellie is a voracious reader of newspapers, magazines and online news sites. She's also a devotee of true-crime podcasts and documentaries and has spoken to me about a desire to create a YouTube channel focusing on the criminal history of Cork.'

Tessa considered this information. 'Is Ellie on the autistic spectrum? I'm not an expert, but from what I saw of her when we spoke last night, she didn't seem to be. She made eye contact, responded to social cues, exhibited a range of facial expressions to express her emotions...'

'No, I'm not suggesting Ellie is autistic,' Cleary said. 'As I said earlier, Kim Peek wasn't – he had something called FG syndrome, a rare chromosomal disorder. But you see, what's interesting is that his having FG syndrome doesn't explain his very special gifts. Most people who present with FG are simply categorised as having physical and intellectual challenges. Science still doesn't understand Kim Peek's abilities.'

'You think Ellie is just... unusually gifted?' Tessa said.

'I do. I think that, because of her very special interests and the focus she applies to them, her mind is joining dots and forming deductions the rest of us would never be capable of making. I asked her father about this once, and he told me there's an online game he plays, something involving a sixty-four-character string of numbers and letters. The game involves you being given a series of conditions and rules, and you have to rearrange the numbers and letters to fit those rules. It is, as you would imagine, incredibly difficult, and most players take hours or even days to solve a single problem. Ellie, apparently, can solve one in seconds. She does it almost on instinct.'

'That's impressive,' Maggie said.

'Very. Do you know, I had her do an IQ test some time ago,

and she scored in the top one per cent of the population? Ellie is, to apply an overused term, a genius. What she's experiencing is, in my opinion, simply an expression of that.'

Danny scratched his head. 'I dunno, Doc. It's a leap. If what you're saying is true, Ellie O'Farrell is a modern-day Sherlock Holmes, except she's a real person rather than a fictional character.'

'I'm acutely aware of that, DI Murphy. I did, after all, use the term "genius" to describe her.'

'Thanks for your time, Doctor,' Tessa said. 'Would it be alright if we get in contact to ask you some more questions once we've had time to investigate the deaths a bit further?'

'Yes, of course,' Cleary said, shaking each of them by the hand once more and patting Pavlov on the head. 'I'm limited, on grounds of confidentiality, in what I can tell you about my sessions with Ellie, but she gave me permission to share my theory on her dreams with you.'

'Does she agree with your assessment of them?' Maggie asked.

Cleary smiled sadly. 'I'm afraid she doesn't,' he said. 'Ellie is convinced her dreams are, for want of a better word, paranormal in nature.'

'Paranormal?' Tessa asked.

'Ellie believes she's having visions,' Cleary said. 'She's of the opinion that she's either psychic or in touch with a higher intelligence.'

'And you've tried to disabuse her of that fact?' Maggie asked.

'Oh, I most certainly have. But she's determined.'

Tessa gave the psychiatrist a hard look. 'We're agreed she's a smart girl – gifted in fact,' she said. 'So why, then, would she choose to believe she has some special powers rather than that she's using advanced deductive reasoning? It doesn't make a lot of sense.'

'Perhaps because she's afraid of what her real abilities mean,' Cleary said. 'If she has the capacity to predict crimes before they're committed, if she can foil the plans and intentions of dangerous men – well, that makes her a real threat to them.'

'Which puts her and her family at risk,' Danny said.

'I believe that's what she's living in dread of,' Cleary agreed. 'Her innate sense of morality brought her to the police station, but her fears forced her to temper the story with a hint of unbelievability. And that has placed her parents in the firing line and resulted in her being detained. Her concerns proved to be wholly accurate.'

'Well, it's up to us to ensure that neither she nor her parents are placed in risk, isn't it?' Maggie said. 'And to get her out of this place.'

'I hope we won't be too late,' Tessa said, looking at the towering blocks that made up the residents' quarters of St Killian's. 'If someone wanted to make a run at her, this would be the ideal place.'

'That's exactly what I was thinking,' Dr Cleary said gravely.

18

They left Dr Cleary and St Killian's and headed towards the three respective locations of the murders Ellie had foreseen.

Tessa called Jim Sheils as she drove west out of the city towards Schull.

'How's it going down there?' he asked after they'd said their hellos.

'Not so well, to be honest,' Tessa told him. 'We're meeting quite a bit of resistance from the local guards and juvenile justice.'

'I'm sure you'll find a way around it,' Jim said. 'Lord knows, I didn't give you the best welcome when you arrived on my turf.'

Tessa laughed. She and Jim had started out as adversaries but had soon warmed to one another, each impressed by the other's dedication to the job and skills as a law enforcement professional. They'd also shared a physical attraction. 'That's true. My charm won you over in the end, didn't it?'

'That and your stubborn refusal to back down.'

'I am a woman with many attractive qualities,' Tessa said, grinning to herself as she drove. 'But I've a favour to ask.'

'Oh. And here was me thinking you'd called because you missed me.'

'I do. I miss having a captain in the coastguard close at hand to help me out on cases.'

'You cut me, Tessa. You cut me deep.'

'Can I send you the details of a death that occurred here a couple of weeks ago? I need to talk to some of the officers who investigated it, as well as any witnesses they've identified.'

'I can make some calls on your behalf.'

'I'd appreciate it.'

'Any idea when you're coming home?'

'To Dublin?' she asked, her tone purposely obtuse.

'You know that's not what I mean. When are you coming back to Wexford?'

Tessa laughed. 'I have no clue. So far, we've achieved a grand total of nothing, so it's hard to gauge how quickly we're likely to turn this one around. Or if we will at all.'

'I have total faith in you.'

'I wish I shared your confidence. Sending you the details of that marine death now.'

She tapped her phone, which was set into a cradle on her dashboard.

'Yeah, got it. I'll see what I can do at this end.'

'Do it quickly – I'm en route to Schull as we speak.'

'No worries. It's not as if I have anything better to do.'

'Sure, don't I know that? Thanks, Jim. I'll try to call later.'

'It was nice hearing from you.'

Tessa smiled. Jim was much better at being romantic than she was, and she liked that he made the effort. It was something she knew she was going to have to work harder at. If she was honest with herself, she found expressing that side of her personality difficult. It didn't come naturally, and when she tried to picture herself making a romantic gesture, she found the mental image embarrassing.

'It's good to hear your voice too,' she said, cringing a little.

They paused, and Tessa tried to push the discomfort aside.

'Okay,' he said after a few long seconds had passed, 'I'd best get calling the West Cork coastguard's office, hadn't I?'

'Please.'

'Talk later, Tessa.'

'We will, Jim.'

And they hung up.

ELLIE O'FARRELL

After breakfast, there was two hours of assessments.

Her therapist, Dr Cleary, came to see her, and he assured her he'd do his best to get her home, which was comforting, but at the same time, he seemed to be part of the assessment process and asked her questions about feelings of aggression, and if she'd ever committed a crime or considered committing one, and if she had violent fantasies and other things that made her wonder if the year she'd spent with him in therapy meant anything. Did he know her at all?

But she supposed it was better to know someone on the inside. Even if they seemed to be playing both ends of the field.

After Dr Cleary, a woman in a trouser suit got her to do what seemed for all the world to be an IQ test, where she had to read a piece of text and answer questions on it and then construct a 3D jigsaw puzzle. She completed both tests in two minutes and thirty-five seconds. The woman looked surprised.

At ten thirty, she was told she could go out to the playing field to stretch her legs, and she gladly did so. She was beginning to find the building, with its stuffy rooms and long, echoing corri-

dors claustrophobic. When she got to the field, a group of girls were playing what looked to be a cross between rugby and American football, which seemed to Ellie to be just an excuse to beat the hell out of one another.

The staff member on duty was buried in their phone and didn't seem to care, so Ellie just dug her hands into the pockets of her coat, turned up her collar and trudged around the perimeter of the field. Some oystercatchers, big black-and-white birds with long orange bills, were digging for worms and bugs at the far end of the pitch, and she headed for those, finding the act of bird-watching comforting and familiar in this strange and frightening environment.

She'd been watching the birds intently, sitting on the grass with her legs stretched out in front of her for about five minutes when she heard a voice from behind her.

'Eleanor O'Farrell?'

She turned to see a girl who she at first thought was seventeen or eighteen, but when Ellie looked closer she could tell was several years older than that, probably early-to-mid-twenties – it was in her eyes. The stranger was slender and tall with dishwater-blonde hair piled in a messy bun on the top of her head and was swathed in a long pink puffer jacket.

'Yes, I'm Ellie.'

'I've a message for ya.'

Ellie didn't say anything, just looked up at the girl expectantly.

'If you don't want to see your mam and dad hurt bad, tell the coppers you got the news about them murders from here.'

The girl handed her a sheet of paper, upon which was written:

http://wearemurderorg77nkq76byazcldy2hlmov-
fu2epvl5ankdibsot4csyd.onion/

'What is this?' Ellie asked, her voice shaking.

'All you need to know is that it's a dark web site. When the pigs go lookin', they'll find all the details you gave and a few for some murders that won't happen at all. The ones you told 'em about will be dated so it looks like they were put there before the deaths happened, and the others will have them chasin' their tails for a good while, long enough for my employers to get on with their business without anyone messin' about in it.'

'But... I've never been on the dark web.'

'When they look at your laptop at home, they'll find a Tor browser installed on it.'

'But how...?'

'It's easily done. Little breakin' and enterin' when you and your folks were in the cop shop. No biggie. Copy that address onto another sheet of paper, and then eat the one I've given you there. It's the best way to destroy it safely. No one's going to go trawling the sewers lookin' for trace evidence.'

'Who are you?' Ellie asked.

The girl squatted down beside her, leaning in close. 'I'm just a messenger. I was asked to give you that bit of paper and the instructions I just shared with you, and to also tell you this: if you do as you're asked, no one will have to spend any time in the hospital. Also, they'll let you outta here once you've come clean and you promise not to go wanderin' about in bad places on the internet again. Everyone will be safe, and everyone will be happy. You know it makes sense.'

'But it's a lie,' Ellie said.

The girl shook her head. 'The first visit my employer's friends make to your family, they'll break bones and maybe cut them up a bit. The second time though...' She shook her head and made a tutting sound. 'The second time, they'll kill 'em. And not fast and clean. Slow. And messy. And once Philip and Cynthia are dead, my employer's people will come lookin' for you.'

She patted Ellie on the cheek and stood. 'I'd think about that, if I were in your shoes.'

And then she turned and walked, slow and unconcerned, back along the field's perimeter and disappeared into the crowd of young people.

19

It took Tessa an hour and forty minutes to get to Schull, which was on the very south-west tip of the island of Ireland. The village, which huddled in the shadow of Mount Gabriel on the Mizen Peninsula, was built along one broad main street with various laneways and alleys running off it. Its inhabitants lived in brightly painted houses and cottages, and lots of old-fashioned pubs and shops tumbled down towards the harbour, picturesque and sheltered, crowded with leisure craft of equally motley colours.

From the waterside, Tessa could see, across the rolling green waves, the dark shape of Long Island, a small, now unpopulated, chunk of rock, about a mile from shore. Somewhere beyond it, not visible from shore, was the slightly larger Cape Clear, an island that still had a small community that called it home.

Jim had messaged half an hour before she arrived at her destination, informing her that his opposite in West Cork would meet her on the dock. She spotted the orange-and-black colouring of the Irish coastguard craft, a large, narrow cruiser, as soon as she steered her Capri onto the waterfront. A short, wiry man in a blue uniform was standing on the boardwalk just below the vessel, waiting for her.

'I'm Sean Kilbarry,' he said, extending his hand. 'Jim told me you're working the Merrill case.'

Kilbarry had a pointed face clean-shaven, and dark-blue eyes. His dark hair was worn long and looked like it could do with a comb.

'The death of Mr Merrill is connected with another case I'm investigating,' Tessa said, 'so I'm just giving it a look over, see if there's any details that might be useful.'

Kilbarry shook his head in puzzlement. 'I don't see how it might be connected with any other cases,' he said. 'It's a pretty open-and-shut case of accidental drowning.'

'I'd be grateful if you'd walk me through it all the same,' Tessa said.

'Jim has helped me out from time to time, and he vouches for you,' the little man said, gesturing for her to follow him along the boardwalk. 'And anyway, we're all on the same side, aren't we? If there's something you see that me or my team has missed, I'd like to hear about it.'

'I'm not going to lie, that's refreshing to hear,' Tessa said. 'We've not been getting a lot of cooperation since we've been in Cork.'

'People here can be a bit protective of their turf,' Kilbarry said. 'Particularly if it seems a team from Dublin has been sent to oversee how an investigation is being handled.'

'They don't call this the People's Republic of Cork for nothing then,' Tessa observed.

Kilbarry grinned. 'They do not. I've been working here for fifteen years, I married a Cork girl and my three kids have all been born here. And I'm still seen as a blow-in.'

They arrived at a boat which, to Tessa, seemed to be along the same design as the one Kilbarry had piloted to the harbour, except this one was black and white, and slightly smaller.

'This was Dave Merrill's cruiser,' the coastguard said. 'She's called the *Strawberry Queen*. Made by the Cayman company in 2018, twenty-seven metres long, fibreglass hull, diesel engine, modified V shape. A fine boat.'

'I'll take your word for it,' Tessa said. 'Can we go aboard?'

'Yes, of course. Follow me please.'

He indicated a chrome-coloured ladder near the prow and scaled it in three rapid movements. Tessa, a bit more stiffly, followed suit. The deck consisted of a single, open space, hemmed in by waist-high rails that had benches attached. The pilot's cabin, which took up the whole front of the boat, was fully enclosed.

'How did the accident occur?' Tessa asked.

'Merrill was an experienced sailor,' Kilbarry said, walking to the stern of the boat and sitting on the bench bolted there. 'He and his friend, Paul Doyle, had gone out line fishing off the northern edge of Cape Clear. Weather conditions had been good, but towards the end of their trip, a bit of a wind came up, and they decided they'd head back in.'

'Back in to Schull?' Tessa asked, casting a glance at the ocean that stretched into the distance before them, broken only by the jagged silhouette of Long Island. Today, the wind was calm, little more than a breeze, and the waves seemed small and friendly, but she could easily imagine how inhospitable the sea could get if the weather took a nasty turn.

'No, Merrill has a house on Cape Clear. They were planning on staying there for the night and heading out again in the morning.'

'Is there much of a community living on the island?'

'It currently has a population of 110 souls,' Kilbarry said. 'It's considered to be the southern-most populated part of Ireland. During the summer months, the number can swell to three times that, of course. A lot of the residents are artists, musicians and writers, and they run summer schools. They get a lot of birdwatchers and marine biologists too.'

'How far away from the mainland is it?'

'Eight nautical miles. It's about a forty-minute trip by boat.'

'Okay. So the wind came up and they decided to head to the island. What happened then?'

'Doyle went into the cabin to pilot the boat in, and Merrill said he'd stay outside and see if he might catch anything by trolling the line – basically, dropping it in the water and leaving it there while the boat moves forward.'

'Had he done that before?'

'It's not uncommon,' Kilbarry said. 'I'd say it's probably used more in lakes. I'm not sure how effective it would be in the ocean, but he probably just wanted to get a final few minutes of fishing in.'

'Where was he standing?'

'Right here.'

The coastguard indicated a space at the railing beside where he was seated.

'So they began the trip back in to the island. How far did they have to travel?'

'Oh, they were only about half a mile out, to the north.'

'Between Schull and the island itself then?'

'That's right, yes. Doyle says he was focused on bringing the boat in. Some rain started to fall, and that can make visibility difficult. He called back to Merrill to advise him to get inside or he'd be soaked and got no answer. He turned around to call to him again, and when he did, he saw the man was gone.'

'What did he do?'

'He stopped the engine and came aft.'

'He assumed his friend had fallen overboard?'

'You're on the boat right now. Where could he have been? There's nowhere to hide here. Yes, he drew the conclusion Merrill had somehow fallen over the railing.'

'Had there been any bumps or jolts to account for that?'

'I asked him that. He said no but figured Merrill had probably had some sort of medical episode and just... passed out or something.'

'Did he turn the boat around?'

'He did, and radioed the coastguard as he retraced his route as accurately as he could, but there are so many currents and riptides around Cape Clear, he knew there was a slim chance he'd find Merrill with any ease.'

'He was found though?'

'Myself and two of my colleagues arrived on the scene forty minutes after he made the call. We'd called for a helicopter, and one was sent from Cork city. Merrill's body was found at 7.36 p.m., three miles beyond the western edge of the island. Which meant he'd been in the water for three hours, more or less.'

'Was there anything about the state of the body that didn't tally with what Doyle thought had happened?'

'There was a wound on the back of Merrill's head. But he could have hit it when he fell overboard.'

'That all?'

'His life jacket was damaged. One of the straps had snapped, which caused the whole thing to hang on him badly. The pathologist says he was unconscious when he hit the water but could have survived if the jacket had acted as it was supposed to. The broken strap caused it to hang a bit askew though, and his face was partially submerged. Due to this, he inhaled a lot of seawater, which slowly drowned him.'

'Aren't things like life jackets regularly checked?'

'Doyle swears it was intact when they put out to sea.'

'Was Mr Doyle looked into at all as a suspect?'

'Of course. But his story was sound, and he didn't waver from it. Also, they'd been friends for years, and he gained nothing from the death.'

'Isn't he the most likely person to have tampered with the life jacket?'

'It could have been damaged in the accident. None of us like Doyle for this. It just doesn't fit.'

'People sometimes snap.'

'They do, but Doyle is known as a moderate, calm, gentle sort of a man. Him walloping Merrill over the head, cutting the strap on his jacket and then tossing him overboard doesn't gel with anything we learned about him. The boat has a GPS, and when we checked its movements, they followed the route exactly as he said – the *Strawberry Queen* turned in for the island then retraced its steps. I know he might have done that to make circumstances look more convincing, but that doesn't sound like the actions of someone who's experienced a psychotic episode.'

Tessa thought about that. 'Did the post-mortem find anything that might have caused Merrill to lose consciousness?'

'He had high cholesterol. High blood sugar. His medical history included sleep apnoea. Any of those might have done it.'

'Can I talk to Doyle?'

'He's an actuary for Zurich Insurance.'

'In Cork?'

'Their offices are on the South Mall in the city centre. I've called him and told him to expect you.'

'I appreciate it.'

Kilbarry waved her thanks away.

'So you and Jim are an item?' he said as he rose from the bench.

Tessa froze – she hadn't expected this line of questioning from Kilbarry.

'It's early days yet,' she said, aware her tone had become stiff, 'but yes, we are.'

'He's a good man is Jim. Took him some time to get over losing his wife. To be honest, I didn't think he'd ever settle down with anyone again. You must be quite the lady to have won him over.'

Tessa shrugged, not exactly comfortable with the conversation. 'Like I said, it's early days yet.'

Kilbarry grinned. 'Well he seems a hell of a lot happier than he was the last time I was talking to him.'

Tessa said her goodbyes and hurried back to her car.

She was surprised Jim would make reference to their relationship when calling his contacts in West Cork. As she drove back towards the city, she mused that there was no reason for him not to, but she had to admit, she was annoyed and embarrassed that he had.

She just wished she knew why.

THE WATCHER IN THE SHADOWS

The driver parked on a hill above the bay, near the Harbour Hotel.

'You can see what she does from here,' she told him. 'You don't need to get out. Unless you want to.'

He thought about that. 'Yeah, probably no need,' he agreed. 'Let's just see where she goes.'

'What's this "let's" business?' the driver retorted. 'I'm just here to drive. I'm not supposed to be doing anything else. You should just be happy I feel sorry enough for your scrawny arse to offer the occasional piece of advice. Don't think for a second you can tell the boss that I contributed to any screw-ups you're responsible for.'

'Okay, okay. I didn't mean anythin' by it.'

'I should fucking well hope not.' She was silent for a time, gazing out the window straight in front of her. 'I'd thought I was finished with all this shit, you know? Then out of the blue he calls me and drags me back into it, and I find I'm babysitting as well as driving getaway. It's not fucking fair, so it's not.'

He snorted and watched as the detective walked along the dock with an officer from the coastguard.

'You know you'll be well looked after for this job,' he said. 'He always makes it worth our while.'

The driver laughed humourlessly. 'Does he?'

'You know he does.'

'Oh, I thought that. I believed everything he told me. I did whatever he asked, never questioned him. But I have to say, things didn't turn out for me the way he said they would. Not even close.'

The detective followed the coastguard onto the boat from which Dave Merrill had fallen to a watery death.

'The boss says we can have the life we want,' the Watcher retorted, 'but we have to work for it. Nothing is guaranteed. He gives us the tools, but it's up to us to use them.'

'He gives us the tools? Do you know what he gave me? A criminal record, that's what. Do you have any idea how difficult it is to achieve any level of success as an ex-con? Very fucking difficult, that's how hard it is. Almost impossible in fact.'

He couldn't see the detective anymore, but there was only one way for her to return to her car, so he kept watching.

'He didn't give you a criminal record. The state did that. The judge or whatever.'

'Me and two others got caught on a job the boss sent us on. He came to visit me. Asked me to take the fall for the whole thing, said that if I took responsibility, the others would be let off with community service. I'd only serve maybe nine months, and he'd look after me when I got out.'

'And didn't he keep that promise?'

'I did two years in Mountjoy Prison, and when I was released, the only job I could get involved me spending a lot of time on my back. If you know what I mean.'

He thought he did, but the idea of it made him flush and feel embarrassed. He'd never been with a woman, not even one he'd paid for. He had no idea how to even talk about sex stuff. He badly wanted to change the subject, but he was fiercely loyal to the boss and wasn't going to listen to her talking shit about him.

'You're saying he didn't help you at all when you got out?'

'He set me up with the guy who ended up being my pimp. I was supposed to get a job in a hotel, but that never materialised. He farmed me out instead.'

The detective was still on the boat. The Watcher kept his gaze on it, looking for any sign of her returning.

'There must have been some kind of mistake,' he said. 'I don't think the boss would have liked you doing that. Did you call and tell him you weren't happy?'

'I was too fucking embarrassed to tell anyone. I did it for a year until I had enough money saved to get a decent place, and then I got out. I was pregnant by then, so I wanted somewhere nice for the baby. Kids cost a lot.'

'Are you married?'

She laughed again, and this time he thought he heard some humour in the sound.

'No, I'm not married. The baby was for one of my "clients" – that's what they liked to be called, though I never thought of them by that name. Fucking saddos. That's what they were.'

He wanted to ask her why she hadn't taken precautions against getting pregnant if she was making a living as a sex worker but didn't think it would be polite.

'How old is your baby now?'

'She's six.'

'What's her name?'

'You know we're not supposed to share stuff like that. The less we know about each other, the better.'

'Yeah. Sorry.'

She shook her head – he could see it in his peripheral vision in the rear-view mirror.

'Ach, it's my fault,' she said. 'I shouldn't be flappin' me gums so much. It's just... you seem like a nice kid. I don't want you endin' up the way I did. You could get away from all this now and start a new life for yourself.'

They lapsed into silence. The detective finally climbed off the boat and slowly walked back the way she'd come, the coastguard chatting to her as they went.

She didn't linger on the quay and drove back towards Cork – breaking the speed limit most of the way, the Watcher noticed.

'Can I ask you something?' he said to the driver after forty-five minutes of silence.

'You can ask. Don't mean I'll answer.'

'If you feel so let down by the boss, why did you come back when he called you?'

She said nothing for a time, and then: 'You know the rules. It's what we agreed. If he helped us, back then, we were bound to him. Any time he calls, we have to answer. I mean, he did help me at first. Made my life a lot easier. It was when I went to prison, that's when it all went to shit. I told him I don't need anything anymore. I'm taking care of myself and my little girl. Not sayin' it's easy, but I'm coping. There's nothing I want from him.'

'He's paying you though?'

'He says he'll give me something. It's never money, you know that. But I expect I'll get helped in some way, whether I want to be or not.'

'You could have said no.'

She shook her head. 'You know what we do for him. What anyone who works for him has done. I'm not going to risk having that turned on me and my little girl.'

She paused and drove for a bit.

'I said yes when he called because I was afraid what would have happened if I'd said no.'

20

It took Danny half an hour to reach Castlemartyr. The village consisted of one long street, at the far end of which were the gates to Castlemartyr Resort, a seventeenth-century manor house that had been converted into a luxury hotel complete with a spa and golf course.

The village had an old-world feel: stone-clad houses, well-maintained shopfronts and a buzz of good-natured community to the people who came and went about their daily business.

Danny found the takeaway, The Balti House, without any difficulty (it had a sign written in large, red block capitals above the door, and someone had painted the name on the restaurant's single large window too, for good measure), but, it being only a little after eleven in the morning, the place was closed. He could, however, smell Indian food cooking somewhere close by and knocked smartly on the door.

His first knock elicited no response, so he tried again, harder this time, and kept knocking until he heard someone shouting within. Momentarily, a tall figure in stained white cook's clothes came from behind the counter, swearing loudly and effusively.

'For fuck's sake, can't you read? We are closed! Orders taken again at 4.30 this afternoon.'

Danny held his Garda ID up to the glass, and the man, whom he could now see was Indian or Bangladeshi, peered at it before throwing his eyes up to heaven.

'What is it now?'

'Can you open the door please? I'd like to ask you a few questions.'

Continuing to complain, though now under his breath, the cook reached up and let Danny in. 'If it's about that guy who got run down outside, I've told you people everything I know.'

'You didn't tell me,' Danny said.

'Isn't it all in a report somewhere?'

The cook had deep-brown eyes, a well-trimmed beard and a full, sensual mouth. There was a look of steely intelligence about him and a sense of pent-up, frenetic energy, as if he was anxious to be off about whatever work he was engaged in.

'I prefer to get my information first-hand.'

The cook sighed deeply and extended his hand at three high stools in front of the takeaway's counter.

'Can we get this wrapped up quickly? I have my sauces simmering, and I need to prep meat and veg for this evening.'

Danny took one of the seats. 'I'm DS Danny Murphy. What's your name?'

'Sharmin. Sharmin Khatun.'

'Okay, Sharmin. You were working on the day Mr McGuinness was killed?'

'I've worked seven days a week every day except Christmas for the last eight years. I own this business. I do all the cooking, box up all the food and keep the place at inspection levels of cleanliness. My brother, Nasrin, does the deliveries. We have a local girl who comes in and works the phones, taking the orders. She's the one you need to talk to. I was out back cooking, so I didn't see what happened. She did though.'

'Does she live in the village?'

'Yes. I can call her. Her house is just three doors up.'

'That'd be good.'

Sharmin reached behind the counter and pulled out an old-fashioned-looking mobile phone (the kind Danny had heard referred to as a 'Blockia'). He fiddled with it for a second or two then placed it to his ear.

'Shauna, yeah, it's Sharm. Can you pop down to the Balti? The police are here again. Yeah. Says he wants to talk to you.' He paused for a moment. 'Now. Okay. See you shortly.'

He hung up and looked at Danny. 'On her way.'

'Thanks. Was Mr McGuinness a regular?'

'Yeah. We saw him once, twice a week.'

'Always the same days? Same times?'

Sharmin thought about that. 'Same time, yes. He usually came after work, I think. Around half past six. Days though – no, they were pretty random. I mean, we'd usually see him at least one day over the weekend, but it could be Friday or sometimes Saturday. Midweek, it was anyone's guess.'

'And it was always him? Never another member of his family?'

'No, always him.'

'He never got his order delivered?'

'No. Always for pickup.'

'Was that usual?'

'Let me tell you a little something about the takeaway food business. Some people go for delivery, some like to collect. The ones who favour collection usually have a complicated order or a fussy person back home – you know, the type who likes to complain if the slightest thing is wrong. People like that prefer to be able to check the order is right before they take the food to avoid grief. Miles was like that. I don't know if it was him or if it was his wife – and this is a small community, so I know the lady from seeing her around – but one of his orders was picky. Didn't want it too spicy, didn't want coriander, didn't want too much garlic on his garlic naan bread. He always went through the order before taking it.'

'Would you describe him as a difficult customer?'

'Nope. Maybe if he'd got the food delivered he might have been – sending it back, lodging complaints, that kind of thing. But he was always very careful everything was as he liked it before he walked out that door. That made *both* our lives easier. He and I never had a cross word.'

The door opened and a stockily built blonde girl dressed in a pink tracksuit with white piping down the arms and legs came in.

'DS Murphy, this is Shauna. She takes the phone orders, gives out the food for collection and deals with any walk-ins.'

The girl nodded and took the stool beside Sharmin.

'Mr Khatun tells me you were here the evening Miles McGuinness was killed on the street outside,' Danny said once the girl had settled. 'I know you've already been through this with the other guards, but I'd like you to tell me what you saw too please.'

'I didn't see very much,' Shauna said. 'Miles rang the order in, as he usually did, while he was driving home from work. It was the same as it always was: a mild chicken balti, no chilli, no garlic and hold the coriander, half boiled rice, half chips, one can of Coke but not chilled, and a chicken tikka masala and chips, with a can of orange Fanta. It was always that. It never changed.'

'What time did he ring the order in?'

'About a quarter past six.'

'And when did he come in to get it?'

'About half past six.'

'Did you notice anything strange about him?' Danny asked. 'Was he agitated in any way? Unusually happy? Did he seem distracted or anxious?'

'No. He seemed the same as always. He wasn't a chatty type – just went through everything to make sure it was all present and correct, then paid, took the bags and left.'

'You saw him when he got outside?'

'I did. You can see the street clearly through the windows.'

Danny had a look out the window and nodded: the window went from just below the ceiling to about a foot and a half from the floor, giving an unimpeded view of the street outside.

'Was traffic heavy?'

'Um... yeah. Deliveries were taking anywhere from forty-five minutes to an hour.'

'When Mr McGuinness left the shop,' Danny continued, 'did he linger on the footpath?'

'No. He looked both ways – quickly, like – then went to cross the road. He got about halfway across and then... well, a car hit him straight on, and he went up into the air, like he'd been scooped up. He actually flew up so high I didn't see him for a second – he went above the height of the window – and then he came down, and I remember I heard a kind of smacking sound. I think it was him hitting the road.'

'And the car?'

'It kept on going. Didn't stop at all.'

'Can you remember anything about the car? Which direction it came from?'

'I don't know much about cars,' Shauna said. 'I think it was grey, but I can't be sure. It came from the right-hand side.' She paused for a moment. 'This is hard to think about, if I'm honest,' she said, her lower lip trembling. 'I mean, I wasn't friends with Miles or anything, but it was still horrible to see him getting hit like that.'

'I know it must be very tough on you,' Danny agreed. 'Your help is appreciated.'

'We look after our own here,' Sharmin said. 'This is bloody

horrible, but if it helps you catch the person that killed Miles, then we're happy to help, right Shauna?'

The girl, nodded, her eyes moist.

'Did you get a sense of the driver?' Danny asked her.

'No. Sorry.'

'Did you go outside after the accident?'

'I screamed for Sharm, then yeah, I did run out.'

'I was right behind her,' the cook said.

'What did you see?'

'Miles was lying in the road, and he looked strange,' Shauna said. 'The way he was lying was wrong. Like his body wasn't the way it was supposed to be.'

'I think his back was broken,' Sharmin said. 'He was... twisted the wrong way. The back of his legs were turned to his front.'

'Pelvic fracture,' Danny observed.

'I suppose, yeah,' the cook said. 'That's what it looked like.'

'Did you see the car?' Danny asked him.

'I saw the back of it briefly. Looked like it might have been a BMW. But I can't be one hundred per cent on that. I'd say it was grey too.'

'Was there anyone else on the street? Any other witnesses?'

'Not that I saw,' Shauna said.

'Me either,' Sharmin agreed. 'It was a wet evening. Not many about.'

Danny nodded. 'Can you take me outside and show me where it happened?' he asked Shauna.

She shrugged and nodded.

'I'll get back to my sauces if there's nothing else,' Sharmin said.

Danny told him there wasn't.

They stood outside the takeaway. Danny looked left and right, as he'd heard the dead man had done on the night of his demise, noting he had a clear view in both directions. The car must have been travelling very fast for McGuinness not to have been able to get out of the way in time. Which made Danny wonder just how heavy the traffic had actually been – heavy traffic was usually slow-moving and would have forced the driver to keep apace with the rest of the cars.

'You think he was about halfway across?' he asked the girl.

'That's what it looked like, yeah.'

There was no traffic at that moment, so Danny scooted out into the road, standing on the white lines in the road's centre. 'Here?'

Shauna looked thoughtful. 'Can I go back into the shop and look from there? That's where I was when it happened.'

'Yeah, that'd be better. If I have to move, I'll go back as soon as the car's gone.'

The girl nodded and went back inside.

Seconds later, she re-emerged. 'He was a bit further towards the other side, I think.'

Danny took a couple more steps, so he was now standing in the lane where cars would be going in the opposite direction to the vehicle that had struck McGuinness. The girl went back inside and returned to the footpath, nodding this time.

'Yeah. That looks more like it.'

'You're certain?'

'You're a lot taller than Miles, and broader, but I remember the way he seemed to be standing next to the "I" in Balti written in the window. I've made allowance for the difference in your size, and I'm pretty certain that must have been where he was.'

'That's great,' Danny said. 'Thanks for putting so much thought into it.'

'I liked Miles,' Shauna said. 'He seemed a sad sort of a man. I don't think he was very happy. He didn't deserve to die like that. In such a stupid, random way.'

'No one does,' Danny said. 'Thank you for talking to me. I'll let you get on with your day. Before you go, though, could you tell me where Miles McGuinness lived?'

The girl smiled briefly then headed back up the pavement, disappearing into a brown wooden door, and the big detective made his way back to his black Volkswagen Golf GTI. As he sat inside, he pondered that if what Shauna had told him was correct, Miles McGuinness hadn't died randomly at all. To have hit him where he was positioned in the road, the speeding grey car would have had to have swerved into the opposite lane.

Which most probably made this death another murder.

21

Maggie and Pavlov sat outside the house of Dominic Wilde, the hotelier whose throat had been cut in his home study, in the large suburb of Ballincollig, twenty minutes west of Cork. The town, the largest in the county, was bustling, its broad main street containing a steadily moving stream of traffic, the shopfronts, as seemed to be the custom in Cork, artfully painted in a mix of bright colours that seemed to complement one another while also managing to appear artfully spontaneous.

Wilde's house was at the eastern end of the main thoroughfare, a long bungalow set in its own gardens, a large gate with an intercom system keeping the public out. The lawn in front of the house had been landscaped carefully, native Irish trees nestling beside heritage shrubs and bushes. It was very pretty, Maggie thought – an oasis of rural charm in the middle of the urban sprawl.

She steered the chair over to the intercom. It was too high for her to reach from her seated position, so with a deep breath, she hoisted herself upright and, leaning against the gate's pillar for support, pressed the bell. It beeped for a few seconds, after which a male voice said, 'Hello, yes?'

'My name is Maggie Doolan. I work for a Garda special task force, and I'd like to ask you a few questions concerning the death of Mr Wilde.'

'Mrs Wilde is in no fit state to talk to anyone just now,' the voice retorted.

'I appreciate that. If you'd be so kind as to allow me inside, I promise to be as gentle as I can.'

There was a pause. 'Is that a wheelchair?'

Maggie smiled. She hadn't seen a camera, but there obviously was one. 'Yes. Is that a problem?'

She heard a whirring sound, and the gates began to crank open.

'No. It's just that you'll need to come to the back door. There are steps up to the front.'

'Thank you. I'll see you in a few moments.'

Pavlov trotted ahead of her as she guided the chair up the winding driveway, the small dog sniffing at this bush and that, gazing intently at a slightly evil-looking garden gnome and barking at a brave song thrush that finally took off from the large stone upon which it had been perched, gazing cheekily at the little dog.

A tall, heavily bearded man was standing at the back door when she reached it, and he stood back to permit her entry.

'I'm Glen Wilde, Dominic's brother,' he said as she executed a tight circle on the tiled floor of a beautifully appointed and very modern kitchen: black cupboards and worktops without visible handles; a sparkling white sink with a single spout; an American fridge/freezer, also in shiny black; a kitchen island in the middle of the room, its top a polished oak chopping board.

Maggie held out her ID card, and the bearded man read it carefully. The dead man's brother looked to be about sixty, his head bald. He was dressed in grey slacks and a light-blue cardigan over a pink shirt, the outfit set off by a purple cravat.

'You're a detective inspector,' he said.

'Relatively newly promoted,' Maggie answered. 'I haven't got used to giving myself that title yet.'

'Who's this?'

'Pavlov,' Maggie said. 'He's a service dog. Sort of.'

The man grinned. 'You're a student of psychology, I see,' he said, referring to the Russian researcher who'd developed an influential theory, 'classical conditioning', by training dogs to respond to the ringing of a bell. Maggie, when asked about her choice of name, usually told people she'd given him the moniker because he'd conditioned *her* behaviour, not the other way around.

Maggie laughed. 'I was at one time. I spent a lot of time in classrooms.'

'None of it wasted, I'm sure. I've told Glenda you're here. She's making herself presentable.'

'Thank you. I'm very sorry for your loss. Yours and Mrs Wilde's. I believe she and Dominic have a son?'

'Yes, Elijah. He's on a college exchange programme in Australia but is on his way back home. He should fly into Cork tomorrow.'

'Did your brother have any enemies, Mr Wilde? Anyone who would have reason to murder him?'

'None that I'm aware of. Dominic was liked by everyone, as far as I knew. The hospitality industry can be tough, but he managed to navigate the day-to-day without rubbing too many people up the wrong way. I always marvelled at his people skills, to be honest. I can be a bit of a curmudgeon, from time to time, but he was always able to find a way through whatever he was doing that made everyone happy. It was his gift, I think.'

'The file I read on the case says there was no sign of forced entry.'

'Yes, that's what I've been told.'

'And he was here alone?'

'Yes.'

Maggie clicked her tongue, and Pav, who'd been wandering about the kitchen sniffing here and there, scuttled over and jumped into her lap. She rubbed the back of his neck and looked up at Glen Wilde.

'Cutting the throat isn't the most common way of taking your own life,' she said, 'but it's not unheard of. Was Dominic in debt or having any kind of difficulties with his business affairs?'

'To the best of my knowledge, Dominic was doing exceptionally well in all his endeavours.'

'Were there difficulties in his marriage?'

'Glenda could be... challenging sometimes. But she and Dom balanced one another out. Their marriage was rock solid.'

'You're certain of that? Lots of couples hide marital problems.'

'Well if they did, they hid them so well I never got so much as a sniff of them.'

'You were close to Dominic?'

'Yes, and to Glenda. She and Dom met through me, in fact. She and I were classmates in University College Cork. We read history back in the 1990s. I was a mature student, before you ask. I did law initially, but it never suited me. People used to laugh at our names being so similar. Glen and Glenda. One of life's weird coincidences.'

'Were you and she ever...?'

'I'm gay, DS Doolan. So you can rest assured, there was no love triangle that might offer a line of investigation.'

'I had to ask,' Maggie said.

'Quite right,' Glen agreed.

The door to the kitchen opened and a tired-looking woman dressed in jeans and a grey woollen jumper came in. Maggie could see she'd just stepped from the shower, and she was without make-up. Regardless, she was a handsome woman, and the fact that her hair was wet and had only had a comb pulled through it did nothing to hide the fact that it was expensively cut and styled.

'Glenda, this is DS Maggie Doolan.'

The woman came over and offered her hand. 'Is this your dog?'

'This is Pavlov.'

The woman rubbed the top of Pav's head and then took a chair at the kitchen table.

'What do you want to know?' she asked. 'I can tell you that I wasn't here; I just found him. I also can't think of anyone who would have wanted to murder my husband, and I can promise you we weren't having emotional problems and we are financially secure. I spoke to our accountant the other day, and he assured me that both our business and personal accounts are all very healthy.'

Maggie rolled over so she was facing Glenda across the table. 'You found his body,' she said.

'Yes.'

'Tell me about that.'

'I'd been out visiting my friend Brid. We get together every second week, watch a movie, usually something old and black and white, and have a little too much to drink and eat our weight in cheese and crackers. My taxi brought me home at about 2.15 a.m. I noticed right away that the light was still on in Dom's office. This wasn't normal, as he liked to be in bed before midnight, and he never left lights on – he had a thing about wasting electricity; his work made him aware of exactly how much money can be saved yearly by simply being conscious of not leaving bulbs burning unnecessarily. I went in to check on him, thinking there must be some kind of crisis going on in one of the hotels. The smell hit me the second I opened the office door.'

'What smell was that?'

'Blood. He'd bled so much the air was thick with it. Like copper. But sweet and... horrible.'

'It's not pleasant,' Maggie agreed. 'Did you see him right away?'

'No. Yes. I... It took me some time to work out what I was seeing, I think. You know how your mind doesn't process something that's so traumatic you don't want to believe it's actually happening?'

'I know that feeling, yes.'

'It was like that. I saw Dom lying there, and I saw the huge stain of blood, and that his clothes and his face were drenched by it. I stood where I was for a few moments and then I think I screamed, and I ran over to see if I could do anything. I suppose... I suppose I hoped he might still be alive. But as soon as I got close to him, I knew he wasn't.'

'Too much blood loss?'

'No. It was his throat – it had been cut so thoroughly, the bones in his neck were exposed. Whoever did it, they'd virtually decapitated him.'

'Do you have any thoughts at all on who might have done that?'

'None.'

'Whoever it was got into your home without breaking in. Which means they must have had a key or they were permitted to enter – or they snuck in at some point when a door or window was open and lay in wait.'

'The thought terrifies me.'

'Does anyone have keys other than you?'

'Me,' Glen piped up.

Maggie looked at him. 'You know what I'm going to ask, don't you?'

'I was with my husband, Derek, all night. He'll vouch for me.'

Maggie nodded. 'Have you lost keys lately? Either of you?

Or misplaced them and found them again somewhere you wouldn't have expected?'

The question was met with headshakes.

'Can you show me the office?' Maggie asked.

Glenda got up without a word and led them through the kitchen door and down a long hallway. The room was big, airy and well lit, with a silver-grey carpet. The wall facing the door was dominated by a big window framed by deep-blue curtains. Heavy plastic material had been placed over the carpet just below this window.

'He was there,' Glenda said, though it hardly needed to be said.

'Do those windows lock?' Maggie asked.

'I don't know,' Glenda admitted. 'I rarely come in here. It was Dominic's man cave.'

'May I?' Maggie asked.

Glenda shrugged.

The detective rolled over, the wheels of the chair making a slight crackling sound as they went over the plastic sheeting. The window was made of one sheet of glass, but two panels had been set into it which could be opened. Maggie once again had to stand to reach the bolts, but when she did, she found the windows could be locked from the inside. One was, in fact, locked. The other was not.

'Did Dominic have the window open much at this time of year?' she asked.

'No,' Glenda said. 'He was as concerned about wasting heat as he was electricity. Couldn't tolerate it. The windows were only ever opened during the hottest months of the summer when the central heating was off.'

Maggie pondered that for a moment, settling back into her chair as she did so. 'Would you say he was security conscious?'

'Well, he checked the doors and windows most evenings, so I suppose he was a bit. But doesn't everyone do that?'

'Perhaps they do,' Maggie said. 'Do you know what he was working on the night he was killed?'

'Something to do with the charity work he was engaged in.'

'Did he do a lot of that?'

'Some. Dominic knew he'd been lucky in business. He wanted to share his success where he could.'

Maggie thought about that.

'I won't take up any more of your time,' she said finally. 'I may need to ask some more questions. I hope that won't be too much of an upset for you, Mrs Wilde.'

The woman said nothing, just showed her to the door.

'Is it okay if I take a quick look about the garden before I leave?' Maggie asked.

'Go right ahead,' Glenda said. 'Just press the release button on the gate on your way out. It's the green one on the wall on your left.'

'Thank you.'

Once outside again, Maggie made her way to the office window. There was a flower bed just beneath it, and there was no way she could get the chair through without ploughing up the bed and all its blooms, so she got out and painfully and stiffly picked her way through the vegetation, thanking God she was having a good day.

When she got to the sill, she leaned her bum against it, looking back down the garden towards the gate and the road. If the killer had used the window to exit the office, Maggie could clearly see an escape path through the garden that would take the assassin right down to the wall, using trees and shrubs as cover. Within easy reach of the high wall was a tree with some branches low enough to use as footholds to aid a person in scaling it and leaping over to the outside and freedom.

She shuffled to her chair and climbed gratefully back in (Pavlov whined in concern as she made the short journey) then rolled through the grass to the tree she'd just been eyeballing.

She parked just beneath it and looked up. Everything in this garden was carefully maintained and well pruned. Yet there, just above her head, was a branch that had been snapped. Part of it was hanging loose, the broken end dangling by a thin shred of bark.

As if someone had broken it trying to climb up in a bid to escape.

PART TWO

ELLIE O'FARRELL

Her parents rang St Killian's office at midday, but she told the staff she didn't want to speak to them. She really did, of course, but was afraid that if she did, she would start crying and not be able to stop, and that wouldn't help her or them.

Now she was in the library, waiting for the next part of her assessment, and was escaping the misery of her situation by sinking into a Lee Child novel. The binary nature of Child's erstwhile hero's morality appealed to her more than ever in her current circumstances, and she wished she had Jack Reacher's self-assurance, not to mention his size, to help her deal with the problems that were coming at her thick and fast.

She so wanted to give in to the tears that hovered at the edge of her vision, yet she knew she couldn't afford to show any sign of weakness – that would be the end. She had to continue to look unfazed. It was the only way to get through this hell.

Reacher never let his enemies see what was going on inside. He showed only courage and fortitude to the world. And so would she until the craziness was over.

The piece of paper with the dark web address written on it was still in her pocket. She hadn't made a copy, and she certainly hadn't eaten it – Ellie was aware of three different poisons that could be soaked into paper and would kill painfully if ingested, and she wasn't about to give whoever was responsible for all of this the opportunity to finish her so easily.

Ellie was scared. Terrified, in fact. But she knew she had one thing in her favour – she was smart, smarter than most people. And that gave her an edge.

If she was going to take the fight to them, she was going to have to use all the skills she had.

In the world of the novel, Reacher was hitching a lift on the outskirts of a small town in middle America. He didn't know where he was going, and he didn't care. The world was his oyster, and he was certain he was the toughest man in any room he walked into. Nothing scared Reacher, and when he encountered problems, he took them as a welcome challenge, a puzzle to solve in a game he was, most likely, going to win.

Because Reacher wasn't just a six-feet-four stack of muscles. He was smart too, and he used his intellect, even in his physical confrontations. Could she do something similar? She didn't think she could. Fear would get in the way. Ellie wasn't made in the same way as someone like Jack Reacher.

And she'd never been in a fight in her life.

Such things weren't encouraged in the Educate Together schools – multi-denominational educational centres designed loosely along the Steiner-Waldorf methodology and strictly against physical conflict in any form – she had attended.

But maybe it was time for her to adopt a different approach. The Child-Reacher philosophy looked like it might be her best hope of survival.

Ellie liked puzzles. She was good at them. Maybe if she saw a fight as a puzzle, it might not be so scary.

'Time for lunch, O'Farrell,' the librarian called to her – she was the only one in the reading room.

'I'm not hungry,' she said. 'Would it be okay if I just stayed here?'

'You can take the book with you. You might feel like eating when you've food in front of you.'

Ellie nodded and picked up the paperback, feeling the heft of its 575 pages. It was, basically, a block made of paper and light card.

But a block for all that.

Lunch was eaten in the same room as breakfast. She took some chicken salad and a couple of slices of wholemeal bread, went to the table she'd sat at earlier and returned to her book. She was coming to the end of the second chapter when a voice broke her concentration.

'I've got my list of stuff for you. The concession store opens at 6.30 tonight, after dinner. You can get my order for me then. Okay?'

She looked up to see Bridie, the girl who'd come at her earlier demanding sweets and nicotine under threat of injury.

'I haven't spoken to my parents,' Ellie said, returning her gaze to her book and hoping the girl would be all talk. She hadn't expected her resolve to be tested quite so soon.

'Then get one of the staff to call them. If I don't have what I asked for tonight, you're gonna be sorry, do you hear me?'

Ellie felt a flash of rage. She was tired of being threatened. She'd done nothing wrong but had still been locked up, treated like a criminal and had violence hanging over her like a dark cloud all morning.

So be it. If it had to happen, better to get it over with. She took a deep breath.

'I will not be speaking to my parents today,' she said, closing the book and clutching it tightly in her right hand. 'Even if I was, I wouldn't be getting you anything. I don't know you, and what I have seen of you, I don't like very much.'

Bridie almost took a step back, so great was her surprise. 'What did you say to me?'

She leaned in close, placing one of her hands on the table in front of Ellie, fingers splayed, grabbing the front of her tracksuit top with the other.

'I think you heard me,' Ellie said and with all the force she could muster smashed the Lee Child book onto the hand the big girl had placed on the table, using the corner of the spine, which she believed would have the greatest structural integrity, as a makeshift hammer, bringing it down between the knuckles of the index and middle finger.

There was an audible crunch, and the girl howled and let Ellie go.

Ellie, sensing she had the advantage, pulled the book up and smashed it down again.

The howling increased in pitch, and the big girl, holding her ruined hand to her chest, staggered backwards. Underneath the wailing, Ellie heard the sound of feet pounding the linoleum floor.

She clutched the now battered book to her chest and sat back, waiting for the staff rushing in her direction.

'What the hell happened?' a large, grey-haired man with a huge, pendulous belly asked her, trying to get a hold of the hysterical Bridie, who was walking in a tight circle cradling her injured limb.

'She told me she was going to hurt me if I didn't get her sweets and cigarettes,' Ellie said. 'When I told her I wouldn't, she grabbed me.'

'So you broke her hand?'

Ellie shrugged. 'I want to see Dr Cleary. I'm ready to tell how I knew about those murders.'

'O'Farrell, you're going to lock-up! Do you understand what you've done?' The fat man's voice had a hard edge to it.

Another staff member arrived on the scene, and Bridie started haltingly asking for her mother.

'Fine. But send Dr Cleary. The police will want to hear what I have to say. Call Sergeant O'Mahoney if you don't believe me.'

'Stand up, O'Farrell, and step away from the table.'

Ellie did as she was asked, and he took her firmly by the arm.

Bridie was transferred to the infirmary, and Ellie, walking between the two male staff members (each looking a little afraid of her now), was taken to what amounted to a padded cell and locked inside.

There was no furniture, but the floor was comfortable enough to sit on. It was quiet and well lit, and Ellie thought it hardly a punishment at all.

Her only regret was that they'd taken her Lee Child novel from her before she'd left the lunch hall.

It was a sacrifice she'd been prepared to make.

And she thought Reacher would have approved.

22

Danny got Miles McGuinness's address from Shauna in The Balti House – he could have checked the files, but she seemed to want to help, so he waited while she scribbled down the details then thanked her profusely.

The house was two kilometres outside the village, up a narrow driveway between tall poplars which formed a canopy above his VW.

The deceased banker's home was modern in design, its front made completely of glass panels so the occupants could view the expertly planned garden, which featured an intricate network of streams and waterfalls, between which had been planted various shrubs and flowering bushes. A path of crazy paving wove its way here and there, going nowhere and everywhere.

Mrs McGuinness was a short, dark-eyed woman with tightly permed hair of a red Danny didn't believe occurred naturally. She met him at the door dressed in a green wool-knit cardigan and purple corduroy trousers.

'DS Murphy,' she said. 'I made us some coffee.'

There was a table and chairs in front of the house, and

Danny saw it had been set with a cafetière of coffee, a jug of milk, sugar and a plate of shortbread biscuits.

'That was very kind of you, Mrs McGuinness.'

'Call me Miriam – please.'

'Thank you, Miriam. I'm Danny.'

They sat, and she pressed the plunger on the coffee pot and filled two mugs that had the image of a castle painted on the sides and looked as if they'd been handmade, Danny reckoned, by a local potter.

'How can I help you?' Miriam asked as he added milk and sugar to his mug.

'Your husband worked at the Allied Irish Bank in Dungarvan?'

'He did. He worked there for the past fifteen years. He'd been in the Waterford branch before that.'

'Was he the manager?'

'Miles was in charge of investment portfolios,' the red-haired woman said. 'He was very good at it. I always felt he had an almost instinctive understanding of the financial landscape. He could see peaks and troughs coming a long way off. He was very much in demand.'

'And he had a good relationship with his clients?'

'He made them a lot of money,' Miriam said. 'So yes, his clients valued him a great deal.'

'I can imagine they would,' Danny said.

'Have you found the man who hit him yet?'

'I'm sorry, no. But his case seems to be linked to another one I'm working, so that may offer new leads.'

'I hope so. That bastard left my Miles lying in the road like a dog.'

'I'm very sorry for your loss,' Danny said. 'It must be very hard for you.'

'I don't know what to do with myself without him,' Miriam said. 'Do you see the size of this house? I didn't want it – we used to live in a four-room cottage across from the hotel. It was Miles that wanted to build this glass display case. Do you know it has six bedrooms? Why do we need six bedrooms? We don't even have a dog!'

Danny shrugged. 'Useful if you're throwing a party.'

'Danny, we have literally never thrown a party here. Not once. Miles wasn't terribly social. He lived for his work. And for me. That was all he needed. But he loved this place, so I came to love it too. It made him happy.'

'Was Mr McGuinness working on anything unusual when he died?'

'Unusual?'

'Maybe something that was causing him stress or anxiety?'

The woman thought for a moment. 'He'd been giving out about some kind of bitcoin investment scheme he was managing,' she said. 'But don't ask me any more about it. I don't understand how all that online currency works, I'm afraid. That's all I can tell you.'

'But he seemed concerned about this particular deal?'

'I wouldn't say he was concerned,' she said. 'More... frustrated. Miles's job was all about advising investors how to use the money they earned from their investment portfolios. Usually, they took his advice and made money, and then they – and Miles too – were happy. Every now and again, he came across one who thought they knew more than he did. I got the impression this was one of those situations.'

'Can you remember who the difficult investor was?'

'Confidentiality was a big part of what my husband did,' Miriam said. 'And he took it seriously. I never knew who his clients were. If he talked about his work, it was always in general terms.'

Danny nodded. 'Thank you for your time, Miriam. Before I go, do the names Dominic Wilde or Dave Merrill mean anything to you?'

'No. I'm sorry.'

'How about Philip O'Farrell?'

She shook her head.

'Thanks anyway. And I appreciate the coffee.'

'You're welcome,' the woman said. 'Please catch the person who killed my Miles.'

'I'll do my very best,' Danny said, and he meant it.

He left her sitting in the ornate garden and hadn't driven more than a mile when he spotted the blue Peugeot EV in his rear-view mirror. He'd noticed it parked up the road from him in Castlemartyr (the model wasn't exactly rare in Ireland, but he'd never seen one that colour) so when he spied it three cars behind him as he was on his way back to Cork, it registered immediately.

Initially he didn't think much of it and continued to listen to Lyric FM, a popular Irish classical music station that he enjoyed while he pondered the implications of what he'd just learned. If Miles McGuinness's death was a murder, just as Dominic Wilde's most certainly was, that meant that even if the drowning of Dave Merrill couldn't be proven to be anything other than an accident, they had enough to suggest something sinister was going on.

What, exactly, he wasn't yet sure, but if he had to guess, it looked to him as if somebody was arranging hits on prominent businesspeople and trying to make them look like accidents. Dominic Wilde's murder didn't fit that pattern, but Danny was prepared to bet something had gone wrong and the murderer had been forced to abandon their plans for some reason and just go for a fast and easy kill. The key to proving this would be to find the connection between the three men. Danny was sure there was one.

His car needed diesel, so he pulled into a petrol station, filled up the tank and got himself a cup of coffee and a whole-meal muffin – Miriam McGuinness's coffee had been very good, and it felt like an age since breakfast. Five minutes later, he was listening to 'O mio babbino caro' by Puccini and sipping his coffee, the muffin already a memory, when he saw the Peugeot in his rear-view mirror again, this time directly behind him. A thin-looking young man in a peaked baseball cap was driving, tapping out a frenetic rhythm on the steering wheel as if he was listening to some very fast drum-and-bass music.

Even if the occupants of the electric vehicle were travelling the same route as him, they should be well ahead by now, as Danny had been in the service station for at least five minutes, probably more.

I'm being followed, he thought. *Now who the hell could that be?*

There was one obvious answer, though he didn't like the implications of it. He tapped the screen of his phone a couple of times where it sat in its cradle.

After two rings, Dawn Wilson's voice came on the line. 'What's up, Danny?'

'Boss, I'm going to call you out a registration number. Can you tell me if it's one of ours or not please?'

'Go for it.'

He accelerated slightly so he had a clear view and read her the plate.

Computer keys clacked, and then Dawn said: 'Nope. Not ours. That number is registered to a Geraldine Doherty. Says here it's a red Mazda3.'

'That is not the car that's currently following me.'

'Are you suggesting someone may have removed the plates from another vehicle and attached them to a car that's currently involved in criminal activity of some kind?' Dawn asked, tongue firmly in cheek.

'I might just be,' Danny said. 'I've got a tail – a blue Peugeot EV.'

Dawn clattered at her keyboard again. 'We've got one

reported stolen from a family in Crosshaven – that's a posh area in Cork – sometime last night.'

'What an interesting coincidence,' Danny observed.

'You okay? Can you handle it?'

'Nothing to worry about, boss. I've got this.'

'Right you be. Keep me posted.'

The big detective maintained his speed, keeping an eye on the vehicle behind. Its driver had a cigarette dangling from the corner of his mouth, and he seemed to be speaking to someone – Danny wasn't sure if he was using a hands-free set or if there was another person in the back. He decided it was best to err on the side of caution, and assume he was dealing with a driver and passenger rather than one shadow until he knew different.

A right turn loomed up ahead, and he took it, easing his Golf down a winding country road. The Peugeot followed.

Well that proves it, he thought. *Let's see if I can engineer a bit of a conversation with my new friends.*

He pressed down on the accelerator, slowly increasing his speed. His tail maintained theirs, not taking the bait. Danny edged ahead, little by little. He didn't know the road, or even where it would lead him, but he wanted a thoroughfare with as little traffic as possible for what he had planned, and this seemed to fit the bill. He reached over and activated Google Maps on his phone, not entering any destination, just getting a map of the road he was on up on the screen.

The app informed him he was in the townland of Lissacrue and showed a bend up ahead, and after that the road ran pretty straight for about half a kilometre.

That was just about the distance he'd hoped for.

Danny began to slowly increase his speed, rounding the bend the map revealed. Now he couldn't see the Peugeot, and they couldn't see him, and he put his foot to the floor, zooming ahead and watching the needle on his speedometer climb: 80 kph, 90 kph, 100 kph. In his rear-view mirror he spied his tail rounding the corner, and as he'd expected, they increased their speed to catch up with him.

He took another bend and covered a couple of hundred metres before turning the wheel hard, putting the Golf into a skid and letting it come to a stop broadside across the road, blocking the way of traffic coming both directions. Pulling his gun, he got out, positioning himself behind the bonnet of his car, his weapon held by his side, so it wouldn't be seen by the people in the oncoming electric vehicle.

Danny waited, his heart beating loudly in his ears.

Nothing happened for what felt like forever but was, in actuality, only a few seconds. Then he heard the building sound of a very quietly approaching electric engine, and the blue car burst around the corner. The driver saw him, and the red-trimmed black Golf blocking his way, and hit the brakes hard. Going at the speed it was, the Peugeot didn't stop but skidded, continuing to slide forward, borne by its own momentum.

It stopped about a foot and a half from the Golf. Danny saw there was, in fact, another, younger-looking man in the back seat, and the baseball-capped driver, whose eyes were locked on Danny's, was talking rapidly to him. The pair looked to be in their mid-twenties. Slowly, Danny raised his police ID and called out: 'I'm informing you that I'm a detective with an Garda Síochána. Could you both step out of the vehicle please?'

The driver didn't move but kept talking. Danny could hear the sounds of the words but couldn't make any of them out. He eyed the driver carefully, trying to gauge if this was another Faceless Man, but the guy behind the wheel seemed to have an intact visage, from what Danny could tell.

'I'm going to ask you one more time,' he said. 'Please exit the vehicle immediately.'

The driver spoke again, and then the rear window of the Peugeot rolled down.

'What's the problem, officer?'

The accent was Cork city, broad and undiluted. As he spoke, the youngster, whom Danny took to be about twenty-three or twenty-four, leaned out the window slightly. Once again, no cosmetic surgery was in evidence. Just a bad case of acne.

'You're driving what may well be a stolen car with what I know for a fact are stolen plates,' Danny said. 'And you're using both sets of items to follow me as I execute my duties. So let me ask you again, and I should advise you, this is the last time I'm making the request politely: could you and your chauffeur please step out of the vehicle so we can have a conversation?'

'And what do you think we have to talk about, Detective?'

Danny, whose patience had run out, began to walk around the bonnet of his own car.

'You'd better show me some ID right now, or I'll have no option but to arrest you on motor theft, interfering with a police officer in the course of his duties and refusal to cooperate with a lawful order.'

He hadn't taken two steps when the driver, still gazing directly forward, slammed the car into reverse. Danny brought his weapon up, but the young man in the back of the car suddenly had a handgun of his own aimed out the window and fired three shots in quick succession. The detective felt one whizz past his left ear and dived forward, sensing the others rip through the air above him. He landed painfully on his side, his leather jacket protecting him from the worst of it, but he still managed to twist his right arm in a direction it wasn't supposed to go.

Gritting his teeth through the pain, he brought his gun up and fired twice, aiming for the reversing car's tyres, but as he did, it spun, turning a full ninety degrees before taking off at speed the way they'd come. Whatever his bullets hit, they missed the escaping car.

Danny pulled his phone from his pocket and called the Anglesea Street squad room.

'Violent Crime Unit.'

'Listen carefully,' he said, speaking as quickly as he could as he pulled himself upright, limped back to his own car and got in. 'This is Detective Sergeant Danny Murphy from the commissioner's task force requesting any cars close to the Lissacrue area be on the lookout for a blue Peugeot EV, registration number 176 C 15223. Approach with caution – the occupants are armed and dangerous. Shots have been fired; repeat, shots have been fired.'

'I'll get an all-points bulletin out right away, Detective.'

'Thanks. I'm in pursuit, but they've got a good head start on me.'

'Report in when you can. I'll tell the sarge.'

'Cheers,' Danny said, and by then he was already speeding down the narrow lane, tailing the men who'd previously been tailing him.

By the time he reached the main road again, there was no sign of them. He considered his options and realised they were gone – he could spend the rest of the day cruising the road between Cork and Castlemartyr and never find them.

He had to hope one of the other cars would pick the errant vehicle up.

Cursing, he turned for Cork, feeling sore and humiliated.

THE WATCHER IN THE SHADOWS

They were following the detective's Capri, still a good hour from Cork when the call came in. The Watcher answered before the first ring was even complete.

'One of the others has been made. Abort immediately. They'll be on the lookout for tails now, and we can't risk any further problems.'

'Okay, boss. We'll pull over, let her get well ahead and then go back to the city by another route.'

'I want you to wait at least an hour before you go anywhere. Fall back as far as you can without drawing attention to your-selves, and when you see the next pub, stop there and get some lunch. Take your time over it. And then yes, return to Cork by as circuitous a route as your driver can manufacture. The nine o'clock news should be playing before you see the River Lee, am I clear?'

'As crystal.'

'Good. I'll call you later. I still have work for you to do. But for now, consider yourself sent home early with pay. I'll trust you to pass all I've said on to your driver.'

'I will, boss.'

The call ended.

'We're to pull back,' he said to the driver and explained what he'd just heard.

The woman said nothing, but the car slowed, and within less than a minute, two other vehicles has passed them.

'I bet I know which of them was made,' she said. 'I told that fuckin' idiot not to steal a car that was noticeable. And electric to boot? The boss is losing his touch if he's working with fools like that young fella. I could tell he was off his head on coke too the second I laid eyes on him.'

'All I care about is that it wasn't me,' the Watcher said.

'That's true, I suppose. Thank heaven for small mercies.'

Another car passed them.

'There's a pub not far from here. We can go there for something to eat, then I'll take you on a tour of the back roads to get us home.'

'Okay.'

They drove on for a while, keeping to 60 kph.

'I don't have any money on me,' he said after a bit.

The woman snorted. 'Looks like it's going to be my treat then.'

'I'm sorry. I didn't think we'd be stopping anywhere today.'

'Me neither. But by some weird coincidence, I brought me purse, and I have a few quid on me bank card.'

'I'll pay you back.'

'It's alright. The boss will make it up to me somehow. Or he won't. It doesn't matter really. I don't mind buyin' you lunch. It's no big deal.'

'Are you sure?'

'I'm positive. My treat.'

He didn't know what to say to that so lapsed back into an embarrassed silence.

23

'You were followed?' Tessa asked Danny incredulously.

'Yeah.' His voice was being transmitted over the speakers in her beloved Capri. 'I spotted them as soon as I was on the way home from my interview.'

'And the bastards drew down on you?'

'They did. I'm fine – just pulled a tendon in my arm. It'll be a bit stiff, but it's not too bad. I'm just warning you to be careful.'

'Did you call Maggie?'

'I will as soon as we're finished talking.'

'I'll keep my eyes peeled. Go on – call her. Let me know if the squad cars catch them.'

'I will. Chat in a bit.'

Tessa was on a secondary road, the R586, which was narrow in this particular spot, lined on each side by ditches of bramble, gorse and sedge, behind which were high trees: oak, hawthorn and ash. There were no cars behind her, so she waited until she spied a gateway on her side of the road, pulled into it and waited. Five minutes passed and a car drove by – a black Hyundai coupé driven by a young woman. She couldn't recall if she'd seen it before or not, so made a note of its make and registration and continued to wait. There was no more traffic for a further ten minutes, and then a tractor cruised by, towing a trailer of what she took to be manure; Tessa thought it unlikely this particular vehicle was tailing her but took the reg anyway, just to be thorough. Three more minutes dragged by and a BMW driven by an elderly man with a similarly aged woman in the passenger seat passed her. Once more, she recorded the car's details.

She waited for forty minutes, taking note of every car that passed – there were fifteen – then continued her journey, keeping her speed low and watching for any of the vehicles she'd seen that might try the same trick and pull over to lie in wait for her.

She spotted not a single one and got back to Cork without incident.

The offices of the Zurich insurance company were just where Kilbarry had said they would be on the South Mall, and the security guard on the reception desk, a grey-haired man who looked like a retired Garda, rang upstairs to inform the actuary the detective had arrived.

The man who arrived in the reception area was about five feet nine, wearing a grey suit over a blue, open-necked shirt. His receding hair, which was still completely dark, was gelled back on his head, and Tessa noted he wore a pro-life badge on his lapel: a small metal representation of a baby's footprint. He was tanned and moved with the easy motion of someone who spent a lot of time outdoors engaged in physical activity.

'DI Burns,' he said, extending his hand. 'I'm Paul Doyle. Captain Kilbarry said you might be calling on me.'

'I thought I might as well do the interview while the details were fresh in my mind after speaking with the captain this morning,' Tessa said. 'I appreciate your taking the time.'

'There's a coffee pod across the street that's quite good. Shall we adjourn to it?'

'Sounds good to me.'

The South Mall was one of Cork's main streets and a busy hub of the city's business community, the Maldron Hotel (the company had renovated several Victorian buildings to create an establishment that combined the best a modern hotel had to offer with the charm of old-world glamour) its most prominent landmark. They crossed the road, dodging cars, and Doyle led her directly to what was little more than a hole in the wall behind which a young woman in a Gorillaz T-shirt made coffees from a lengthy list written in chalk on a board beside her window.

Doyle ordered a soy latte and Tessa a cup of hot water into which she dropped a Barry's teabag, her favourite brand. This got her a hard look from the barista, to which the detective simply smiled beatifically in response. She and Doyle took a seat on a bench just a few yards up the pavement.

'How can I help you, Detective?' Doyle asked as he crossed his legs and watched the crowds of people filing past.

'I don't know. Kilbarry seems to be satisfied Mr Merrill's death was an accident.'

'Are you not?'

'I'd like to hear a little more about it is all. An experienced seaman fell overboard and drowned. I know things like that can happen, but it still seems worth looking into, wouldn't you say?'

'No harm in double-checking,' Doyle agreed, taking a sip of his soy latte.

'Talk to me about Dave Merrill's life jacket.'

'Neither of us were ever on deck without one – they're essential kit and can save your life. His malfunctioned for some reason.'

'They're designed to keep you floating upright in the water, aren't they?'

'Yes, but when they found him, David's jacket was damaged. He'd been floating with his face partially submerged and had inhaled quite a bit of seawater as a result. Which is why he drowned.'

'Did you know his jacket was damaged before you put out to sea?'

'It wasn't when we got on board.'

Tessa looked at the dapperly dressed man. 'You're certain of that?'

'Yes. Absolutely positive.'

'How so?'

'I checked it myself. I do a thorough examination of the boat's engines and safety equipment every single time we prepare to leave shore. There's a record of it in the cabin on the *Strawberry Queen.*'

'And both jackets were in good condition when you checked them?'

'Yes. Both were safe to be used.'

'How do you think his got damaged then?'

Doyle pondered the question. 'The only thing I can come up with is that after he lost consciousness and fell overboard, one of the straps snagged on some part of the boat, leaving him hanging there for a while. The rise and fall of the vessel in the waves would have, sooner or later, caused the strap to snap, and this could have caused him to lie semi-submerged in the water.'

'What is there on the end of the boat that he might have got caught on?'

'There are several protruding hooks and rods.'

'He was only out of your sight for a few minutes though, wasn't he? Is that enough time for the strap to rip or tear?'

'The wind had really come up at that stage of the afternoon, and we hit a couple of big swells. Either would have been enough to cause him to swing back and forth, straining the material and buckles. He wasn't a small man. His weight could have caused the strap to come apart.'

Tessa drank some of her tea. Her friends always said that Tessa's only real addiction was her devotion to Barry's tea, which she consumed in vast quantities on a daily basis. She found that just having a cup of the brew in her hands helped her think more clearly.

'Do you or the company you work for stand to gain anything from Dave Merrill's death?'

'Quite the opposite, Detective. Dave had life insurance with us. We're going to have to pay out and pay out substantially. His passing is going to *cost* Zurich.'

'Do you have any kind of axe to grind against your employers? Any disputes?'

'None. Zurich has been very good to me. My parents couldn't afford to send me to university, but once I hired on with Zurich, they paid for my education. Do you know how difficult it is to get on to an actuarial course?'

'No idea.'

'Well, I can tell you it's damned hard. Zurich Ireland recognised my abilities and ensured I secured a place. I'm very grateful to them.'

'Does Dave leave behind a spouse? Children?'

'No. He was single.'

'So no girlfriend? Boyfriend?'

'None I know of.'

'What about old flames?'

'He's had girlfriends, if that's what you call them at our age. But no one recent, by which I mean none within the past year. And none of them would have any reason to wish him harm. He always managed to end his romantic relationships on good terms.'

'His fruit company has been one of the most successful in

the country for two decades. Did he ever mention clashes with competitors? Any investors he's had disagreements with? Members of his board who might want him out of circulation?'

'Detective Burns, David and I were friends our entire adult lives, and the reason for the longevity of our comradeship was that we hardly ever discussed business.'

'So he never complained about having a tough day?'

'He might indicate he'd had to overcome some difficulties, but I never asked for details, and he rarely offered them. To be frank, I'm not sure anything he told me would have meant much anyway. I spend my days calculating probabilities and risk. I'm a statistical mathematician. I've never been privy to the ins and outs of business at the level at which Dave operated.'

'You're telling me your best friend never bitched with you about his day job?'

'The only thing that comes to mind actually had nothing to do with his work.'

'Go on.'

'He was involved in raising money for a charity and was concerned some of the monies, which were supposed to all go to the people they were meant to be helping, were being skimmed, siphoned off.'

'What was the charity?'

'I don't recall, though I did tell him what he was describing is, in fact, standard practice. Even the best charities have to pay for overheads. Fundraisers usually understand that. Dave tended towards idealism in his thinking.'

'Did that ease his mind?'

'I believe so. He never mentioned it again.'

'He didn't seem stressed, worried, anxious in the weeks before his death?'

'Not at all. He was his usual self.'

'Thank you for your time, Mr Doyle,' Tessa said, draining

her cup and tossing it into the bin Cork City Council had placed next to the bench.

'You're quite welcome.'

She stood and was about to say goodbye when something occurred to her. 'Was there anything unusual about your fishing trip that day? Anything that struck you as out of the ordinary or strange?'

Doyle, who was still sitting, placed his carboard cup on the bench in the space Tessa had just vacated and fished a pink plastic vape from the inside pocket of his jacket. He took a drag from it, exhaling sweet-smelling vapour from his nose.

'There was nothing odd in terms of the boat or what we did,' he said, 'until I noticed Dave was missing of course. But there was... well, I didn't actually see it, but I suppose it merits a mention.'

'Go on,' Tessa said.

'It's probably not relevant,' Doyle said, taking another pull on his vape.

'I'll decide that,' Tessa said. 'Please, what were you going to say?'

'About half an hour before we turned back in, Dave spotted something strange in the water. He gave a kind of shout and pointed, but I was reeling in a fish, and by the time I turned to where he was indicating, the thing had gone. But he was deter-mined he *had* seen it.'

'What did he say he'd seen?'

'He said he'd seen a man swimming, just off our starboard bow.'

Tessa gave Doyle a hard look. 'How far out were you?'

'Nine miles from Schull, probably three from the island.'

'Is the sea safe for swimming around that area?'

'Good heavens, no. There are currents, reefs and riptides. I mean, I suppose some of those guys who do cross-Channel races might be capable of it, but when I looked, there was no one there, and a deep-sea swimmer would have had a support craft with him. I thought David must have been mistaken, that he probably just saw a seal. People have been mistaking those for all kinds of things since time immemorial.'

'Perhaps,' Tessa said. 'Did you tell Kilbarry or any of the other detectives about this?'

'No. It only came back to me when you asked if there had been anything strange about the trip. I hadn't thought about it since then.'

'You didn't think him seeing a man swimming past your boat was important?'

'In that patch of water, without a support boat? I thought it impossible so dismissed it.'

Tessa sighed. 'But you felt to tell me.'

'Well, you did ask.'

'That I did,' Tessa replied. 'That I did.'

THE WATCHER IN THE SHADOWS

The pub consisted of a small bar that contained only a couple of small tables with low stools to leave room for a dartboard and pool table, and a lounge that was only slightly bigger but had five tables, each of which could seat four diners. The menu was short, consisting of traditional Irish fare.

'What's tripe and drisheen?' the Watcher asked the driver.

'It's a Cork speciality,' she said. 'You've never eaten in the English Market, I take it.'

He flushed. 'I've never eaten nowhere fancy.'

'Would you call this place fancy?'

'No, but...'

She looked at him over her menu, and he saw there was no ridicule in her eyes and relaxed somewhat.

'I've never eaten anywhere except a takeaway before, alright?' he said. 'I grew up in care, and the units where I lived, we didn't get all that many treats.'

She lowered the menu and smiled at him. 'Lad, I grew up pretty much the same. I didn't eat in a restaurant until I was twenty-five, and when I did finally get to one, I didn't know three-quarters of what was on the menu and was too scared to ask what all the fancy stuff was. So I ended up ordering chicken and chips.'

'Was it good?'

She laughed. 'Probably not much better than I'd had before, and three times as expensive.'

He laughed too, and the tension left him, and maybe a little went from her too. He hoped so anyway.

'Tripe and drisheen is actually what they call peasant food,' she told him, 'which means it used to be something only very poor people would eat, but it's become trendy now for posh people to like that kind of stuff.'

'Why?'

She laughed again. 'Because some of it is really good, once you don't mind eating weird bits of the animal.'

'Weird bits?' the Watcher asked, aghast.

'Oh yeah. Tripe, for example, is the lining of a cow's stomach. They cook it for a long time, then mix it with a creamy white sauce that has herbs and onions in it. It's not bad, once you stop being scared of it. The tripe is soft, not unlike a kind of meaty pasta if it's cooked right. Drisheen is black pudding, but not like you've had before. It's not made with oats and breadcrumbs, just the blood, so it's a bit like a mousse. They usually don't spice it, so it's got a very mild flavour.'

'It doesn't sound all that nice,' the Watcher observed.

'I quite like it, but I'm not going to risk trying it in a place where I haven't eaten it before,' the driver said. 'It's a very easy dish to fuck up badly.'

'I think I'll just have the bacon and cabbage,' he said.

'Good choice. I think I'll have the beef-and-stout stew.'

They ordered.

'Thank you for buying me lunch,' he said. 'I... Well, no one's ever done that for me before.'

'You're welcome,' the driver said. 'We have to look after each other, people like you and me. Maybe one day you'll be able to do the same for some other young lad who needs a friend.'

He nodded. 'I hope I will.'

She had a glass of Diet Coke in front of her and took a sip from it. He had an ale shandy and drank some too.

'Do you know what this whole business is about?' she asked. 'This thing the boss is mixed up in?'

He shook his head. 'All I know is that this girl who's in Killian's seems to know more than she should about some jobs the boss had contracts for. She went to the cops about it, and these detectives from Dublin were sent down to check into it. The woman I was following, she's in charge of them, and she's supposed to be shit hot and tough as they come. The other two aren't exactly lightweights either. The boss isn't happy.'

'Do you know the girl?'

He shook his head. 'She's not like us. Comes from a good family.'

'How the hell is she involved in this kind of shit then?'

'I don't know. But she's in Killian's now. So he can get to her if he wants to. I'd say this'll be wrapped up soon enough.'

'Which doesn't mean anything good for the girl,' the driver said. 'Poor wee lass, whoever she is.'

The Watcher looked at the woman across the table from him, puzzled. He hadn't thought of Ellie O'Farrell as anything other than a mark, a name on a piece of paper, someone to watch and report back on. That she might be scared, hurt or sad hadn't occurred to him. Suddenly he remembered the expression on her face in the yard of the police station the previous evening; recalled the genuine pain and terror in her voice as she said goodbye to her parents. And he felt awful for not being aware of it before now. He'd been so scared he'd thought he might die many times and had no wish to see that kind of misery visited on someone else. Yet he'd allowed the boss to make him an instrument of such things and worse more often than he wanted to remember.

'Do you think he'll kill her?' he asked, the words out of his mouth before he even knew he'd spoken.

'Will you keep it down?' the driver hissed, looking about her to make sure they hadn't been overheard.

Luckily, there was no one else in the lounge at that moment. Even the barman had stepped out.

'You have to be careful,' she said. 'You never know who's listening!'

'Sorry,' he said, almost whispering now. 'But... do you think he would?'

'I don't believe the boss would think twice about it if he thought it would help him, even in a small way.'

At that moment, a door behind the Watcher swung open, and the barman emerged carrying a tray laden with food.

It was probably the best meal the Watcher had ever had, even though he couldn't get Ellie O'Farrell out of his mind throughout it. She seemed like a nice girl, from what he'd seen.

He hoped nothing bad would happen to her.

24

Tessa had tried to call Kilbarry as she drove, but he hadn't picked up and didn't call her back until she was pulling onto Anglesea Street.

'I've just a quick question for you,' she said as she reversed the Capri into a parking space.

'Fire ahead.'

'The waters around Cape Clear – does anyone do any deep-sea, open-water swimming around there?'

'No one in their right mind,' Kilbarry said. 'It's a particularly treacherous stretch of sea.'

'So there aren't any of those Ironman types out there doing distance training or anything like that?'

'No. To be honest, event organisers are having to rein a lot of that kind of nonsense in. There used to be a contest where contestants had to run a half-marathon, cycle seventy-five kilometres and then swim across Galway Bay. They nearly lost a couple of their competitors last year during the swimming section. You can train to swim the distance in a pool, which is what the majority of those who were in the race did. But it's a whole different ball game once you're in the ocean. Nothing can prepare you for the currents and swells.'

'There are people who swim from England to France and that type of malarkey though, aren't there?'

'Cross-Channel, yeah. No one would attempt that without a couple of support boats shadowing them. Too much can go wrong.'

'I just spoke to Paul Doyle, and he told me Dave Merrill thought he saw a swimmer three miles off Cape Clear.'

'He never told me that.'

'He said he thought it was irrelevant, as such a thing was impossible. Reckoned Merrill must have seen a seal.'

'Yeah, or a porpoise maybe.'

Tessa switched off the engine. 'I'm sure that's it.'

'Right you be. Catch you again, I hope.'

Tessa ended the call.

It was, of course, most likely Dave Merrill had been mistaken, but she couldn't kick the feeling there was more to his death than met the eye. For instance, after she'd spoken to Doyle, she'd checked the specifications for life jackets. Their straps were made to withstand pressures of more than a tonne. Merrill should have been able to dangle from a hook for days, even in a very rough sea, without the strap of his jacket giving way.

And as an experienced sailor, one who actually had a house on Cape Clear, shouldn't he be able to tell the difference between a seal, a porpoise and a human being, even if just glimpsed for a second in the water?

Something wasn't right.

And she was going to find out what it was.

25

The team had been given a corner of Anglesea Street's squad room to work from, and they gathered there at 3 p.m. to pool their information. The room, cluttered with desks and filing cabinets, boxes of old paperwork lying here and there about the floor, was almost empty mid-afternoon, most of the detectives who had their desks there out working cases.

'Let's take it chronologically,' Tessa said when everyone was seated. 'Earliest death first, so that's me. Dave Merrill, according to the coastguard and the report from the medical examiner, fell overboard due to a medical crisis – he was a man of a certain age who didn't look after himself. The scenario that seems to have been accepted is that as he fell, his life jacket snagged on a piece of metal on the stern of the boat, causing it to tear, which in turn caused him to float low in the water with his face partly submerged. Due to this convergence of circumstances, he inhaled seawater and drowned.'

'A genuine accident then?' Danny said.

'Maybe so, maybe not,' Tessa said. 'The likelihood of him getting caught as he fell, not to mention the odds of the life-jacket strap tearing, are infinitesimally small. And he told the guy he was with that he'd seen someone swimming past the boat shortly before the accident that killed him.'

'Did his friend see this mystery swimmer?' Maggie asked.

'Nope. But this is the same friend who checked the life jacket and deemed it to be in prime condition.'

'Does the friend have a motive?'

'Not a single one.'

They all looked at one another.

'So what we have is a series of circumstances that don't add up very well,' Danny said.

'I can't believe it's just been accepted as an accident,' Tessa said. 'If this were me, the case would still be open.'

'In fairness, there's no motive, no witnesses, and from what you've said, he wasn't a well man,' Maggie said.

'He's a hugely successful businessman,' Tessa said. 'I bet that if we start digging, we'll find half a dozen motives for murder within the first hour. Danny, you're up next. You've had quite an adventurous day.'

Danny told them about his conversation with the staff of The Balti House.

'And to be frank,' he concluded, 'the situation is very like yours, Tessa. It could have been an accident, but if it was, the driver who hit him was in the wrong lane.'

'Could have been drunk or stoned,' Maggie said.

'And yet they got away,' Danny said. 'When I got back here, I checked the traffic cams in the area and looked at the reports of the squad-car drivers who went looking for them. The car seems to have just vanished. I'm not sure a person who was so drunk they killed a guy who was on the other side of the road to the one they were supposed to be on would have had the soundness of mind to get the car off the road that quickly and that thoroughly.'

'But the witnesses didn't know for sure what make or model it was, did they?' Tessa asked.

'Sharmin, the cook and owner at The Balti House, thought it was a BMW. He and Shauna, the girl who saw the accident, both said they thought it was grey. And it would have had Miles McGuinness's DNA on it. He was pretty messed up. No, whoever hit him got the car and themselves undercover fast, and I'm absolutely certain that vehicle has been disposed of. It'll be little more than scrap metal now, if it's even that.'

'So you're thinking this was a murder too then,' Tessa said.

'I am. And, just like you, I'm wondering why the hell the guards aren't tearing the place apart looking for the driver of that car.'

'Speaking of cars and drivers, you had a bit of bother on the way back to Cork?' Tessa said.

'Just a small bit, yeah.'

He told them again about the Peugeot EV and its two passengers, and how one of them had opened fire on him when he'd confronted them.

'You didn't think to call for backup before you decided to go all Dirty Harry on them?' Maggie said disapprovingly. 'Particularly after me and Tessa being attacked by trained fecking assassins?'

'This didn't feel like that,' Danny said. 'And I could tell as soon as I got a look at them, these were local hoods. The one that shot at me was little more than a kid. Early twenties, at the oldest.'

'Any word on the car since then?' Tessa asked.

'They put out an APB, but I've heard nothing,' Danny said.

'They probably disappeared into the back roads,' Maggie said. 'That part of Cork is a maze once you turn off the dual carriageway.'

'Both the car and the plates were stolen,' Danny said. 'But I did get a decent look at both the driver and the passenger. I've been going through mugshots, but no joy so far.'

'Keep at it,' Tessa said. 'It'd be good to know who those guys are, and why they were following you.'

'You think they were just trying to scare me off? The shots came damn close if that was their plan.'

'I'm not saying that kid wasn't trying to kill you once you rousted them,' Tessa said. 'But before that, I'm pretty sure you were being watched, which makes me think we all were.'

'I didn't spot anyone,' Maggie said. 'I spent an hour driving the most obscure route back from Ballincollig, but no one was behind me.'

'My guess is that the others pulled out when Danny spotted he was being followed,' Tessa said.

'Why tail us though?' Maggie asked.

'They want to know how we're approaching the case,' Tessa said. 'What we're learning. Who we're talking to. Whoever is behind all of this didn't expect a team to be sent from Dublin. We're an unknown quantity. They want to get to know us. What better way than to watch us at work?'

'We'll have to be extra careful going forward,' Maggie said.

'Damn right we will,' Tessa agreed. 'How did you and Pav get on?'

'This scene doesn't make sense either. The killer managed to get into the house without leaving any evidence of how they gained access, then made the most godawful mess. Blood everywhere. It's as if almost pathological subtlety disintegrated into complete chaos.'

'Any sign of how they got out?'

'I'm pretty sure it was by the window in the office, which wasn't open but had been left unlocked. I wondered if they might have gotten in that way too, but Glenda insists her husband was a stickler for closing windows and doors, so it doesn't seem likely. I was able to work out the killer's path through the garden and onto the street. Only thing is that they'd have been covered in blood.'

'Unless they changed at the scene,' Tessa suggested. 'They had time. There was no one alive in the house, remember.'

'No clothes were found, or any sign of someone washing up.'

'They might have just pulled a coat on over their clothes, so all they needed was some... I dunno, some wet wipes to get the blood spatter off their hands and face,' Danny said. 'Probably took the used wipes with them.'

'That sounds plausible,' Maggie said.

'On the face of it, this one doesn't look like the others,' Tessa suggested.

'I bet it was supposed to be just like them though,' Danny said. 'It was meant to look like an accident. Something happened. The killer got spooked, and that made them get sloppy.'

'What could have spooked them though?' Maggie asked.

'Could have been anything,' Tessa said. 'Maybe Wilde spotted them and tried to fight. Or they thought he was going to spot them. I agree with Danny. This one was a botched job.'

They sat for a moment, considering all they'd learned.

'That leaves us with two questions,' Danny said.

'Why these three men?' Tessa said, voicing the first one for him.

'And how did Ellie know they were going to die?' he finished.

Tessa's phone buzzed. She picked it up. 'Tessa Burns here. Oh, hello, Doctor.' She listened for a moment. 'Yeah. I'll be right there. Thanks for calling.'

She hung up and looked at the others. 'Well, what do you know?' she said. 'My night visitor was right.'

'You've lost me,' Maggie said.

'Me too,' Danny concurred.

'Ellie O'Farrell has just informed Dr Cleary where she got her information about the murders.'

Danny and Maggie looked at her expectantly.

'And?' Danny pressed.

'They wouldn't tell me over the phone. They are, in fact, calling an emergency case conference.'

'Your Faceless Man said we'd receive an explanation of what happened,' Danny said. 'I never expected that would come from Ellie herself. I mean, are you sure this is what he was talking about?'

'Only one way to find out,' Tessa said. 'I'll go and hear what Cleary has to say. Danny, will you keep checking those mugshots, and, Maggie, I'd love to know if there's a connection between our three deaths.'

Her team mates nodded, and they all went to work.

26

The case conference was chaired by Gary Wilton, the manager of St Killian's. He was a well-built man in his late fifties, his head shaved to the point it shone under the light of the electric bulb overhead. He was dressed in designer jeans and an open-necked shirt and had a well-trimmed, grey goatee. Wilton began by going over the details of why Ellie O'Farrell was in the unit then gave an assessment of how her time at St Killian's had gone.

'Ellie's stay with us has been short but eventful, and not in a particularly good way,' he said to the group who'd gathered in the unit's meeting room, which seemed to be designed so that no one felt comfortable: it looked like a playroom that someone had started to adapt and then stopped before the task was complete. The walls were adorned with a mural of a sunny day with clouds, a smiling sun and various colourful birds. There was a low table in the middle of the room that Tessa thought might have once been used to put games on when the kids were doing floor play.

There were plenty of seats, but they were all at different

heights, and two of them were little more than beanbags. Tessa had taken one of these and sat cross-legged in it – she'd been posted in Afghanistan when she was in the army and was used to sitting on low seats and cushions as a result. It didn't bother her in the slightest.

Another young woman, whose name was Janet Reece, sat in the other one, though she didn't look at ease. Ms Reece was in charge of Ellie's floor in the unit. She was, Tessa guessed, in her late twenties, heavyset with tightly permed hair, and looked as if she would much rather be somewhere else.

Philip and Cynthia, Ellie's parents, sat opposite Tessa, Cynthia on a high stool and Philip on a chair that looked like it was meant for four- or five-year-olds in a school's junior class-room. Behind them, leaning against the wall with his arms folded, was Conor Stokes, their lawyer, today wearing a dark-blue suit with a narrow charcoal pinstripe over a starched, open-necked white shirt. Dr Cleary sat next to Cynthia, perched on a wooden, straight-backed kitchen chair. Beside the therapist was Sergeant O'Mahoney, sitting with his knees together on a three-legged stool, and next to him was a social worker, Alannah Guthrie, tall, thin and waspish, a Joni Mitchell haircut framing a serious face with prominent cheekbones.

'Could you expand on the word "eventful" please?' Alannah Guthrie said, making inverted commas in the air with her fingers.

'She hasn't been an easy resident to deal with,' Wilton said. 'She's been oppositional, has done everything in her power to separate herself from the other young people, and when one of them approached her with an offer of inclusion, Ellie responded with violence.'

'What?' Cynthia O'Farrell asked, the anger clear in her tone. 'Ellie isn't a violent child! She's never raised a hand to anyone in her life.'

'If she'd just raised a hand, we wouldn't have such a problem,' Janet Reece interjected. 'She used a weapon.'

'A weapon?' Philip gasped. 'What kind of a weapon? And where the hell did she get it?'

'Does it matter?' Guthrie asked mildly.

'I would say it matters a great deal,' Tessa said, speaking for the first time since the meeting had begun.

'I fail to see how,' Wilton said.

'Then you're probably in the wrong job,' Tessa said mildly. 'I mean, did she hit some kid with a bar of soap inside a sock, or did she carve up someone with a shiv made from a razor blade and a toothbrush?'

'She... well, she used a book,' the manager said.

Tessa gazed at Wilton incredulously. 'Ellie whacked some kid with a book? You're having a conniption because of that?'

'She did a little more than whack someone. The girl she assaulted suffered multiple fractures to her hand. Two of the knuckles were effectively separated.'

'And this was done without provocation?' Philip asked.

'Well... Bridie, the girl who was attacked, can be a bit of a hard case, but that doesn't excuse the assault.'

'I should remind you at this point that, under Irish law, a verbal threat constitutes an assault in itself,' Stokes growled from his stance against the wall. 'Ms O'Farrell, by the sounds of it, was acting in self-defence.'

'*Did* Bridie assault Ellie first?' Tessa asked.

'The incident is being looked into.'

'I trust somewhere like St Killian's has lots of security cameras?' Stokes said.

'Of course,' Wilton agreed.

'I'd imagine an examination of the relevant footage will show exactly what happened then.'

Wilton seemed to sense he was fighting a losing battle and cleared his throat before changing the subject. 'After the... um... altercation with Bridie, Ellie asked to speak to Dr Cleary. Doctor, would you like to share with the group what Ellie told you?'

The doctor sat up a bit straighter and opened a hard-backed notebook, running his finger down the page as he spoke. 'I left St Killian's to return to my private practice around midday and had just arrived at my office when I received the call that Ellie had asked to see me urgently, and that she was prepared to divulge where she acquired foreknowledge of the three deaths. I immediately returned to find Ellie had been placed in a time-out room, due to an incident with another resident, which Mr Wilton has just been good enough to inform you of.'

'What's a time-out room?' Cynthia asked.

'It's... well, a room designed to protect the residents when they become overstimulated,' Cleary said.

'Like a sensory room?'

'Not exactly. It's a bare room where the walls and floor are constructed of soft material so the resident can't harm themselves.'

Cynthia's eyes became wide and her tone shrill. 'A padded cell? You put my daughter in a padded cell?'

'It was for her own protection,' Wilton said. 'Our policy when a resident becomes violent is very clear: they must be isolated for their own safety and for the safety of others.'

'Even when you're dealing with a child with no history of violence, and one who's committed no crime?' Stokes asked. 'I'll be having a very close look at these policies of yours.'

'I cannot believe you people!' Cynthia shouted.

'Mrs O'Farrell, can I please continue? What I have to say may help us in getting Ellie out of here once and for all.'

Cynthia fell into a tense silence.

She's close to breaking point, Tessa thought. *It's not going to take much to push her over the edge.*

'When I spoke with Ellie, she was quite calm, and delivered

what she had to say clearly and directly. I have to say, I find her story quite convincing.'

'What *did* she say?' O'Mahoney asked pointedly. 'We've all dropped everything to be here, and so far there's been a lot of dancing around the point.'

'Ellie says she's been visiting a site on the dark web for some time. The page is called "We are Murder" and seems to be a message board where people who are planning on killing someone post details of their intentions, and where others can offer advice on how they might... um... well, how they might improve on their schemes and make them more effective.'

'I've heard of the dark web,' Cynthia said, 'but I don't really know what it is.'

'The internet is divided into two parts,' Tessa said. 'There's the surface web, which is indexed and can be searched using engines like Google or Bing, and what's known as the deep web, which isn't indexed, meaning you have to know what you're looking for and have specific addresses and possibly passwords to make your way around. There are apps you can get to help you navigate it though.'

'Why is it unindexed?' Cynthia asked.

'Because whoever created the sites doesn't want the general public accessing them. There can be good reasons for that – in the case of company intranets and government websites, for example – but sometimes it's because the content of the sites is illegal, and that part's called the *dark* web,' Tessa explained. 'A chat forum like the one Ellie described would just be the tip of the iceberg there. People go there to buy weapons, hire hitmen, upload child pornography or torture videos, arrange drug drops... the list is endless. An old captain of mine used to say that if you can imagine it, no matter how sick or bizarre, you'll find it on the dark web.'

'How would Ellie know anything about this kind of stuff?' Philip asked, sounding appalled.

'Mr O'Farrell, your daughter is a fan of true-crime books and podcasts,' Cleary said. 'It's most likely her interest became piqued by listening to or reading something that referenced this aspect of the online world. Once she'd heard about it, it wouldn't be that difficult for her to find her way there. The page she found allows you to search according to geographical area. Ellie, of course, looked for entries referring to her hometown.'

'And once there, she would have encountered some very dangerous people,' O'Mahoney said. 'The dark web is a hotbed of unpleasantness.'

'I would guess there were a lot of fetishists on the page,' Cleary said, 'people who are excited by the idea of violence but probably won't ever commit a crime. It seems, though, that Ellie was able to pick out, on a subconscious level, the ones that were genuine. And they gave her nightmares.'

'So her telling us about what she'd seen, and going to the police, was all really a cry for help?' Cynthia asked.

'I would say that's true,' Cleary said. 'She may have even repressed the fact she'd ever been on the dark web. It all became too stressful for her, but she needed to assuage her guilt by informing the Gardai about what she'd learned.'

O'Mahoney snorted. 'Has she handed over the web address for this site?'

'She wrote it down for me,' Cleary said.

'I'd best have our tech guys look at it.'

'Maggie can do that for you,' Tessa said. 'She's an excellent researcher.'

'I'd prefer to use my own people,' O'Mahoney growled.

Tessa shrugged and smiled at Ellie's psychiatrist. 'Dr Cleary, I'd appreciate that web address too please.'

The therapist nodded. 'To conclude, I think it's clear we're not dealing with a young woman of criminal intent,' he said. 'This was simply the act of a curious mind, and one that acted honourably once its owner realised the mistake she'd made. I, for one, would like to petition that Ellie's time here be concluded. Immediately.'

'Her assessment isn't yet complete,' Wilton said. 'Her behaviour doesn't support your conclusions. I look at Ellie and I see a very angry young woman. One who's shown she has a capacity for violent acts.'

'Mr Wilton,' Tessa said, 'every single person in this room has the capacity for violence, though most people never have the need to access that capacity. By placing Ellie in a unit like this, she was put in a position where she had no choice but to act or else allow herself to be preyed upon. That's not her fault.'

'Whose fault is it then?' O'Mahoney asked.

'Yours probably, Sarge,' Tessa said. 'I told you it was a bad idea sending her here.'

'You say that despite the fact we have results?'

'I do. There are other ways we could have got them.'

The sarge snorted again and lapsed back into silence.

'I don't think Ms O'Farrell belongs here,' Alannah Guthrie, the social worker, said. 'I have to say that I have some concerns about her though.'

'And what are they?' Cynthia asked primly.

'I wonder if you're as connected with your daughter's interests as you might think,' the social worker asked. 'A girl with her intellect and unregulated access to the worldwide web can find herself in a lot of trouble. People tend to forget that online activity *can* cross over into the physical world. I believe you've had an object lesson in that these past few days.'

Cynthia looked at the woman with an expression of utter disdain, but Philip, placing his hand on his wife's smaller one, said, 'Thank you for your advice, Ms Guthrie. I assure you, we'll be keeping a weather eye on Ellie's online activities from here on.'

'I'd be watching your back around her too,' Alannah said

dourly. 'Anyone who can do that amount of damage with a paperback is someone I'd be very feckin' careful of.'

'I'd be careful what you say about my daughter,' Cynthia said through gritted teeth.

Alannah eyed the woman with an expression that was approaching a smile. 'I see the apple doesn't fall far from the tree.'

'I'd also be careful about stepping into the realms of slander,' Stokes rumbled.

Alannah turned and threw him an evil glare.

'I don't think this type of exchange is helpful,' Cleary said, sounding more than a little uncomfortable with the scene that was unfolding.

'May we have a vote on Ellie being returned to her family while the website is investigated?' Tessa asked in an attempt to defuse the situation.

'All in favour of sending Ellie O'Farrell home?' Wilton asked.

Only Wilton himself and the sarge didn't raise their hands.

'That's passed then,' Cleary said. 'Mr Wilton, will you record the findings of the panel and report them to the department?'

'I will,' Wilton said. 'Mr and Mrs O'Farrell, if you come with me, we can fill out the necessary paperwork, and you can take your daughter home.'

The couple, looking somewhat dazed and confused, stood – though not easily.

'Don't go leaving town,' O'Mahoney said as they moved towards the door. 'We're a long way from done.'

'As are we,' Stokes said.

O'Mahoney got up and walked over to the lawyer so they were nose to nose. 'Do your worst. I've dealt with your type before. You might represent this bunch of tree-huggers, but I know who you are. And you don't scare me.'

Neither Philip nor Cynthia uttered a word. At that moment, it didn't matter to them what Sergeant O'Mahoney said.

Ellie was going home.

27

Danny and Maggie worked side by side in the squad room in Anglesea Street, Danny using one of the station's old desktop computers, Maggie the laptop attached to her chair.

'Any joy?' she asked after forty-five minutes had passed.

'I think this guy might be the driver,' Danny said, turning the screen slightly so Maggie could have a look at the photo and accompanying rap sheet.

'Josh Haughey,' she read. 'Twenty-eight years old. Been involved with crime since he was in school.'

'He's been in and out of St Killian's a few times, I see,' Danny pointed out.

'No known gang affiliations,' Maggie said. 'So why was he tailing you then?'

'Just because he didn't have gang links doesn't mean he hasn't found any,' Danny pointed out. 'The last stretch he did inside was for driving the getaway car after the robbery of an armoured van carrying cash to ATM machines. That was eighteen months ago.'

'He's fresh out of jail then. We should pay him a visit.'

'We should. How about you? Anything linking our deceased pals?'

Maggie grinned. 'I couldn't find anything when I searched for them individually,' she said. 'Even when I put the three names in together, I got no hits. It looked as if the three of them really didn't know one another. I tried a few trawls using standard business and finance topics for each in turn and got the standard articles and mentions in the Sunday *Business Post* and the like, but nothing that offered us anything useful.'

'I have a sense you're getting to something,' Danny said.

'Oh, I am. It wasn't until I'd given up on the dead guys completely and was researching the O'Farrells' lawyer, Conor Stokes, that I hit the jackpot.'

She turned her own computer screen around so Danny could look. On it was a photo of a black-tie event. According to the caption, it was a fundraiser for HuTec (Humanitarian Technology) International, Philip O'Farrell's company. The photo showed a group of men, all with their hands resting on one of the oversized cheques that were used for photo opportunities to demonstrate how much money had been raised – in this case it was €150,000.

The caption named only Stokes – he'd raised the money by climbing Mount Kilimanjaro in 2017. He was, according to the web page, pictured with members of the HuTec board.

Danny picked out Stokes in the group immediately – his facial scarring was clear, even in the slightly blurred online photo. It took him a little longer to identify the other people in the shot, but he soon picked out Philip, and then, to his surprise, Miles McGuinness, the banker who'd been killed in the hit and run in Castlemartyr. He recognised the man's bald pate and prominent ears from the photo on his file. As his eyes ran along the group, he spied Dominic Wilde and then Dave Merrill. There were two other people Danny didn't know in the shot as well. But that hardly seemed to matter.

'These three were on the board of Ellie's dad's company?' Danny asked, open-mouthed. 'How the hell did the investigators miss this? It throws things into a completely different light!'

'The reason they missed it is that that caption is incorrect,' Maggie said. 'They weren't on the management board.'

'No? What's their involvement then?'

'They were all part of a group dedicated to raising funds for the company.'

'Still, I would have thought that was relevant.'

'This incarnation of the fundraising committee officially disbanded a month after this photo was taken. Those groups usually have a fixed time in which they're active, then they drop out and others replace them. It's common practice in charity work. It prevents compassion fatigue, sustains energy and keeps ideas fresh. Also, most people don't publicise their involvement in groups like this. It makes you look like you're only doing it for the kudos.'

'I bet loads of people do make a big deal out of it on their social media,' Danny observed.

'Not at this level. Stokes did with his Kilimanjaro climb, by the looks of it, but only to encourage a few local businesses to contribute. It was all low-key really. This is a staff page for HuTec itself, so not available on the web without a password.'

Danny grinned. 'How'd you find it then?'

'I just asked nicely and the site opened up for me.'

'Of course it did.'

'Did you find out anything about Stokes?'

Maggie sighed. 'He's quite the character. With quite the story.'

'Do tell.'

'Conor Stokes was, up to December 2010, a mob lawyer.'

'What changed in 2010?'

'That's the thing – no one knows for sure. I've read a couple of articles that speculate. It seems he vanished for three months.

When he reappeared, he had the facial scars and began working solely for registered charities and NGOs. It seems that whatever happened caused him to realign his moral compass.'

'The articles that speculate...' Danny said, 'what are their hypotheses?'

'That Stokes fell foul of one of his employers, who decided to remove half his face as a sign not to mess with them.'

'That's pretty much what I was thinking,' Danny said. 'So we have three dead men just so happening to be ex-fundraisers for Ellie's dad, and a former mob lawyer mixed up in all of this. Curiouser and curiouser.'

'When I was speaking to Dominic Wilde's widow, she indicated he was working on some sort of charity project the night he was killed.'

'That's a bit of a coincidence,' the big detective said.

'I say we head out to visit the driver of the car that followed you and swing by Mr Stokes on the way back. I'll call Tessa and let her know where we're going.'

Danny nodded and sent the page on Josh Haughey to be printed. He was standing to go to the room's printer, which was in the corner at the back of the squad room, when the door opened and three men in plain clothes came in.

And that was when everything took a very disturbing turn.

28

Tessa sat in the reception area of St Killian's with Ellie while her parents went to sign the papers for her release. Stokes skulked about near the counter, doing something on his phone.

'What made you decide to come clean about the dark web?' Tessa asked the girl.

'I'd had enough of this place,' Ellie said, looking sullen and sulky.

'Fair enough. Why not just tell your folks right away? Why all the cloak and dagger?'

'I didn't want them to take my computer away. Or my phone. I expect they'll both be gone now.'

'Maybe. Maybe not. How did you get the web address for this page you visited?'

'I found it on a true-crime page I visit.'

'Yeah? Which one?'

Ellie blinked. 'I can't remember.'

'I call bullshit,' Tessa said gently. 'But okay, I'll play along. A page like that isn't going to be accessible using Chrome. Which browser did you download to navigate your way about the dark web?'

'Tor. I used Tor.'

'And where did you learn about Tor?'

Ellie blinked at Tessa.

'Online.'

'Which site?'

'I... I don't recall. Just one about how to use the dark web.'

'Just a random site?'

'Yeah. You know. There's loads of them.'

Tessa shook her head. 'You weren't on the dark web, were you, Ellie?'

The girl just stared at her.

'Who told you to say you were?'

It was Ellie's turn to shake her head this time. 'I was,' she said quietly. 'I was on the chat forum. That's how I know what I know. That's all *you* need to know.'

'This won't be the end of all the scary stuff,' Tessa said, leaning in close to the girl. 'If we don't know what's going on, we can't stop it, and if we can't stop it, it'll just keep happening. These people, once they have their claws into you and your family, they won't let go.'

'Come on, Ellie – let's go.'

Tessa looked up to see Stokes towering over her and the child.

'What?' Ellie asked.

'Your mum and dad have asked me to take you home. They've signed the papers permitting you to leave, but they've got to talk to the management and social workers and whatnot. Your mother doesn't want you to stay here a moment longer than you have to, so I said I'd drive you back to Douglas and wait with you until they get back.'

He held out a hand. Ellie looked dubious for a moment, but then she took the scarred man's much bigger hand in her own and allowed him to lead her towards the door.

'Ellie, before you go,' Tessa said, and ran over and gave the girl her card. 'Just in case you need to reach me.'

Ellie nodded and slipped it into her pocket before following the lawyer to his Saab.

Tessa watched them drive away, wondering why it felt like she shouldn't have let the kid out of her sight.

29

In the squad room at Anglesea Road, Danny was pulling on his jacket when the biggest of the three detectives who'd just come in said in a voice he and Maggie were obviously supposed to hear, 'Seems they're giving anyone a badge these days. Fuckin' wokeness gone mad, if you ask me.'

Danny froze.

The man who'd spoken was perhaps two inches shorter than his six-feet-four and had a developing paunch. His hair was greying and cut in a standard short back and sides, and he was wearing a cheap blue suit with a white shirt and red tie, which was askew about his neck.

The other two were shorter, one probably just over six feet, the other smaller again. The taller one had the broad shoulders of someone who lifted a lot of weights. The other guy was slim, and Danny figured he was a runner. He had the loose, elastic movements of someone who was comfortable in their body.

'I know exactly what you mean,' the runner said, laughing loudly. 'Makes the rest of us look like fuckin' jokes. I hope the union kicks up some shit about it.'

Maggie must have seen the expression on Danny's face,

because she said, 'Danny – leave it. They're just assholes mouthing off.'

He threw her a look and tried to quell the anger that was bubbling in his gut. 'Let's get out of here,' he said.

'My thoughts exactly.'

The three men were clustered around a desk just to the left of the door. The big one made an exaggerated show of opening it to allow Maggie through.

'Thank you,' she said dryly.

'You're welcome. Just let me know if you need help with anything else. Well... I'm not gonna wipe your arse, but I'd say you've got big boy here for that.'

Danny had grabbed the man by his lapels before he even knew he'd done it and slammed him hard back onto the desktop.

'I'm giving you one chance to apologise to my friend,' he said. 'If you don't, I'm going to enjoy teaching you some manners.'

The big man didn't utter a word. Instead, he delivered a headbutt directly into Danny's nose, driving him back and causing blood to gush forth. Danny staggered against the still-open door, effectively wedging Maggie between it and the door frame, and as he did, the other two charged in. Half blinded by tears, he managed to punch the weightlifter in the shoulder, but the runner, whom he'd known from the start was probably going to be the most trouble, came in with some kind of martial arts kick, catching him in the throat and cutting off his oxygen supply for a few moments.

Maggie was unable to move either forwards or back. 'Boys, for God's sake, what is wrong with you?' she bellowed.

Danny could hear Pav growling, a low, rumbling sound, and knew the hair all along his back would be standing up.

'I need to get back in there,' Maggie said to the dog. 'Go and help Danny.'

Pavlov didn't need to be told twice – he rounded the door at speed and flung himself at the runner, who'd followed up his karate kick with three driving punches into Danny's stomach, pushing whatever air he'd had in his lungs out and making him feel light-headed.

Pav sank his teeth into the man's calf, shaking his head back and forth to deepen the wounds. The runner cried out and went to kick the dog, but Pav shimmied out of the way then launched himself at him again, aiming for his groin. Danny, his breath returning, pushed himself away from the door, releasing the pressure on Maggie's chair and allowing her to reverse back in. She grabbed the can of mace from its scabbard as she did so.

'Is everyone finished?' she shouted. 'You're like a pack of schoolkids! Cop yourselves on, for the love of God!'

'Fuck you, you retarded cripple,' the tallest man said and drew his handgun. 'Here's what my report is going to say: the big boy there lost control. Pulled his weapon. We had no choice but to defend ourselves.'

Maggie didn't hesitate. She tossed the can into her left hand and sprayed the man full blast in the face while whipping out her extendable baton with her right. This she lashed across the wrist of his gun hand, causing the shot he fired to go wide.

Danny, fully recovered, caught the bodybuilder by the hair and slammed his head full force into the wall, letting the unconscious body drop to the floor. He turned to see the runner had drawn his own weapon and was aiming it at Pav, who had him by the other leg.

'Hey!' Danny shouted.

The man looked up reflexively, and Danny punched him full force in the forehead. He dropped like a stone.

Danny and Maggie paused, both breathing heavily.

'What the fuck just happened?' Maggie asked as Pav jumped up into her lap.

'I haven't got a clue,' Danny said. 'But I think we were just set up.'

That was when the door burst open again, and two detectives, one male, one female, both with flak jackets over their shirts, rushed in, guns drawn.

'Get on your fucking knees, hands behind your head!' the male detective said.

'Um...' Maggie looked a bit sheepish. 'Can either of you see a problem with that request?'

PART THREE

THE WATCHER IN THE DARK

He was lying on his bed staring at the ceiling when his phone buzzed. It was a withheld number.

'I want you to round up some of the boys you've worked with in the past. Reliable ones, mind. I don't want anything to go wrong. We're at a crucial stage, and things are already hanging in the balance. Can I trust you to do this?'

'Of course, boss.'

'Good. I'll text you an address. Take them there and wait for my instructions.'

'Okay.'

'If things go as they should, you'll be handsomely rewarded.'

'Okay, boss,' he said. 'Boss, can I ask you something?'

'Go right ahead.'

'You told me you'd arrange for me to go to college. I know you're busy and all, but I was just wonderin' if there's any news on that?'

There was a pause at the other end of the line, and he could hear the man breathing.

'Have I ever let you down?'

'No, boss.'

'Haven't I always come through for you? Even when everyone else in your life hasn't?'

'Yes, boss. Always.'

'Well then trust me. Put your faith in me as I have done in you. Do as I ask and all you wish for will come to you.'

'Okay. Sorry, boss. I was just wonderin' is all.'

'That's quite alright. Now go and get me some workers, and we'll talk again soon.'

The Watcher hung up and sat on the edge of his bed.

He'd been waiting for the boss to get him a college place for more than two years. He wanted to learn programming, or coding, as he'd heard other people call it, so he could make games for the PlayStation or the Xbox or even for PCs – he'd prefer to work on stuff for games consoles, but he'd do PC work to begin with, if he had to.

The Watcher had lots of ideas, and once, when he'd smoked a few joints, he'd told a couple of lads who were staying in the squat he'd been living in at the time about one of the games he was working out in his head, and they'd told him they thought it sounded brilliant.

He just needed a chance. If he had an opportunity to make his dreams come true, he'd grab hold of it with both hands – he knew he would.

He didn't have a good Leaving Cert, the exam all students took to complete their secondary education in Ireland – he'd hated school and skipped more classes than he'd attended. When he'd sat down to fill out the college application forms, he'd panicked. He couldn't make head nor tail of what they were even asking him.

The boss had said he'd help. Take care of all of that for him.

In his heart, he wanted to believe the boss would come through. But he couldn't help thinking about what the driver had told him. About how the boss had absolutely not come through for her.

Then there was the fact that he was starting to feel bad for Ellie O'Farrell.

She seemed like a kid who didn't deserve to have bad stuff happen to her. Not that anyone did, but he had a feeling she'd always done the right thing and tried to be the best person she could be.

The Watcher didn't want to bring fear and pain into her life.

He stood up and put on his coat.

He didn't want Ellie to feel worse than she already did. But he had a feeling it might be too late to stop the tidal wave that was already making its way towards her.

Tessa sat opposite Sergeant O'Mahoney in his office.

Dawn Wilson was on speakerphone.

'Commissioner, I don't think I need to tell you how absolutely horrified I am at this turn of events,' O'Mahoney was saying. 'I have never, in more than thirty years of service, seen this kind of conduct in any of my houses. I know some of the lads can play a bit rough sometimes, but I have three officers in A&E as we speak, and a bullet hole in the wall of my squad room.'

'Maggie Doolan informs me your men were behaving inappropriately towards her, and Danny came to her defence,' Dawn said patiently. 'It was, according to her, *your* man who discharged his weapon. I'm assuming ballistics will reflect that.'

'I've been led to believe he did so in self-defence. That brute Murphy, whom I've learned is on probation for seriously assaulting a suspect, drew first.'

'Detective Murphy's weapon wasn't fired, Willie – it was still in its holster, in fact. You know that. Please tell me there are cameras in the squad room.'

'There are not. I meant to have them repaired, but it didn't seem a priority. You know how it is with budgets. It seemed more important to maintain the ones in the interview rooms.'

'For fuck's sake, Willie,' Dawn said, all patience gone. 'This is just a "he said, she said" situation then. What do you want me to do?'

O'Mahoney laughed. 'Oh, I can tell you what I want. Take your task force off this case. Well, I say your task force, but it's become somewhat depleted now.'

'How, exactly, has it been depleted?' Dawn asked.

'Danny and Maggie are in cells,' Tessa said. 'The sarge is insisting charges are brought against them.'

'Willie, is that strictly necessary?' Dawn asked. 'No one was seriously hurt.'

'One of my lads has a broken jaw, a fractured nose and has lost three teeth. I'd say that was serious enough, wouldn't you? He'll be drinking through a straw for the next three months.'

'I would take it as a personal favour if you allowed me to deal with my own people,' the commissioner said. 'I promise you, I will get to the bottom of what happened.'

'I already have,' O'Mahoney said. 'Your man ran amok. End of story. And his pal in the wheelchair wasn't exactly slow to throw down either. She fractured a man's wrist with that stick of hers and half blinded him with pepper spray. I have to question your judgement letting that woman go about with a chair packed with weapons! What are you thinking? This isn't the Wild feckin' West, you know.'

'Maggie Doolan is a highly respected member of the force who does not utilise those weapons frivolously,' Dawn said. 'I know for certain that she must have been sorely provoked.'

'Danny Murphy is going to remain in custody until we can get him to trial,' O'Mahoney said. 'I'm acting within my rights, and you know it. I'm charging Maggie Doolan and will be recommending she not be permitted back on active duty until she's received a full mental-health assessment. I'm not convinced she's fit for active duty. It's feckin' embarrassing seein' her goin' around the place with that mongrel.'

'Pavlov is a hell of a lot more than just some mongrel,' Tessa said testily. 'I have personally had reason to be glad he was part of the team – he has *literally* saved lives.'

'He's vicious and needs to be destroyed if you ask me,' O'Mahoney said. 'One of my men is going to need stitches from the injuries your mutt gave him.'

'Pavlov would only attack to protect members of the team,' Tessa said.

'I've put a call in to the dog warden,' O'Mahoney said. 'Luckily he doesn't work nights, so my advice is to not have the mutt here when he arrives tomorrow. If the animal is on site, he'll be removed pending euthanasia.'

'What the fuck is wrong with you?' Tessa asked, unable to control herself any longer. 'You've gone out of your way to make this case difficult from the moment we arrived.'

'You heard me, Detective Burns,' O'Mahoney said. 'He's currently locked up in the family room. Don't say I didn't give you fair warning.'

'I'm answerable to the commissioner, and no one else,' Tessa seethed. 'You should remember that before you start issuing orders.'

'Tessa, take it easy,' Dawn said. 'Willie, you've made your position clear. You leave me no choice but to remove Tessa and her team from the case, effective immediately. As for Danny, you're right, there's nothing I can do until I've had a chance to fully investigate what happened, and you, sir, can't block my doing that. However, until then, Detective Murphy will have to remain in custody. You can charge Maggie, and I suppose you have grounds to hold her too, pending an assessment. But let me tell you – I'm not going to be taking this lying down. I don't know what's going on in your house, Willie, but I have to tell you, I don't like it. And when I find out what it is, there will be repercussions. And serious ones. Don't say I didn't give *you* fair warning.'

'I have nothing to hide.'

'We'll see about that, won't we?'

'Good evening, Commissioner. Detective Burns, take your animal and get out of my police station.'

'Nothing would make me happier,' Tessa said.

ELLIE O'FARRELL

At first she thought her dad's lawyer was taking a circuitous route home, heading back into the city rather than going through the Jack Lynch Tunnel. But she soon realised they weren't heading for Douglas.

'Where are we going?' she asked Stokes.

'I have something I need you to do,' he said in that rasping voice of his. 'It's very important. Your family's future depends on it.'

Ellie looked at the man. From where she was sitting, in the front passenger seat of the Saab, all she could see was his profile, the network of scars and striations that made up the left side of his face. She could tell, even through the healed injuries, that Stokes had once been a handsome man. It was a cruel kind of beauty, but it was there nonetheless.

'What is it you want me to do?'

He smiled. 'You had the chance today to throw the police off our trail. I do believe you wanted to do it. You tried. But in the end, it looks as if Detective Burns saw through your façade. So we need a backup plan. I'm going to entrust something very important to you. As long as it gets where it's supposed to safely, all will be well. If you make things difficult, and don't do exactly what I tell you, then bad things will happen. Not just to you. To your parents too. Particularly your father. Do you understand, Ellie?'

The girl felt herself shrinking back into the seat. She'd thought she was safe. It felt like she was trapped in a nightmare, and every time she woke up, she found she was still dreaming. For a second, she felt like screaming, but then she pushed the terror back down. It wouldn't do her any good. She had to stay calm and think.

'Please,' she said, fighting to keep tears from her voice. 'I don't want any of this. I just want to go home.'

'I know you do,' Stokes said. 'Do this one thing for me, and you'll be home soon.'

But in her heart, Ellie knew he was lying.

She was in terrible danger, and the only person who was going to get her out of it was Ellie herself.

31

Tessa sat on the narrow bed of Danny's cell, the big detective perched beside her, looking far too big for the tiny windowless room.

'What the fuck happened, Danny?'

'We were set up,' her partner said. 'They riled me into losing my temper – probably hoped I'd pull my gun.'

'But you didn't.'

'My temper's bad, but not that bad. They didn't account for Maggie being as tough as she is, or Pav for that matter. Once it was clear we weren't going to go down easy, it looked to me as if the plan was to just shoot us.'

'You're serious?'

'I wish I wasn't. If Maggie hadn't been as quick as she is, I'd be dead now.'

Tessa sighed and shook her head. 'They're planning on holding you until a trial. Which leaves you completely at their mercy.'

'The commish knows I'm here,' Danny said. 'If I end up dead in a cell in Anglesea Street station, it'll bring all kinds of hell down on them. You can't explain that away.'

'That's true,' Tessa said.

'I think what they really wanted was to get us out of the picture. Whatever's happening here, someone high up is involved in it. We're stepping on too many toes. I mean, I've been thinking: who knew we were booked into that hotel? Our rooms were booked by the administrators in Harcourt Street. So how did that faceless killer know to find you there?'

'I've been wondering that myself.'

'We've thought before there was a mole of some kind in our own house. I think this proves it.'

'I'll talk to Dawn. We need to get you out of here. And Maggie.'

'I'm sure she's working on it right now,' Danny said, although he didn't sound optimistic.

'I'm not going back to Dublin until this is sorted anyway,' Tessa said. 'I'll dig around and see what I can find out. There are so many threads, I don't know where to start pulling, but I hope that if I can get hold of one, the others will unravel.'

'Good luck,' Danny said. 'Maggie found out that the dead men knew each other.'

He told her what they'd discovered during their research session and that he'd identified the driver of the car that had followed him.

'Charity work?' Tessa said. 'Dave Merrill was having some issue with a charity too.'

'Looks like that might be the connecting factor then,' Danny mused.

'Do you still have the printout of your tail's address?'

Danny shook his head. 'They took it from me when they brought me in here. But the name was Josh Haughey. Address was an estate right here in Cork city. You'll find it on the system. He's got a record.'

'Thanks, Danny. I'll follow it up.'

The big man sighed. 'I never thought I'd end up back in here.'

'Hang in there,' Tessa said. 'We're down but not out.'

'I'll try to keep that in mind,' Danny said dolefully.

32

Maggie grinned when her cell door was opened and Pav scampered in, accompanied by Tessa. The space being as small as it was, they'd taken her chair so she was lying on the bed. She sat up to pet her dog and give Tessa somewhere to sit.

'Good to see one of the prisoners has been released,' she said. 'How's Danny doing?'

'Not in the most jovial frame of mind I've ever seen,' Tessa said.

'I imagine not.'

'Maggie, what are we not seeing here?' Tessa asked.

'Well, let's look at what we have.'

'Okay. But it's a mess.'

'I know, but the answer is in there. It has to be. So, Ellie comes to the police because she knows a man's going to die. She's right about that – and has predicted deaths before. The previous two looked like accidents, but when we went to look at them, we reckon they were, in fact, murders, although the local Gardai had pretty much closed the books on them.'

'The same guards who set you and Danny up,' Tessa said.

'And who probably would have killed us if we hadn't thwarted them,' Maggie agreed.

'Thwarted,' Tessa said. 'I like that.'

'It's a good word. Ellie's family have no criminal connections – or so we thought. But today we learn that the lawyer who represents Philip O'Farrell's charitable company used to be mobbed up to the gills. And that he knew the three men who died. As, in fact, did Philip O'Farrell.'

'Something he failed to mention,' Tessa pointed out. 'Add to that he works for a charity, and two of the dead men were experiencing some kind of stress due to charity work at the time of their deaths.'

'Which is a bit curious,' Maggie agreed. 'Then the Faceless Men tried to stop us coming here and, when that didn't work, went to the bother of trying to warn us off.'

'The guy who broke into my room told me some of us would die if we didn't leave.'

'And he was nearly true to his word. Danny and I were almost killed this afternoon.'

'And O'Mahoney has been trying to get rid of us from the get-go.'

'What happened at your meeting?' Maggie asked.

'Ellie told Cleary that she'd got her info from a dark web chat forum. It was enough for them to release her, but when I asked her to talk me through how to get on the dark web, she hadn't a clue. She was lying.'

'So someone got to her in St Killian's.'

'Looks like it.'

'This whole town is like a spider's web of criminality,' Maggie said. 'I thought O'Mahoney was supposed to be a supercop of some kind. He seems to have lost his touch.'

'I dunno. You didn't see him with Stokes. There's no love lost there. I don't think O'Mahoney is crooked. It looks like he's stuck in the middle of a force that is though. Could be he's fighting an uphill battle.'

'And doesn't know who to trust.'

'So he distrusts us on instinct,' Tessa said, thinking out loud.

'It'd be nice to think we might change his opinion,' Maggie suggested.

'One can but try,' Tessa agreed.

33

Tessa called in to O'Mahoney's office before leaving the station. 'Sarge? Can I have a quick word before I go?'

He glared at her but sat back expectantly. 'What do you want, DI Burns?'

She sat down in the sparsely decorated room. 'To speak plainly.'

O'Mahoney narrowed his eyes at her. 'DI Burns, I never speak any other way.'

Tessa smiled. 'I kind of figured that might be the case.'

'I'm a busy man,' O'Mahoney said. 'Can you get to the point?'

Tessa took a deep breath. 'Sarge, I'm a guard. It's... it's who I am. I'm proud to be a member of the force, and I recognise my fellow officers as brothers and sisters. Family. I take that very seriously, and so do Danny and Maggie.'

'You wouldn't think it from their behaviour.'

'With respect, Sarge, you haven't seen their behaviour, not really. I work with them day in and day out. I know what makes them tick. They're good people. Honest. Loyal. Kind. Those qualities we would all want to see in a fellow officer. I think you can tell from the work they did on those guys in the squad room, they're tough too.'

O'Mahoney gazed at Tessa unflinchingly. 'Why are you telling me all this?'

'Because I think I recognise those qualities in you. I think you're a good copper who's found himself in a very tough posting. I think you feel isolated and you don't know who you can rely on.'

'You do, do you?'

'I do.'

'You've got a fucking nerve. Where do you get off making those kinds of allegations?'

'I'm making them because I care, Sarge. I care about the force, and I care about my fellow officers. And that means, despite everything that's happened between us, I care about you. I think you're in trouble, and I want to help.'

Tessa thought she saw a slight softening in the older man's eyes. It was a small thing, but she was sure it was there.

'What makes you think I'm in trouble?' O'Mahoney asked.

'Me and my team, we wondered why you hadn't climbed higher up the ladder after the miracle you worked in Limerick, and I think I've worked out why that is. It's because you're not a political player. Politics is all about compromise, and you won't. You know what needs to be done, and you know what's best for your people, and you won't stray from that. And that got you put in a station where you have an impossible task. In fact, I think they put you here because they don't believe you *can* fix things.'

O'Mahoney said nothing, which Tessa took as a sign she might be right. She pressed on.

'Your people are compromised, aren't they?' she asked.

O'Mahoney sighed. 'Have you been sent to bring me down?'

'No. Me and my people are here to help Ellie O'Farrell.

That, and only that, is what we're about. But if we can help you while we're here, we'd be happy to do so.'

The sarge got up, walked behind Tessa and closed the door. Then he went back to his desk, opened a drawer and took out a bottle of Scotch and two glasses. He poured a generous amount for each of them.

'I'm going to tell you something,' he said. 'It goes no further – am I clear?'

'Anything you tell me I'll share with Danny and Maggie. And with the commissioner. If you aren't happy with that, don't tell me.'

O'Mahoney nodded. 'Very well. You're honest. I appreciate that.'

'I won't lie to you, Sarge.'

'I don't believe you will. Okay, when I got here, I worked out within the first three months that there was a group of my top detectives who were taking bribes from a very well-resourced gang. The money they were taking assured their turning a blind eye to certain activities occurring locally, and, in instances where investigations had to occur, these would be so half-hearted as to be hardly worth anyone's time. No prosecutions would ever come from them.'

'Which is exactly what happened in the cases of Merrill, McGuinness and Wilde.'

'Yes. And countless more. I've tried to worm these rotten apples out of my basket, but they're protected by the rest of the rank and file. So my city falls deeper and deeper into a crime wave I can't hold back, and my house spins more and more out of control.'

'I believe I can help.'

'How?'

'We're obviously on to something with the Ellie O'Farrell case. They wouldn't be putting so much effort into warning us off if we weren't. Let me and my team continue working it, and we'll share any information we turn up that can help you.'

'It sounds like you just want me to let your friends go.'

'You know Danny and Maggie were only defending themselves,' Tessa said. 'They were attacked because we're getting close to something this gang is involved in. And let's be honest, they could have killed your guys – easily. They were gentle with them. Our enemy is your enemy.'

'Maybe.'

'Let them go. If we can get to the bottom of the Ellie O'Farrell case, it could very well blow the lid off things. And that can only help you.'

O'Mahoney nodded and sipped some Scotch, tilting his head back to let it roll down his throat.

'Okay. I'm going to take a leap of faith,' he said. 'I'll have to process the paperwork on Danny, which means I won't be able to release him until tomorrow, but you can take Maggie now.'

'Thank you, Sarge.'

'Don't make me regret it.'

'I won't.'

The old cop grinned and extended his arm. Tessa clinked glasses with him.

'You're a pain in the arse, DI Burns,' he said. 'But you might be the first honest copper that's passed through this station in a while.'

'Thanks, Sarge,' Tessa said. 'And you're quite a pain in the arse yourself, if you don't mind my saying so.'

O'Mahoney laughed. 'Seeing as we're speaking plainly.'

'I never speak any other way,' Tessa said, and then they were both laughing.

HERCULES DONNELLY

The Twisted Snake Tattoo and Piercing Parlour, Est. 2001, Proprietor Hercules Donnelly was situated down a side road off Patrick's Street, which was a source of satisfaction to its owner and one and only tattoo artist, Hercules. Hercules (he pronounced it the French way, with a silent H, though he mistakenly wrote it in the English manner with the S present) was of the opinion that a tattoo parlour should be off the beaten track. The tattooist was a big believer that ink had always been the remit of outsiders and freaks, and he didn't for one moment appreciate the current trend of bored housewives and bespectacled fucking accountants getting flowers and butterflies and goddam pug dogs etched on their asses.

He couldn't see the point in it: three-quarters of the idiots who arrived into his shop, loaded up on the overpriced cocktails some of the local bijou drinking establishments served, would be calling their cosmetic surgeon of choice to have his work lasered off within a week of him putting it on (which was really annoying, as he always gave one hundred per cent, regardless of how stupid the request).

What made him really sick though was the reality that,

despite such strong feelings, Hercules had bills to pay and an ex-wife who wasn't prepared to lower her maintenance demands to appease his principles. So even though it made him want to puke, he always played nice and feigned respectful interest with each and every wuss who staggered through his door, adorning their sagging flesh with pictures of the Little Mermaid to the best of his ability.

At eight thirty on a Thursday night in September, Hercules was doing just that: a skinny, acne-faced student from University College Cork, half drunk and reeking of Red Bull, was sprawled in his chair, making little squealing sounds every now and again. The kid had asked for a picture of the fish-tailed redhead from the Disney cartoon with his girlfriend's name, Shannon (Hercules secretly wondered if the girl in question knew she was this kid's girlfriend, but he kept the thought to himself) written above it, like a rainbow.

'Are we nearly done, sir?' the kid asked in a wavering voice, his eyes clenched tight against the needle's activity.

'Nope,' Hercules answered truthfully.

'Oh,' the youngster said, although Hercules reckoned he probably wanted to say a whole lot more.

'Y'know, it's not too late to change this into something less detailed,' the tattooist offered, taking pity on his client. 'Does your girlfriend like sharks?'

At that moment, the door of the Twisted Snake banged open, and a tall, scarred man in a tailored suit stalked in, dragging a girl by the arm. Four guys who looked like stars from the TV show The Young Offenders, *all with bowl haircuts shaved at the sides, clad in ill-fitting tracksuits, followed.*

'I have a job for you, Hercules,' the man in the suit said, pronouncing the S, which always annoyed the tattooist – although almost everyone did until he told them not to, and even then, most forgot and continued to do so.

Somehow, though, this wasn't a man Hercules thought he would correct.

He'd never seen him before, but he'd seen his type. This was someone who was used to being obeyed. Someone who didn't tolerate anyone disagreeing with him.

The man was perhaps six feet two and slimly built, but what was most striking about him was the intricate pattern of scarring across the left side of his face. It looked as if someone had gone to work on him with a cheese grater.

Hercules sat back as soon as the man spoke, taking the tattoo gun away from the student's arm.

'We're done,' he said to the youngster. 'Have a think about whether or not you really want ink and come back to me if you decide you do.'

'But—'

'The man told you to leave,' the scarred newcomer said, his voice like rusty metal being dragged across gravel.

He spoke quietly, but there was something in his tone that told the kid that he didn't want to linger. Without a second glance, the youngster leaped from the chair and bolted out the still-open door.

'Give her this,' the scarred man said, pushing the girl towards the chair and pulling a piece of paper out of the inside pocket of his suit.

'I don't want a tattoo,' she said, and Hercules had no doubt she was telling the truth.

The girl looked to be in her early teens, maybe younger, with hair shaved on one side and shoulder length on the other. She was pretty but had been crying, and there was anger and fear in her eyes.

'What age is she?' the tattooist asked.

'Old enough to know she wants to be tattooed this evening.'

'Please – I don't!' the girl implored.

Hercules looked at the scarred man. His associates had taken *up positions at various points around the small studio and were watching them with bored expressions on their pocked faces.*

'She's my niece. I promised her this as a birthday present. Now could we get on with it? I have places to be.'

The girl made a lunge towards the door, and Scar caught her by the scruff of the neck. She fought him, pulling against his grip, but it was pointless. He was too strong for her.

'How am I supposed to ink her if she's gonna thrash around and sound off?' Hercules asked.

Scar nodded at his four compatriots, and within seconds, the girl was on the chair the college kid had so recently vacated, held firmly in place by eight tracksuit-clad arms.

'Now get to work.'

Nodding, Hercules swiftly prepared his workstation and began, the sounds of the girl's cries and imprecations resounding in his ears as he made his mark on her right shoulder. The kid sounded utterly bereft – if Hercules hadn't been so focused on his work, not to mention so nervous under the watchful gaze of the five people he was sure were stone-cold killers crowding his place of work, it might have upset him. Finally, her sobs became too intrusive, and he glanced up at Scar's weathered visage.

'I'm sorry – her crying is puttin' me off my game.'

Without a word, the man nodded and produced a Ruger SR9 handgun from inside his jacket, bringing it to within centimetres of the girl's temple.

'Child, be silent,' he snarled.

'I hate you,' was the girl's response, but she lapsed into scowling quietude after that.

An hour later, it was complete. Hercules wiped down the marked skin on the girl's arm. It was a wolf, howling at the moon, done in shades of black and grey.

'Excellent,' the scarred man said.

He took something from his pocket and handed it to the

tattooist. 'Could you administer this please? Use one of the craters in the moon as the entrance point.'

Hercules looked at the tool the man was holding and then up at the terrifying face. 'That what I think it is?'

'Probably not. But put it in her anyway.'

'It's not what I usually do.'

'I'll pay you extra. A lot extra.'

Hercules nodded, took the implement and did as he was asked.

'Good,' Scar said. 'You do excellent work.'

Hercules smiled. 'I thank you.'

'What did you just do to me?' the girl hissed.

'Get her out of here,' Scar ordered, and she was carried to the street, kicking and screeching all the way.

'That is one unhappy lady,' the tattooist said, the words out before he even realised he'd spoken.

Shocked at himself for daring to express an opinion in front of a man who clearly didn't encourage independent thought, he got up and began to tidy his work area, putting needles in the medical waste container and stowing bottles of ink back on their shelves.

'She needs reminding of who she is and who she belongs to,' Scar purred. 'Ellie still has a role to play, and it's about time she faced up to her responsibilities to her family.'

'Well, that's between you and your niece,' Hercules said. '"T'ain't none of my business.'

'No,' Scar said. 'You're absolutely right.'

And in one smooth movement, he raised the Ruger and shot the tattooist in the head at point-blank range.

* * *

Stokes paused for a moment, studying the blood spackling the *white walls of the room and giving the framed photographs of happy customers a nightmarish look.*

The tattooist had been knocked forward by the blast, tumbling across the tattoo chair before landing on the tiled floor with a sickening thud, and Stokes looked thoughtfully at the body before once again concealing his gun. Then he took a phone from his pocket, dialled a number and waited.

Finally, someone on the other end spoke.

'It's done,' he told them.

The line went dead.

After straightening his jacket to make sure the bulge of the Ruger was completely obscured, Stokes followed his men and the furious girl out into the night.

Tessa went to get Maggie's chair so she could leave the station with some dignity.

It had been placed in a storage room to the rear of Anglesea Street, and when Tessa got there, she couldn't believe what she found. There, amid stacks of chairs, some old recording equipment, riot gear and a couple of old heavy bags, was her best friend's pride and joy, and someone – probably more than one someone – had gone to work on it with what looked to be crowbars.

The wheels were buckled, the laptop smashed, the seats torn, the armrests bent and warped, and the engine removed and battered to pieces. Many of its component parts lay in various states of damage about the floor. Tessa knew the chair wasn't a part of her friend, but it was a piece of kit that Maggie had worked long and hard to modify to her exacting standards and needs, and seeing it like this made the detective want to sit down and weep. It was an act of calculated cruelty.

She went back downstairs to the sergeant's office. 'Some of your guys have done a job on Maggie's chair.'

The older man's face dropped. 'How bad?'

'Catastrophic.'

'Show me.'

When he saw the extent of the damage, O'Mahoney shook his head in shame. 'If there was ever an image that sums up how bad things are here, I would say this is it. What kind of a blackguard does this to a fellow officer's vehicle?'

Tessa liked him for that. Really liked him. 'Do you have a manual chair she can use until we can get this one repaired?'

'Yes, of course. I'll go and get it.'

He went with Tessa to explain to Maggie that she was free to go.

'And there's bad news too,' Tessa said. 'Those fuckers – they smashed up your chair.'

Maggie sighed, looking at the one O'Mahoney was pushing. 'So I'm going old-school for a while?'

'It's the best I can offer for the moment,' O'Mahoney said. 'They took your baton and mace too. But here's a fresh can from supplies and a baton I used to use myself. I'd take it as an act of kindness if you accepted it as a gift.'

Maggie smiled. 'I'll use it with great pride then, Sarge.'

'Then it'll be expertly used, by all accounts.'

'They have your phone at reception,' Tessa said. 'Let's tell Danny we'll see him tomorrow and then get back to the hotel.'

THE WATCHER IN THE SHADOWS

They were walking back to the boss's car when he saw the driver.

She was on the other side of the street, near an adult store, dressed in a short denim skirt with a low-cut top. She'd told him she'd managed to get herself out of sex work, but it appeared, from how she was dressed, where she was standing and the other girls she was with, that she hadn't.

Her coming back to work for the boss made sense now. He'd probably promised her that he'd get her something better if she did this one last job for him.

Maybe she needed something for her child. It didn't matter. She was still trapped doing something she loathed, and the boss hadn't helped her.

As he wouldn't help him.

He looked at poor Ellie O'Farrell, who was walking near the front of the group, a hoodie to her right and left, hemming her in. She looked scared. Really scared. The Watcher didn't blame her. She'd been through a terrible ordeal, and he suspected things were only going to get worse for her if the boss continued to hold her.

He'd been walking at the back of the group, so he quickened his pace so he was beside her.

'I'm going to cause a distraction,' he hissed at her. 'When I do, run. Run as fast as you can and don't look back.'

She didn't look at him, just whispered, 'Thank you.'

Those words made him feel warm inside. She didn't know him. Knew nothing about him. But she would remember he helped her. No matter what happened to him, she would know he'd done this one good thing.

He looked over his shoulder. He could still see the driver. She was talking to a fat man in a suit. As the Watcher looked, he put his arm around her. As he did, her eyes met the Watcher's, just for a second. Each saw the other, and there was a moment of shared recognition. Then the group moved on, and the Watcher couldn't see her anymore. He wished he could help her too. She'd been kind to him. And she'd told him to pay that forward.

Which was what he was trying to do now.

Without slowing his pace, the Watcher shoved the hoodied young man to Ellie's left out into the road, right into oncoming traffic. The youngster swore, falling on his ass, a car slamming to a halt just in front of him. The car behind, unable to deal with the sudden stop, ran right into its rear end, and the car behind it did the same.

Horns blared, and people turned to look.

'Go!' he hissed at Ellie, who turned and disappeared into the crowd.

The boss turned a smouldering gaze on the Watcher. 'What have you done?'

'I've seen you for what you are,' the Watcher said.

'It'll be the last thing you do see,' the boss said.

He turned to one of the other hoodies. 'Go and find her. I need her back.'

Then he took the Watcher by the arm. 'You and me are going for a ride.'

They walked through Cork's narrow side streets until they reached the car park at Lapps Quay, where the boss's Saab was parked. The Watcher got in without a word.

He watched the river as they drove along it, following its twists and turns until they reached the docks. The Watcher knew where he was being taken. He'd taken people here himself, so it seemed fitting.

Gradually, the buildings and machinery became less frequent, and they were driving between ruined, unused containers and old, rusted forklifts.

When the car stopped, he got out without being told to do so and walked towards the water's edge, where he kneeled down, looking at the water.

'I would have got you that college place, you know,' the boss said.

'It doesn't matter. It's not right what you're doing with that girl. I couldn't do it no more.'

'You've outlived your usefulness.'

'No. I helped her. That's something.'

'By the time your body is underwater, we'll have her back.'

'I helped her. I done something right.'

'You did something meaningless.'

'Not to me.'

'Have it your way.'

He heard a shell being jacked into the chamber of the boss's Ruger and said, 'Boss?'

'What now?'

'My name is Jason. Jason Kelly. I thought you were a good man. I think I even loved you. I was wrong.'

'I don't care.'

And the boss shot Jason Kelly in the back of the head, and his body tumbled into the ever-moving River Lee.

35

Tessa helped Maggie get comfortable on the bed, put a new laptop they'd bought at a DID on the way back to the Isaacs in her lap, then made them both some tea and put some water down in a bowl for Pavlov.

'What now?' Maggie asked.

'We keep digging,' Tessa said. 'The gang Stokes represented – what do we know about them?'

'He represented three. It was rumoured he was the leader of one of them himself – they were a loosely organised conglomerate of some of the youth gangs from around Cork's inner city. He seemed to have the ability to channel them, make them do stuff for him. He tended to use them as enforcers to get things done. You know what they say about child soldiers. They'll do anything for you and are as vicious if not more so than adults.'

'These are kids?'

'Late teens to early twenties. So pretty much, yes.'

'The other two?'

'One is one of the longest-running criminal syndicates in the south of Ireland. They make their money from selling drugs, prostitution and counterfeiting, and they're currently run by a matriarch, Mama Frida. She is, from what I've read, utterly terrifying. She's got a degree in chemical engineering and likes to use toxins she's cooked up herself to torture and kill her enemies.'

'Nice.'

'Very. The others are the Cadogan crew. They started out as members of the Irish National Liberation Army, a Marxist group determined to drive the British out of the six counties. Since the ceasefire, however, they've had to find other ways of earning a crust, and they've branched out into organised crime, mainly gunrunning, drug importation and sale, and, of course, mercenary work.'

'So how do the Unattested fit in with that motley crew?'

'Well,' Maggie said, taking some tea, 'didn't you say they were a guild rather than a gang? A guild is like a trade union; it has people from lots of different groups as members. We've only seen one Faceless Man since we've been involved in this case. He could work for either Mama Frida or the Cadogans.'

'It's still a mess,' Tessa said. 'But I suppose it's our mess.'

She sighed and her phone buzzed. An unknown number.

'Hi. Tessa Burns here.'

'Tessa, it's Ellie.'

'Hi, Ellie. Is everything okay?'

'No. It's not okay at all. Mr Stokes tried to take me away. One of the boys he had with him helped me to escape, but I'm scared. I've been running and running, but I still keep thinking I see those boys in the hoodies he has working for him. Can you come and get me?'

'Of course I can. Where are you?'

'I'm outside a pub called the Nine of Diamonds. Do you know where that is?'

'I'll find it. You need to be in a place where there's lots of people – it'll be harder for them to take you in a public space, so go on into the pub. Get a drink if you have any money. Make it a soft drink and tell the barman you're with your mam and dad – pick a couple that look the same age as your parents and sit near them and don't move. I'm coming.'

'Okay, Tessa. I have some money – they gave me back my money and phone when I left St Killian's.'

'Thank heavens for small mercies.'

'Yes. Please hurry.'

Tessa looked at Maggie when the call ended. 'Did you hear that?'

'I did.'

'Stokes, as we suspected.'

'Well, he does look like a Bond villain.'

'He's certainly perpetuating the stereotype.'

'Go. Take Pav. Ellie will need the comfort.'

'Are you sure?'

'He'll be more use to you out there than me cooped up in here.'

'Thanks, Maggie. Stay by the phone – I'm going to need you. Come on, Pav. We've got work to do.'

The dog, his tail wagging furiously, scampered out of the room with Tessa. He looked very happy to be going on an adventure.

36

Google Maps took her to the bar without any problems. It was a big, old-style country-music venue just off the river, with a large car park out back. The outside of the bar was painted in black and red, the words 'Nine of Diamonds' emblazoned in old Western-style lettering over the door.

Tessa left Pav in her Capri – he would draw too much attention to her in the pub – and made for the front door. Inside, an acoustic trio of guitar, five-string banjo and double bass were performing Kenny Rogers' old classic 'Lucille' on a small stage. A lot of people were up dancing, others standing or sitting on the outskirts of the dance floor, drinks in hand, singing along.

Tessa stood in the middle of the throng, gazing about her, trying to spot Ellie. She didn't seem to be anywhere in the dance-hall part of the bar: Tessa saw lots of couples, plenty of men in cowboy hats, a few women in suede jackets and boots, and as she scanned the crowd, her eyes fell on three young men in tracksuits and hoodies. Which seemed a little at odds with the rest of the clientele.

Falling back so she was hugging the wall, the detective watched the three youngsters. It didn't take her long to realise that the trio weren't in the Nine of Diamonds for the music. She moved in a parallel arc to them, keeping to the shadows, and soon spotted that they were homing in on a specific area of the bar, an alcove close to one of the exits. There were three tables in that small space, which seemed to Tessa to have been constructed for regulars who wanted to have a few drinks while remaining separate from those enjoying the band. The fact that the space was slightly recessed protected it somewhat from the sound – she noted that a middle-aged couple, who were at one of the tables in the alcove, were able to have a conversation even with the band in full swing. A couple of guys Tessa took to be truckers were at a second table, and in the middle, at a table on her own, was a small figure in blue jeans and a hippyish-looking patchwork jacket.

God love you, Ellie, you stick out like a sore thumb, Tessa thought before turning her attention back to the three hoodies. Was it possible they weren't here to interfere with Ellie at all? Tessa had never been to the Nine before. Maybe their intentions were innocent; surely it was possible to be a country-music fan and still sport a hoodie? After her ordeal, Ellie could be experiencing some quite understandable paranoia.

In the fourteen months after she graduated from Templemore, the Garda Training College, Tessa had worked a beat in Finglas, an area in Dublin with a lot of youth crime. Her partner at the time, a large, red-haired youngster from County Clare called Floyd Barnes, would always carry out a kind of audit when they arrived at any crime scene. Floyd might have looked like he didn't have much brains, but anyone thinking that would have been mistaken.

'Tessa,' he would ask, 'what's wrong with this picture? What's out of place?'

Identifying the element that didn't belong, Floyd believed, would always set them on the path to solving the puzzle – it was like a mechanic establishing which bit of the car wasn't working properly.

As she watched the young men closing in on the exact location where the girl she was sure was Ellie was sitting, Tessa ran a checklist in her head.

1. Were there any other guys dressed like that in the bar? She did a quick scan. There were not. They stood out from the very country-music crowd as much as Ellie did. The trio looked like they would be at home in a rave but seemed completely out of their element here.
2. Did any of them have a drink? No, and nor were they approaching the bar. They were clearly looking for someone or something. And that someone seemed to be Ellie.
3. Was it possible Tessa was wrong, and the girl sitting along drinking a Coke in the alcove wasn't Ellie, but was, in fact, a friend of theirs? That didn't seem likely. Tessa had encountered many girls who associated with young men like the ones she was now observing, and none of them dressed like the girl these guys were homing in on.

Then she saw the girl spy the three hoodies, and her body language told Tessa everything she needed to know – she recognised them immediately, and that recognition was accompanied by fear: the girl stood and made to bolt for the door.

But she never got to make good her escape.

One of the boys rushed over, grabbed her by her auburn hair and dragged her backwards. The girl said something Tessa couldn't hear, and made as if to strike her assailant, but he caught her by the wrist and began to haul her towards a door to their left, which Tessa knew would lead to the car park at the rear of the pub. Not to be dissuaded, the girl kicked out, aiming for the groin, but the man turned his hip, catching the blow on his thigh. One of the truckers who were also seated in the alcove stood and made to move towards the scuffle, but the other two hoodies were suddenly there, making a loose circle around the man and the girl he was restraining, and, raising his hands in submission, the trucker sat back down. The girl was thrashing about frantically now, knocking a table over, but despite her protestations, the three interlopers swiftly moved out the door.

And Tessa slipped out after them.

By the time Tessa was outside, the three hoodies and their captive had crossed the car park and were standing about a dusty Honda Civic. The car's boot was open, and one of the hoodies was trying to force Ellie, who was fighting hard and uttering a stream of invective, into it.

Just for a second, Tessa froze.

She suddenly realized that the second she moved against those three and rescued Ellie, she was in breach of a direct order from her superior officer. All her experience in the army and the Gardai had conditioned Tessa to follow orders to the letter. Now, for the first time in her career, she was going to disobey a command.

The Burns Unit was, after all, off the case. Anything that happened here was no longer about Tessa executing her duty; it would be a fist fight between civilians in the car park of a bar on the outskirts of Cork city. Tessa might try to rationalise that she was a cop, and therefore all crime was within the remit of her job, but she'd been expressly told to leave the O'Farrell case alone.

It would be seen as rank insubordination.

A much larger part of her, though, the part that wasn't Tessa the soldier or Tessa the cop, the part that was just Tessa Burns, could not turn and walk away when someone was being abducted. Let alone a child.

It might be detrimental to her career in law enforcement, but that didn't matter. What mattered was the welfare of the child who needed help.

In the instant she realized this truth, she began assessing how she was going to take on three assailants without Ellie getting hurt in the struggle, and before she knew it, a part of Tessa that she tried hard to keep buried stretched and shook itself awake. It was the part that had fought every injustice she'd experienced in the care homes where she'd grown up. The part that raged at bullies and abusers and oppression. Tessa felt that presence step forward, and as soon as it did, she knew it was too late to back away.

'I don't think the young lady wants to take a ride with you this evening, boys.'

She didn't speak the words loudly, but they cut through the girl's curses nonetheless.

The three hoodies paused, looking at the new arrival as if she'd just appeared out of thin air. Tessa stood a little away from the group – maybe five yards separated them. She knew they were trying to work out how much of a threat she was, and she allowed them to carry out their assessment. Tessa was very aware she didn't look like much – she was shorter by at least a head than all of them, and she had no obvious weapons – she did have her Sig of course, but drawing it would only lead to further problems (the last thing she needed was a witness dialling 999 to report that a woman had drawn a firearm on three young men). No, her sidearm would have to stay where it was – holstered.

But that suited her too. These were young men who were

used to striking fear into everyone they came up against. They seemed deeply confused that she wasn't afraid. And she intended to use that confusion to her advantage.

'Fuck off, skank,' the one trying to force Ellie into the boot said.

'Help me, Tessa!' the girl shouted, her eyes wide and sweat beading on her brow from the exertion of the struggle. 'Please don't let them take me!'

Tessa made an expansive move with her hands. 'Well, fellas, I have to say, after hearing that, I'm obligated as a detective with an Garda Síochána to intercede. Now why don't you just let her go, and then you and me can have a talk?'

It was obvious to Tessa that the thug who had his hands on Ellie was the leader and probably the brains of the operation. Up close, Tessa saw he was several inches over six feet and was in good shape. The other two seemed less sure of themselves, and she got the impression they were waiting to be told what to do.

'Why the hell would we want to talk to you?' Brains asked.

'Well, that's a good question,' Tessa said. 'Let's just say, I think you might benefit from a little education, and I reckon I'm the woman to do it. See, I don't like guys who pick on young women. And three against one just isn't fair. So I'm asking one last time, nicely, for you to let her go. If you do, I'm prepared to let you go on your way. Someone else can catch you another time for whatever shit you'll be up to.'

The three goons followed this exchange open-mouthed. The reality that anyone, much less a complete stranger – and a woman to boot – was standing up to them seemed to befuddle them completely.

'Will you boys deal with her while I get this bitch secured away?' Brains said.

Tessa had been watching Brains' two colleagues as they had their short conversation: one was all muscles – probably a steroid junkie, and moved awkwardly, as if his absurdly swollen limbs got in the way. The third one was so skinny it looked as if someone had poked drinking straws through the sleeves of his tracksuit. Yet his eyes were sharper than his friend: he was probably going to be the most dangerous.

'I don't have any argument with you fellas,' Tessa said as the pair advanced on her. 'I just want the girl.'

'You should stop talkin', missy,' Steroids said. 'Your mouth has already got you in a pile of trouble.'

'Well, don't say I didn't give you a chance,' Tessa sighed.

They came at her head-on, Steroids on the left and Skinny on the right. As always happened in situations like this, time seemed to slow. Tessa felt her body relax and her breathing become deep and regular – she moved into an easy, balanced stance, her mind emptying, her vision becoming sharp and clear.

Tessa had already been in plenty of fistfights before she ever joined the Gardai – growing up in care, she'd been forced to learn how to protect herself at an early age. These childhood confrontations had all been messy, uncoordinated affairs: the antagonists would as likely as not end up rolling around on the ground, delivering blows into one another's ribs that were largely ineffectual at such close quarters. Tessa now knew that fights like that, which often had no clear winner, weren't really fights at all. They were just displays that sent a message that you weren't afraid to get physical if the situation demanded it.

Then she'd joined the army.

Military combat training had taught her two important lessons: that real fights have winners and losers, and that the winner is usually the person who's prepared to do whatever it takes to win. This last point was a lesson Tessa had seen proven time and again during her military career – anyone can win a fight, but what stops most people is their natural reluctance to do the horrible things necessary to claim that victory. The average Joe simply doesn't have the stomach for it.

Tessa had stopped being average a long time ago.

By the time she joined the Irish police force, she wasn't just a seasoned brawler; she was a highly trained one. The three hoodies who were trying to take Ellie O'Farrell were about to experience the fruits of that training first-hand.

In a movement that looked slow and easy but was still somehow too fast for anyone to avoid, she kicked Steroids as hard as she could in the testicles.

The man stopped dead and made a high-pitched keening sound, then fell forward onto his face. As he did so, Tessa stepped to the left and punched Skinny, who'd produced a flick knife from somewhere, directly on the Adam's apple in one short but powerful motion. The man immediately dropped the blade and brought his hands to his throat, gasping for breath (the punch served to paralyse the muscles in the throat, making breathing impossible for about thirty seconds, which was alarming but not fatal), and when he did so, Tessa floored him with a right hook.

Kicking the blade under the nearest car, she looked at Brains – who was still holding Ellie half in and half out of the boot – shaking her head and tutting. 'Your friends will be okay. The guy I kicked in the nuts might need a hospital – but usually putting a bag of frozen peas in the affected area does the job.'

'What the fuck do you want?' Brains asked, looking more than a little distressed.

'I've already told you. Let the girl go and be on your way. I don't have the time or the inclination to deal with you now. Count yourself lucky.'

The man opened and shut his mouth as if the words just wouldn't come out, and that was when the girl took her chance, sinking her teeth into her captor's ear and whipping her head back and forth like a shark, ripping flesh and cartilage as she did so. It had the desired effect: roaring in pain, he released his grip, and Ellie drove her knee into his gut. He doubled over in pain, and Ellie took the chance to rush over to Tessa, hugging her tightly.

'We have to get out of here *now!*' she said and, grabbing Tessa's hand, took off towards the road at a sprint.

38

'Can you tell me what's going on?' Tessa asked her as they reached the road.

'I will, but not right now,' Ellie said. 'We have to keep moving.'

'I've got transport,' Tessa said. 'I'm parked just up the road.'

'Let's go then,' the girl said. 'Stokes will be on his way by now, and he'll have more people with him.'

They covered the distance in a couple of short minutes and bundled into the Capri, with Pav climbing onto Ellie's knees and lapping her face giddily.

'We need to get to the police station,' the girl said.

'It's not safe,' Tessa replied.

'What do you mean it's not safe? It's the police station.'

'Whatever's going on, some of the guards are in on it,' Tessa said. 'We can't go there. We have to find somewhere to lie low.'

Tessa turned onto the motorway and headed west. The girl kept on glancing into the rear-view mirror as they drove.

Finally Tessa said, 'You don't need to keep doing that. I'd know if we were being followed.'

'You'll have to excuse me,' Ellie said, 'but every single adult I've dealt with in the past two days has lied to me.'

Disdain was dripping from her voice.

'I'm a police detective, and before that I was in the army. I spent quite a lot of time in the engineering corps.'

'An engineer? So you built bridges and stuff? How does that help us?'

Tessa sighed. 'I wasn't *that* kind of engineer. I was attached to the Irish Army Rangers. My job primarily involved demolition and reconnaissance.'

'Meaning?'

'Okay – so what I did, most of the time, was drive specialist vehicles to somewhere dangerous and blow stuff up when I got there. A pretty big part of that was making sure I didn't get shot or blown up myself on the way.'

The girl was listening now. 'Really?'

'Really.'

She seemed to be studying Tessa, trying to work her out. 'How did you learn to fight like that?'

Tessa grinned. 'Product of a misspent youth.'

The girl laughed. 'Is that what I'm having now?'

'No,' Tessa said. 'No kid I've ever worked with was in trouble because of anything they did themselves. Kids get dragged into messes made by the adults around them. It's the job of me and my team to get them out of it.'

'Do you think you can get me out of this mess?'

'That depends,' Tessa said. 'Do you know what the mess is exactly?'

'Not all of it. But I know some. I tried to pretend I didn't – I didn't want to believe my dad was involved in anything bad. And I thought that by getting him and my mam to take me to the police station, they might ask for help themselves. But it didn't work. It just made everything worse.'

Tessa reached over and patted Ellie on the back of her

hand. 'Maybe you could tell me while I do what I've been trained to do and get us where we're going in one piece?'

Ellie smiled, and Tessa saw some of the worry and dread leave her, and even though she was so young, and despite the danger they were obviously in, Tessa could tell the girl had already calmed down and was thinking straight. She admired her for that.

'Once upon a time,' she began, 'there was a little girl called Ellie, and she had a mam and a dad, and she was really happy.'

As Tessa drove, Ellie told her how that happiness had been brought to an end by a man her family had believed they could trust.

39

'I know I told you yesterday that my dad was kind of a saint,' Ellie said. 'And there was a time that was almost true. I mean, he was always nice to me, and we have a fine place to live, and he and my mam love one another.'

Tessa continued to drive west. Pav sat in the back seat, his tongue lolling out, watching the river of lights that flowed past them as they travelled.

'You and your dad were pretty tight then?'

'Oh yeah. We like a lot of the same things. We'd watch sci-fi on the TV – *Doctor Who* and *Star Trek* and *The Mandalorian*. And he used to love me to do these number games on his computer with him. He found them hard, but for me... well, they were easy. He used to get all excited when I solved them.'

'Kind of like sudoku?'

It was Ellie's turn to laugh. 'No. These were sort of like logic problems using alphanumeric chains. You get sixty-four characters and a set of rules, and you have to use the rules to reorganise the figures into a new order.'

Tessa remembered Dr Cleary mentioning those. 'Sounds *very* hard.'

'Not for me. Once I know the rules, I can just sort of... see it. I've always been like that.'

'So things were good,' Tessa said. 'But they didn't stay like that.'

'Stokes, the lawyer for his company – he's where things began to go wrong.'

Tessa glanced over at her. 'Does your dad know he used to represent criminals?'

'I don't know for certain. But I did hear my mam and dad talking about him once, and Dad said that the ethos of HuTec is that everyone deserves a second chance. So I'd say he knew.'

'So, Stokes was where things started to go wrong.'

'He started visiting the house a lot. Not many of Dad's work colleagues ever did – he always used to talk about having a work/life balance, and that after he clocked off, that was his time. But about a year ago, Mr Stokes started to call over in the evenings, and they'd go into Dad's office and be in there for a long time together.

'I remember one evening – it must have been a Wednesday because I was listening to a podcast I like in my room, and the new ones get uploaded on a Wednesday – I heard my dad shouting. And that was weird, because Dad never shouts. Like, ever. He sounded scared more than angry. It was upsetting. I remember going out onto the landing, and my mam was standing in the hallway, looking at the office door, and she looked so frightened.

'After a few minutes of shouting, the office door opened and Stokes came out, and he stopped in the hallway. He looked back in and told my dad that whatever he was proposing would benefit everyone, and that it had been my dad's idea to begin with, whether he wanted to accept it or not. I remember Stokes saying: 'You can either be in it, and on the winning side, or you can fight us and lose. And if you lose, you'll lose more than you can imagine. Think about it. Think long and think hard." And then he walked out.'

'Sounds ominous,' Tessa said.

'He went out the front door without so much as looking at my mam. Dad didn't come out for a few minutes, and when he did, he tried to make light of it. "Bit of a work tiff," he said. But it wasn't. I knew it wasn't, and I think Mam did too.'

'I take it Stokes came back.'

'He did. About a week later. My dad had been jumpy all that evening, and when Stokes rang the doorbell, I knew why. Dad didn't say anything, just took him into the office, and when they came out, he looked... awful. Just awful.'

'Awful how?'

'Tired. Pale. Sad. He looked as if someone he cared about had died.'

Tessa signalled and moved into the left lane to join a merging road which was signposted 'Timoleague'.

'My mam and dad never fought,' Ellie said. 'But after Stokes's visits started, I'd hear them rowing.'

'What about?'

'They never fought when I was in the room. It would be in his office or in their bedroom. Dad started to sleep in the spare room quite a bit. They didn't think I knew – tried to hide it from me – but I did.'

'You never overheard anything?'

'She kept telling him it wasn't too late to stop it. That it was within his power to do so.'

'Ellie, your dad works for a tech company – what exactly is it that he does for them?'

'He's a software developer. A lot of the countries his company sends people to don't allow social media, so my dad helps develop apps and programs that can be used as an alternative.'

'You've lost me.'

'Places like, say, Turkmenistan for example, block platforms like Instagram, Twitter or TikTok because they don't want their citizens to be able to communicate on a large scale for fear it might cause some kind of uprising against cruel governmental policies. My dad and his colleagues have developed simpler social-media formats, ones modelled on old-school systems like Bebo or MySpace, that can operate under the radar. It helps give the people there a voice.'

'So your dad has computer smarts.'

'He does. He started out in finance, but he was always interested in computers and what you could do with them. So when one of his old college friends came up with the idea for HuTec, he took a pay cut and joined the company. My mam supported him in it. She went back to work, reopened her bakery. They were really happy.'

'Ellie, do you think your dreams might be linked in some way to Stokes and whatever he's doing?'

'Well,' Ellie said. 'They started about six months into my dad being involved with him. And Mr Stokes, when he took me, he told me he knew about the girl who gave me the dark web address. Told me that you knowing I was lying meant he had to have another plan. So he took me to that tattoo place.'

'A tattoo place? Whatever for?'

The girl pulled off the sleeve of her jacket and showed Tessa the wolf-and-moon on her shoulder. 'After they'd done it, the tattoo guy injected me with something, I think.'

'Like a drug? Do you feel okay?'

'I feel fine. I didn't get sick or woozy. I don't know what it was.'

Tessa wondered what possible purpose tattooing the child could serve. Was he branding her in some way, marking her as property? Was it a fetish, some kind of sexual thing? Was it meant as an insult to the buttoned-down, safe eco-liberalism of

Ellie's parents? Realizing she was just making stabs in the dark, she said:

'Come back to the dreams for a moment. Do you know the three guys who died were all involved in fundraising for your dad's company?'

Ellie shook her head.

'When my friends and I spoke to Dr Cleary, he told me he thought you had a special gift. An ability to link facts and ideas you'd picked up subconsciously, maybe things you're not even aware you heard but your mind registered. Is it possible you heard your dad talking about the men who died, maybe even to Stokes or to your mum or to someone over the phone, and you didn't register it at the time, but somehow it all added up in your head and you worked out what they were planning?'

Tessa looped back down onto the motorway, but this time, she was headed back for Cork city.

'Are you saying you think my dad was involved in killing those men?'

'I hate to say it, but he's involved in something bad. I haven't worked out what it is yet, but my friend Maggie is trying to do just that as we speak.'

'So what can we do to help her?' Ellie asked.

'Do you know where Dr Cleary lives?'

'Yes.'

'Good,' Tessa said. 'I think it's time we got to the bottom of how you knew what you knew. And I reckon he has some ideas on how to do that.'

The psychiatrist lived in a renovated cottage near the airport.

He answered their knock in his shirtsleeves, a glass of something that looked very like whiskey in his hand.

'Detective Burns,' he said. 'You'll have to pardon me, I wasn't expecting visitors.'

'That's okay, Doctor,' Tessa replied, glancing about quickly to make sure no one had followed them before pushing Ellie inside ahead of her. 'Things have reached something of a crisis, and we need your help.'

'Come into my study,' Cleary said, leading them down a short hallway to a large room, the walls lined with books, a fire burning in a small hearth. An old blues song was playing quietly over speakers set on the corners of a large desk that had a laptop and lots of papers spread across its top.

A two-seater couch nestled in the corner, and Cleary motioned for Tessa and Ellie to take it, while he brought his own chair from behind the desk and sat opposite them.

'I take it something has happened since the case conference,' he said.

Tessa and Ellie took turns filling him in. When they were

finished, the therapist shook his head and sat back, pinching the bridge of his nose, his eyes closed. 'And you wish for me to definitively establish how Ellie was able to predict the death of the hotelier, Mr Wilde?'

'And Merrill and McGuinness, yes,' Tessa said. 'I think it's vital, at this stage, that we know. You had some pretty firm theories when we spoke earlier today. Is there a way you could prove their accuracy?'

Cleary opened his eyes and looked first at Tessa, then at Ellie. 'There might be. I could use hypnosis to help Ellie follow the threads of logic back to their points of origin. I'm not sure it would stand up in court, but it would give you an answer.'

'It doesn't need to stand up in court,' Tessa said. 'Ellie isn't on trial.' She looked at the girl seated beside her. 'Are you willing to give it a go?'

Ellie nodded. 'It'd be good to know.'

Cleary got up and left the room, returning with an old-fashioned wax candle in a silver candlestick holder. He lit the wick with a kitchen match and placed it on the floor between him and Ellie.

'I want you to focus on the candle's flame,' he said to the girl. 'Follow its ebb and flow, its rise and fall. Watch as it dances, as its colour alters. And as you do, I want you to begin to relax. Feel the weight of your body on the couch, and as you do, allow all the tension and anxiety you've been experiencing to flow out of you, down through the couch and into the floor and from there to be absorbed by the earth. Let your breath become steady and easy, let your eyes close and allow my voice to become your sole focus. We're going to go on a journey, you and I, and I want you to know you are completely safe. You feel warm, content and secure.'

Ellie looked to Tessa as if she was asleep, but then Cleary said, 'Ellie, you told the police that you knew Dominic Wilde was going to be murdered. Do you remember that?'

'Yes,' Ellie said, and her voice was firm.

'How did you know Mr Wilde was going to be killed, Ellie?' Cleary asked.

'I calculated the likelihood,' Ellie said. 'The facts indicated this eventuality would occur.'

'Please outline the facts that led you to this conclusion,' Cleary said.

'Mr Wilde was working with my dad's company. He'd been co-opted back onto the fundraising committee in the role of chairperson, so he saw all the funds coming into the company from each money-raising initiative. It was a position that gave him access to a lot of information.'

'And this put him at risk?' Cleary asked.

'I heard Mr Stokes ask my dad on one occasion if Mr Wilde was "easily controlled". Dad said he believed Mr Wilde "would want to avoid confrontation". Then, several days later, I over-heard him tell my mam, "Dominic's asking questions. He suspects something." Mam asked him if Mr Wilde "would stay quiet", and Dad said he was worried "he might cause a fuss".'

'And what did you understand that to mean?'

'That he was asking questions about the source of monies going into the HuTec accounts and where some of that money was going.'

'What caused you to draw that conclusion?'

'At that time, I was in my dad's office most evenings playing the game we both liked. One time I saw accounts on his desk. It was obvious that money was coming in from unnamed sources and that portions of this money were being redirected into numbered accounts.'

'So you believed Mr Wilde would see this too?'

'If he was a good businessman, yes.'

'And was he a good businessman?'

'Mr Stokes came to visit one evening. My dad wasn't home yet, and Mam showed him into Dad's office to wait. He made a phone call while he was waiting, and I heard some of it as I was on my way upstairs. He told the person he was speaking to that: "Wilde has to be removed from his position. He knows too much and has become a liability. Do it like the others, and get it done this weekend."'

'Why did you interpret that to mean he was to be killed?'

'Mr Stokes used to work for gangs in the Cork area. I've listened to three podcasts in which he was mentioned as a key player, and one that focused on his disappearance and theorised as to what happened to him during that time. That show also questioned whether or not he'd actually left the criminal life at all and proposed his working for charities may be a cover. It seemed clear to me that they were right, and that he was using HuTec as a front to raise money.'

'Did that not also incriminate your father?'

'I chose to believe he was being coerced.'

'Was he made aware of Wilde's approaching assassination?'

'Two days later he was driving me back home from chess club, so it was around ten thirty at night when he received a call. I'd fallen asleep, but I opened my eyes for a moment and could see from his phone screen that it was from Mr Stokes. He uses handsfree so the entire exchange was easy to hear. When I thought about it later, I thought it must have been a dream.'

'But you know it wasn't.'

'No. I think I wanted to believe I had imagined it.'

'What was said?'

'Stokes told him that he'd arranged "for Wilde to be put down, and that it was to be made to look like he'd done it himself". My dad told him no one would believe that, that Mr Wilde was happily married and had everything to live for. He pointed out that Mr Wilde rarely socialised and is either at work or at home, which means he's never alone. Mr Stokes said that wasn't my dad's concern, but if it would make him sleep easier, his "man was good at close quarters and it could be made to look like a botched robbery".'

'Close quarters?'

'I took it to mean he'd use either a ligature or a blade. Blades use less energy and are quicker.'

'Is that it?' Cleary asked the girl. 'That's how you reached the conclusion you did?'

'Yes.'

Cleary looked at Tessa. 'Do you need me to go through that for Merrill and McGuinness, or do you have enough?'

'More than enough,' Tessa said. 'Thank you, Doctor.'

Cleary nodded. 'Ellie, I'm going to begin counting backwards from twenty. As I do, you're going to slowly start to come back to full consciousness. When I reach one, you'll be fully aware of what we just spoke about, and you'll feel well rested and relaxed.'

When Ellie opened her eyes, she looked at Tessa. 'It looks like I'm not psychic,' she said.

'No,' Tessa said. 'Just very, very smart.'

41

When they left Cleary's home, Tessa headed west again, turning off the motorway at the sign for Timoleague once more. Shortly after she did, she spotted the lights of a roadside inn, The Halfway House.

Tessa managed to get a room at the back of the inn and pulled the Capri around so it was hidden from the road.

'We're in number twenty-three,' she said. 'We can have a good rest, I can make the calls I need to make and we'll review the situation tomorrow over breakfast.'

'Don't you want to make sure it's safe in there first?'

Tessa stopped in the doorway and gave her a funny look. 'What makes you think it's *not* safe?'

'Don't you think it would be better to make sure?'

Tessa scratched her head and looked down at Pav, who was watching them both with great interest. 'Would you be more comfortable if I did?'

'I think I'd feel more secure. I'd certainly sleep better.'

Tessa shrugged. 'Okay then. What am I looking for exactly?'

'I don't know. You're the detective.'

The room wasn't unlike the one Tessa had occupied in

Cork city, except this one was painted in pale blue while the other had been decorated in cream hues.

'There you go,' Tessa said after checking the shower room for hidden intruders. 'All clear.'

'I know I'm being silly. Thanks for looking.'

'You've been through quite a scare,' Tessa said. 'It's normal to be a bit freaked out.'

'You're very understanding,' Ellie said, sitting on the bed.

'We're thirty miles and then some from where we left the guys who tried to snatch you. No one followed us to or from Dr Cleary's – I can guarantee you that. I took an elaborate route to get here, and I made sure to avoid as many traffic cameras as I could – even though, to be honest, there's no reason in the world anyone would suspect we'd travel this direction. No one is going to be looking for us here. I promise.'

'You swear?'

'I do. Now, let's order some food, and then I'll make those calls. See if you can find something light to watch on the TV. We might as well enjoy the break while we can.'

They ordered plates of pasta – vegetarian carbonara for Ellie, spaghetti bolognese for Tessa and a couple of burgers cooked very rare for Pav – and watched a rerun of *Friends*, during which Ellie pointed out every joke that wouldn't be allowed in a contemporary comedy due to its political incorrectness.

It was a pleasant respite from the stress they'd both been under, and the hotel room echoed with their laughter.

42

After they'd eaten and watched TV for a bit, Tessa said to Ellie, 'I'll pop out now and make my calls. Will you be okay on your own for a short while?'

'I'll holler if I need you,' Ellie said.

'Do,' Tessa said.

She went out, sat in the Capri and called Dawn. 'I've got Ellie O'Farrell,' she said.

The commissioner heaved a sigh on the other end of the phone. 'I should be furious with you, DI Burns.'

'I know. She was taken by Stokes, the O'Farrells' lawyer, who's in on whatever scam is being run.'

'Are you somewhere safe?'

'For now, yes.'

'Good. Willie is processing the paperwork to have Danny released. Whatever you said to him, it worked.'

'Thank heavens for small mercies. Are we back on the case then?'

'I'm afraid not. I got an email from the minister's office. You're to return to base while there's a proper inquiry into your handling of the whole Cork debacle.'

'Who initiated that?'

'It's coming from the Cork branch of the Garda union. They're alleging your team is allowed to act with impunity, that Danny and Maggie were promoted inappropriately, that I'm playing favourites... There's a long list of grievances.'

'I'm not coming back yet, boss. I can't. Ellie is still at risk.'

'I know. Luckily you're a favourite of mine, so run along and do what you have to.'

'Do you have anything for me?'

'I do have one thing, as it happens. Since Maggie found the link between the deceased men and HuTec, the forensic accountants have been taking a look at their financial dealings. In the past six months – and it's been happening very gradually, so you'd need to have your eye on the ball to see it was happening at all – there's been an increase in monies going to HuTec from charitable donations. When you add up the difference between where they were last year at this time with where they are this year, we're talking about a three-million-euro bonus. If the trend continues, with donations going up a bit each month, by this time next year we'll be looking at about sixty million, if the increase continues to scale.'

'And where are these donations coming from?' Tessa asked.

'That's the thing. Our people have chased them down to a series of shell companies. And do you know which large companies are linked to these aforementioned non-existent businesses?'

'Merrill Fruits, owned by Dave Merrill, and South Coast Hotels, owned by Dominic Wilde, would be my guess,' Tessa said.

'And the bank that handled the transfers is the branch of Allied Irish Banks Miles McGuinness worked for,' Dawn replied. 'He handled the paperwork.'

'Now isn't that a thing? The money they're getting – do we know where *it's* coming from?'

'Our people are looking, but they can't find a source. It's as if this cash is appearing out of thin air.'

'Great way to launder money,' Tessa mused. 'Charitable donations are all tax deductible.'

'That they are,' Dawn said. 'Only thing is, no one has filed any returns on them.'

'No?'

'Not a one. So it doesn't look like a laundering scam.'

'What then?'

Dawn laughed. 'You're the fuckin' detective, Tessa. Go and detect. I'm hoping Danny will be out by the morning. Maggie is working from the hotel. Is there anything else I can do for you?'

'No thanks, boss. Once Danny is out and with me, I'll feel a lot better, but in the meantime, I'm good.'

'Okay then. Sit tight.'

And Dawn hung up.

Tessa sat back in the driver's seat and thought for a few moments. Despite her confused feelings, she realised that she really did miss Jim Sheils. She wanted to hear his voice.

He picked up after just one ring. 'How's it going down south?' he asked.

'Oh, you know,' she said. 'The odds are against us. Lives hang in the balance. The usual.'

'Kilbarry was telling me you dropped by. Was he any help?'

At the mention of Kilbarry's name, Tessa felt irritation rise in her gut. She fought it but knew her voice had lost some of its lightness. 'He was actually. Thanks for the introduction. He spoke highly of you.'

'Ah, he's a good old boy. Um... Tessa, you sound a bit off, if you don't mind my saying.'

'I'm tired, Jim. It's been a long couple of days.'

'Fair enough. I won't keep you if you need to rest.'

'Okay.'

'Any idea when you'll have things sorted down there?'

'No. Not a clue.'

'Oh. Well... thanks for the call.'

'No worries. Chat soon.'

And she hung up, wondering why, when she'd wanted to talk to him so badly, the mention of Kilbarry and her annoyance at him knowing she and Jim were an item still rankled with her.

Especially when all her friends knew, and that didn't bother her at all.

Ellie was already asleep when Tessa got back to the room. She read for a while on her phone – she always had a couple of books on the go and was currently reading one called *Last of the Giants: The True Story of Guns N' Roses* by a guy called Mick Wall. It was pretty good, but before long, she found herself drifting off to sleep, with Pavlov snoring at the end of her bed.

A strange sound woke her sometime later.

At first she thought it was an engine, but she quickly realised it was Pavlov growling.

'What's the matter?' she asked, pushing herself up on her elbows.

The dog had climbed down off the bed and was standing on the floor beside her, making a low, rumbling noise deep in his throat.

'What is it, boy?'

She was just about to get out of bed when the door exploded inwards in a cloud of splinters.

Tessa didn't have time to count how many were in the group that charged through the newly formed entrance, but she had a sense it was three or four. The only advantage she had was that she had some familiarity with the room while her opponents didn't. Close-quarters combat in low visibility was something she'd always been told to avoid where possible, but she couldn't risk shooting in such a confined space, so there was no option. She'd been taught in the military to keep low and go in fast and hard.

So that was the plan.

'Pavlov, let's go,' she hissed, and the dog immediately launched himself at the nearest figure, who swore and fell back beneath the animal's snarling – Tessa guessed the intruders had no idea she and Ellie had a dog with them, which also meant they didn't know what size he was, making a sneak attack by Pavlov in the dark a scary thing.

But there was no time to think about such considerations. There was work to be done.

Tessa put her head down and charged, bringing her elbows up and using them as a battering ram. She felt herself collide with something and turned slightly, using her shoulder to knock the person off balance. At the same time, she lashed out with her right leg, hitting something soft and hearing a satisfying exhalation – she'd got someone in the stomach and winded them.

Just then a light came on – it was Ellie using the torch on her phone. The room had been invaded by three youngsters in hoodies – Tessa only had a quick look, but they seemed to be a different three to the ones she'd dealt with outside the bar. At a glance, Tessa saw that Pavlov had one guy by the throat, and the other two were down but not out.

A thought flitted across her mind: *How did they find us? I was really careful!*

Then one of them was on his feet and there was no more time for such questions. Tessa grabbed the guy by the hair and slammed his head against the wall. By then the other had pounced on her back, but Tessa drove her elbow hard into the man's gut – once, twice, three times. She felt him sag and threw herself and him backwards onto the floor, using her bodyweight to disable him for a moment before butting her head backwards and breaking his nose.

'Tessa, look out!'

She heard the cry from Ellie, but it was too late.

Something exploded in her head, a black hole opened beneath her and she sank into it.

ELLIE O'FARRELL

During the fracas, Ellie hadn't been idle.

She'd woken to the sound of the door shattering open, and slid from her bed and scuttled underneath it.

As soon as the fighting started, she peered over the top of her mattress and turned the torch on her phone on in an attempt to give Tessa and Pav the upper hand before grabbing the lamp that sat on the locker beside her bed and smashing it across the head of the thug the tenacious little dog was biting on the neck.

She thought they'd won the hour until she saw a strange man step into the room. He was dressed from head to toe in black, and his face looked as if it had been made from playdough. There was something about this man that led Ellie to believe things were about to get very bad indeed.

She called out in warning, but it was too late. The strange-looking man was carrying a sawn-off shotgun, and before Tessa had a chance to move, he clubbed her square in the back of the head with the butt, knocking the detective senseless. He then levelled the barrels of the gun at the fallen woman's head.

Ellie was so scared, she thought she was going to be sick.

Terrified or not, however, she wasn't going to allow this awful man to kill Tessa.

'Hey, mister, you've got me,' she said, raising her hands. 'I'll come quietly.'

'My employers wish for Detective Burns to be retired,' the Faceless Man said in a soulless voice, thumbing back the hammers on his weapon.

'She's down,' Ellie said. 'Please don't kill her.'

'I have my orders.'

The man's finger tightened on the trigger, but before the shot was fired, Pavlov sailed across the room like a projectile, knocking the shooter off balance. The deadly spray went wide, tearing a chunk out of the plaster on the wall above the bed.

The Faceless Man landed on his ass on the floor, while the dog, his teeth bared, stalked towards him. Tossing the shotgun aside, the downed man pulled a Glock 9 from inside his jacket and aimed it at Pavlov, but as he pulled the trigger, the dog sprang, literally leaping over the bullet's path and landing on his attacker's chest. The assassin tried to bring the handgun up to shoot the dog in the belly, but seeming to sense this, Pavlov sprang aside, then lunged forward and sank his teeth into the blank palette of the man's face.

The Faceless Man screamed and tried to wrestle the dog off himself, but the more he struggled, the more the teeth ripped the flesh of his cheek. The assassin sat up, as if intending to stand, but when he did, Pavlov allowed himself to hang, suspended by his teeth, and the man lay back down again to relieve the pressure and pain. As Ellie watched, one of the tracksuited thugs grabbed Pav about the neck and tried to drag him off. This seemed to only cause the animal to redouble his efforts – meaning he bit down harder.

'Reload the fucking shotgun!' the youngster whose nose Tessa had broken said in a muffled voice. 'Shoot the damn thing!'

'I don't got no shells!' the kid trying to pull Pavlov away said.

'Grab the Glock then!'

'Where is it?'

'It's in his hand.'

'I can't fucking see it! You grab it seein' as how you're so full of ideas!'

The broken-nosed kid scuttled over and tried to get his hand under Pavlov's body, which caused the dog to release the assassin's face momentarily so he could lunge at this new threat. The Faceless Man, his visage a mask of blood, moaned in misery and tried to push himself away, but before he could, Pavlov attached himself to his throat.

'Will one of you shoot him or put a knife in him or something?' the Faceless Man hissed, an edge of fear creeping into his dry, monotonous voice.

Broken Nose picked up the shotgun and began to club Pavlov about the head, an action that caused the dog's victim to make a gurgling sound.

'You might hurt the dog, but you're also going to break Faceache's neck,' Ellie said urgently.

'Can you call him off?' Broken Nose asked, pausing mid-strike.

'I will if you give me your word you'll let him and Tessa live.'

The youngster nodded. 'Make sure he doesn't go for me then!'

'Only if you promise not to shoot him.'

Broken Nose nodded again, more urgently this time. 'Cross me heart.'

'Pavlov, let him be.'

The dog didn't move. Ellie swallowed hard and took a breath before saying more firmly, 'Pavlov, please let go.'

The dog opened his jaws and sat up, growling low in his chest. The Faceless Man was deathly pale and trembling, his face a mess, blood flowing from several holes in his neck and a vicious-looking tear in his cheek, though the fact that he was still breathing seemed to indicate that Pavlov had been gentler than it might have appeared.

'Get off him, Pavlov,' Ellie said.

The dog gave the prone man a hard look then padded over to where Tessa lay and sat down beside her.

'Mister, are you alright?' Broken Nose asked.

'No, I'm not alright.' The voice that answered was thin and trembling.

'We oughta get outta here,' Broken Nose said. 'We got the girl. You maybe should see a doctor or something.'

'I want you to shoot that dog,' the Faceless Man said, still flat on his back. 'And then the woman.'

'Stokes needs me,' Ellie said sharply – her heart was pounding, but she sensed she might have the upper hand. This weird-looking person didn't want to upset her. 'If you hurt either of my friends, I'll do whatever I have to to make sure you pay dearly.'

The Faceless Man raised his head and tried to aim the Glock that was still in his hand. The movement caused blood to pour in even greater quantities from the wounds in his throat, and the gun barrel bobbed and weaved drunkenly.

Ellie stepped in front of the weapon. 'You've got me. Let's go.'

Seeming to sense he was beaten, the wounded man let the gun fall to the floor.

'Help him up,' Ellie said to the others, and they scuttled over and helped their fallen comrade to his feet. He had to be half carried outside.

Ellie looked back at Pavlov before following them. 'Watch over her, boy,' she said.

The dog looked back with big eyes then put his head on his paws.

'Mr Stokes can't wait to see you,' the Faceless Man said to

Ellie as they got into a van that was parked outside. 'And he's not in a happy mood.'

'What makes you think I care?' Ellie asked.

She was sitting in the back of the van between Broken Nose and the other kid. She could see the strange man's mutilated face in the rear-view mirror. 'Do you think you're going to be even uglier now?' she asked him.

The man made a gurgling sound that could have been a laugh, and the van pulled away.

44

Tessa woke with a start, sitting bolt upright and lashing out at imagined attackers.

She immediately saw that she was alone and lay back down on the floor for a moment. Her head was pounding, and a little investigation told her she had a bump the size and shape of a tennis ball coming up on the back of it.

'Pavlov?'

The dog hopped down from the bed and nuzzled her gently.

'They got her, didn't they?'

Pavlov sat down beside her, making a non-judgemental whine.

'How long have I been out?'

The sun was coming up, which told her it had been at least a couple of hours – there were no other guests staying on this side of the property, so the noise of the altercation hadn't aroused any attention. She didn't know what time she and Pavlov had been disturbed by the attackers, but she reckoned it was about three in the morning. Sitting up a bit more carefully, she looked at the wall clock and saw that it was ten after six.

'They've got a head start,' she said to Pav. 'And we don't have any way of tracking them.'

She walked gingerly out to the Capri and climbed in, fumbling around in the glove compartment until she found some paracetamol.

'Of course,' she said to the dog, 'we do have one advantage. We know who took her, even if we don't know why.'

Pavlov looked at her with an expression that suggested he wasn't sure how this helped.

'Let's go and pick up Danny and see if we can't get her back.'

To that, Pavlov was in full agreement.

While she was en route, she called Maggie.

'They've taken her again,' she said. 'We got hit during the night.'

'Are you okay?'

'I'll live to fight another day. Maggie, I'm wracking my brains trying to work out what's going on here and why they want Ellie, so I'm grabbing at anything I've got. Do you remember Dr Cleary telling us about those sixty-four-character puzzles Ellie's dad used to get her to do?'

'Yeah, I remember. She could solve them in seconds, or so he said.'

'She mentioned them again last night when we were talking. She said her dad used to get excited when she solved them. Do you think there might be anything in that?'

'Hold on.'

Tessa heard laptop keys clacking.

'Shit,' Maggie said.

'Go on.'

'I can't believe I didn't think of this earlier,' Maggie said.

'What is it?'

'Crypto-mining.'

'I don't know what that is.'

'Philip's had his daughter mining for cryptocurrency online. Those puzzles she's been doing? Every time she solves one, he gets tens of thousands of euros – it's a system the international financial world has designed to promote cryptocurrency as a real fiscal force. If she could solve, say, three a night even, he could easily be earning over a hundred grand.'

'It's all starting to make sense,' Tessa said. 'The money appearing in those shell corporations – it was from the work Ellie's been doing, except she didn't even know it *was* work. She thought she was playing games, doing tricks to make her dad happy.'

'And the gangsters want her because she is, literally, the goose that lays the golden eggs,' Maggie replied.

'Danny is out today. I know you're without your chair, but you can still research and act as support.'

'Just tell me what you need. What's the plan?'

'It's a pretty simple one,' Tessa said. 'We're going to get Ellie back, and we're going to shut this whole operation down.'

45

Danny was so excited to get out of the cells that he was almost hopping from foot to foot.

'I see Sergeant O'Mahoney's had a change of heart,' he said as the Garda in charge of the cells handed him back his belt, jacket, ID and sidearm.

'Just a bit,' Tessa said. 'His back is against the wall, and I think we might have experienced some of his misdirected anger.'

'So how have things been going?'

She told him, and his face fell.

'So what's our next step?'

'We need to know where they've taken Ellie.'

'Any thoughts on where that might be?'

'None.'

'Do you have a proposal as to how we could find out?'

'I do, as a matter of fact.'

'I'm listening.'

'This might have started with Conor Stokes, the lawyer, but from what Ellie told me, her father's key to whatever's going on. Whatever they're doing, which seems to involve putting large amounts of funds through his fundraising initiative, Philip O'Farrell is pivotal to it all.'

'So even if he doesn't know exactly where his daughter is, he'll have a fair idea of where we might start looking.'

'That's what I'm thinking.'

'Okay. So where do we find him?'

'I think we should try his home in Douglas. I have a strong feeling Philip O'Farrell didn't show up for work today.'

Tess and Pav took her Capri, and Danny followed in his Golf. It took them twenty minutes to reach Douglas, and when they did, they made straight for the O'Farrells' gated residence. Tessa parked out front and pressed the buzzer. No one answered.

'No one home?' Danny called from the Golf, which was idling behind her Capri.

'My guess is they're holed up inside scared out of their wits,' Tessa said.

'Maybe we should park in that estate over yonder and climb over the wall?'

'Pav will have to stay in the car.'

'I'm sure he won't mind missing what'll probably be a short conversation,' Danny said.

'Is that a hint of sarcasm I detect?' Tessa asked.

'Me? Never!' Danny said primly.

'Let's park and get in there.'

They left the vehicles in a small housing estate called Belgard Downs then jogged back across the road. Danny gave a quick run, jumped and grabbed the top of the wall with both hands, hauling himself up with consummate ease. He turned and offered Tessa his hand, but she was already pulling herself up.

There was no answer to their ringing of the doorbell, so Tessa opened the letter box and called through, 'Philip and

Cynthia, this is DI Burns. Please open up. It's very important. Your daughter's safety is all I care about. We can deal with what you chose not to share with the Gardai at a later date.'

She waited, still peering through the letter box. Finally, she spied movement, and saw a very dishevelled-looking Cynthia O'Farrell come down the stairs and pad up the hall.

'What do you want?' the woman said.

'To come in for a moment please,' Tessa said.

The woman opened up and stood aside, and they went into the same living room she and her team had sat in two days ago, although it felt like a month had passed.

'Where's your husband?' Tessa asked.

'At his *work*,' Cynthia said.

She spoke with very little inflection or emotion, and Tessa could tell she was in shock.

'You know Stokes took Ellie?' Danny said.

Cynthia looked at the big detective, her expression sagging. 'They won't give her up. I don't know how you're going to get her from them.'

'We can be pretty persuasive,' Danny said. 'And if that doesn't work, I can be just a bit ferocious.'

Cynthia smiled weakly. 'You'll need to be.'

'Can you tell us where she is?' Tessa asked.

'Stokes has a mansion – Faoin Tuath, it's called – in the countryside just outside Youghal. That's where Philip has gone, so that's where they'll have taken her.'

'Why do they want her?'

'It's because of what she can do. She's... she's special. Philip knew that.'

'How does her giftedness help Stokes?' Tessa asked. 'I know money is being channelled through HuTec, using shell corporations owned by men who were part of a fundraising initiative. I know the money seems to have been appearing out of thin air, and that Ellie has been finding it online for Philip through that game they were playing. It's called cryptocurrency.'

Cynthia nodded. 'But there's more to it than that. Philip created a highly complex algorithm that mines for cryptocurrency automatically – it finds the codes and then works to crack them. He could set it to run for the day, and when he checked, there'd be a pile of bitcoin waiting for him, and it's worth a *lot*. Right now, one bitcoin is worth about €35,000.'

'Did it work?' Tessa asked.

'It did, but not as effectively as he'd hoped. To mine bitcoin, you start with a sixty-four-character alphanumeric code. Whichever platform you're on sets a series of criteria you have to match, and you need to rearrange the sixty-four letters and numbers to solve the puzzle before any of the other miners do it. Whoever wins gets the bitcoin reward. But each time the set is solved, the next one gets harder. Most people don't make any kind of big money consistently doing it. And neither did Philip's program. As the puzzles got harder, it slowed down, and in the end could take days to crack one.'

'But Ellie could still do it quickly, no matter how difficult,' Tessa said.

'Exactly. The algorithm Philip wrote tried to compensate for the difficulty,' Cynthia said. 'But it wasn't foolproof – sometimes he won and sometimes he didn't – but one evening, he was using the algorithm in his office, and Ellie popped in to tell him our evening meal was ready. She happened to see the blockchain on his laptop. And within a second of seeing it, she'd solved the puzzle.'

'Just like that,' Tessa said.

'Philip thought it was a fluke,' Cynthia said. 'So after dinner, he brought her in and asked her to see if she could do it again. And she did.'

'Did you know she was so gifted?' Tessa asked.

'Dr Cleary believed she was,' Cynthia said. 'He was always

talking about how she was a Rain Man-level savant. I preferred to treat her as a normal child, but when she did this, which involved complex mathematical calculation, along with a lot of instinctive guesswork, all in her head, I couldn't pretend any longer that she was just a normal, albeit intelligent, little girl. Philip had created highly advanced software to perform this task, and it still got it wrong a lot of the time. Ellie was able to beat the system *every* time.'

'Your husband told Stokes about the software, didn't he?' Tessa asked.

'He did. It was starting to bring us in a bit of extra money here and there, and making our lives a lot easier. He wasn't earning a huge wage at HuTec, and my bakery was doing alright, but the money from the bitcoin mining was getting us holidays, nicer cars. Philip wanted to put the software to good use – share our good fortune with those who really needed it.'

'Couldn't you just have donated some cash here and there?' Danny asked.

'Philip didn't want any credit for it,' Cynthia said. 'He wanted to be transparent about it, have it all above board. So he asked Stokes to come over one evening so he could tell him about his algorithm and the cryptocurrency we could earn. I was proud of him for doing it. At that stage, he hadn't mentioned Ellie – he was just going to hand over the software to Stokes and let it earn what it could, and whatever money it made would go to HuTec. But you see, there are periods of time when the returns are thin on the ground. The problems become almost impossible to solve. There had been several weeks where nothing was coming in, and Stokes came to Philip quite angry about it. He said the software was faulty, had bugs in it or something to that effect. Philip scoffed at him, and told him that he and Ellie had been doing some mining just that evening and she'd cracked the chain three times. Stokes stalked out, but he came back a week later and insisted that if Ellie could do this for us, she should be doing it for HuTec as well.'

'Were you getting the impression that all the money this software was earning for HuTec might not be going directly into the company?' Danny asked.

'Philip asked some of his friends to look into that. They learned that money was certainly going to HuTec, but it was being siphoned off into two other accounts from those shell corporations too. It was Dave Merrill who was the first to suggest that Stokes might not have left his criminal affiliations completely behind.'

'And I'll bet his death occurred shortly after he made that statement,' Tessa said.

'It did,' Cynthia agreed. 'After he died, Miles said he was determined to get to the bottom of things. He called Philip on the day he had his accident. Told him he needed to stop the use of the software at HuTec, as it was going to cause us to be audited. And Dominic Wilde found that the shell corporations had been set up in his and Dave Merrill's names to redirect the funds.'

'Stokes was covering his tracks,' Tessa said. 'What did Philip do?'

'He did what Miles suggested. He erased the software from the HuTec database.'

'But you still had a copy of it here.'

'He removed it from our system too. He was afraid someone would hack into our computer and steal it.'

'He kept a copy somewhere though, didn't he?' Danny said.

'On a SIM card in his office.'

'And did that SIM card happen to go missing over the past couple of days?' Tessa asked.

'It vanished two days ago. On the day we were all taken to the police station.'

Tessa nodded. 'Why did you take Ellie to the Gardai when your husband was so deeply involved in all of this?'

'Would you believe it was his idea?' Cynthia said. 'She was so upset, he thought going to the police would set her mind at ease. With a story like the one she had, that she was dreaming all of this, he thought they'd never take her seriously.'

'I think I know where the missing SIM card is,' Tessa said. 'Come on, Danny. Let's go and get Ellie back.'

'We're bound for Youghal?'

'We are. But I think we need to get some firepower first.'

46

Tessa made a call as soon as she was back in her Capri. 'Wallace, it's Tessa.'

'Hey, Tess. Long time no hear.'

Allan Wallace had been in care with Tessa in a unit in Dublin during her last year in the residential system before she left to join the army. They'd shared an interest in military history, and when it came time for Tessa to leave and sign up for service, Wallace had assured her he would follow. Their paths, however, weren't destined to cross within the Irish armed forces: Tessa had been recruited to the Irish Army Ranger Wing, while Wallace had quickly been diverted into the intelligence service's counter-terrorism unit, where he still worked.

'Wallace, I'm in Cork and I need weapons. I was wondering if you might know someone who can help me out.'

'What do you need?'

'My partner and I are about to storm a gangster's stronghold. We don't know how many men we're going up against, but we have to assume at least twenty. Probably with automatic weapons.'

'I see. Is this anything my people should take an interest in?'

'These are organised criminals rather than terrorists.'

'Okay. Well, I do know a guy in that neck of the woods. He provides a service for us when we're working in the south of the country. I'll give him a call and ask him to help you out off the books.'

'Thanks, Wallace.'

'You owe me, Tessa.'

'You know I'm good for it.'

'I wouldn't be helping otherwise. Be safe.'

'I'll do my best.'

'Please do. I'm sending you an Eircode.'

The coordinates took Tessa and Danny to a shop called Doolan's Shootin' & Fishin', situated on a long country lane, a byroad off a byroad. Google Maps informed Tessa they were near the town of Bandon, but the location seemed to be about as close to the middle of nowhere as she'd ever been. Why anyone would set up a business here was absolutely beyond her.

The shopfront was utterly unkempt: peeling paint and rusted hinges, appearing to have been shut for some time, but when Danny knocked, an elderly man opened the door a crack and peered out.

'I'll be with you in a jiffy,' the oldster said, undoing a chain and opening the door to allow them entrance.

'Mr Doolan, my friend told me you'd be expecting us,' Tessa said, offering her hand to him.

'Always happy to do business with a friend of Mr Wallace. Who are your pals?'

'This is Danny and Pavlov.'

'That's a fine dog,' the man said. 'You use him for huntin'?'

'No. He's just a friend.'

'He gun-shy?'

'Not in the slightest.'

The shopkeeper shrugged. 'Well how can I help you today?'

Inside, the shop belied its external façade: it was spick and span, typical for its type: wooden cabinets with clear glass frontage displayed knives, guns and fishing equipment of all kinds. The head of a red deer, its enormous antlers extending from it like tree branches, sat above the door, and a large pike, so big it looked as if it could consume a small child, hung over the counter.

'I'm a... a collector and would like to purchase some weapons,' Tessa said.

'You got ID?' the man asked, his tone deadly serious.

Tessa stared at the man for a second before he exploded into guffaws of laugher.

'Oh, don't mind me,' the old man said. 'You can call me Doolan – everyone around here does.'

'It's nice to meet you, Doolan.'

'You too. So – what are you looking for?'

'If you happened to have load for a Sig Sauer P226 in stock, that would be really wonderful.'

'You mean the Mark 25?'

'Ideally, yes.'

The old man walked past Tessa and pulled a metal box from atop a high shelf. He took a key from his pocket, opened the box and took out a large box of bullets. 'Is this what you're looking for?'

Tessa nodded. 'Thank you, Doolan. That's all I need.'

She looked at Danny.

'Do you need extra load for your sidearm?'

'That's it?' the oldster asked. 'You only want lead for your peashooters? Mr Wallace said to put whatever you need on his account. I've got lots of weapons here – you sure you don't want anythin' else?'

Danny tutted and took his partner aside. 'For God's sake, Tessa,' he said quietly, so Doolan wouldn't overhear. 'We're in Willy Wonka's factory and all you ask for is a tube of mints? Come on – show some imagination!'

Tessa gave her partner a hard look. 'Danny, we may be working this one as private citizens, but I have no intention of going Dirty fucking Harry. So far, we've got by without spilling any blood at all. I don't need an armoury.'

'I know, but isn't it always better to have and not need than need and not have? We haven't a clue what we're going up against. If they have machine guns, we won't hold them back with pistols.'

Tessa heaved a deep sigh. 'I suppose you're right.'

'Good. Now, Mr Doolan, I was hoping you might have an FN P90,' Danny said.

The old man paused. 'That's a military weapon.'

'I am aware of that.' The big detective sounded slightly offended.

'If I did have such a thing, it would be against the law to sell it to you.'

Danny looked crestfallen.

The oldster cackled again. 'I'm only joshin' with you. I might have one or two of those guns.'

'I heard there were some modified versions on the market,' Danny said. 'For collectors.'

Doolan seemed to weigh up that proposal. 'You ain't lookin' to do nothin' circumspect with it, are you, son?'

Danny smiled, trying not to look guilty. 'I'm generally a straight-ahead kind of person,' he said. 'I wouldn't know how to begin being circumspect.'

Doolan nodded, as if this confirmed an opinion he'd already formed. 'Lock the door again for me there, lad, and turn that sign back around to "closed".'

Danny did so.

'Let's go out back. I might have somethin' that'll suit your needs.'

A door behind the counter led to a low-ceilinged storeroom,

cluttered with boxes, shelves and several workbenches. The old man moved some packaging to reveal a wooden crate.

'Take that crowbar and open this baby up.'

Tessa did as the old man asked. Inside was packed with dry straw.

Doolan reached in and pulled out a bundle wrapped tightly with oilcloth. 'St Nick just came early,' he said, passing the parcel over.

Inside, Tessa found four FN P90 tactical assault subma-chine guns – they had the familiar, rectangular shape she'd seen during her military service, making it look as if someone had started to carve a gun out of a block of iron but had stopped before they were finished. It looked clumsy and hard to manipu-late but was actually quite the opposite.

'That is one fine carbine,' the old man said warmly. 'The unusual design makes it compact and ergonomic, and it comes with a thumbhole polymer stock and ambidextrous operating controls. The top-mounted detachable magazine has a fifty-round capacity. There isn't a single weapon like it available today when it comes to accuracy or stopping capability. Which is why most of the world's special forces units use it.'

'It certainly is pretty,' Tessa agreed. She took another one out and tossed it to Danny.

'Well, if you're collectors, they'll look damned nice in a glass case in your hallway.'

'I couldn't agree more,' Danny said. 'It'll fit in perfectly above my mantlepiece.'

'Well, that's in the bag. Can I do you for anything else?'

'Do you happen to have a Heckler & Koch pump-action?' Danny asked.

'I most surely do.'

'I'll take one and a box of shells please.'

The old man went to a shelf and removed a leather case, which he passed across to Danny.

'And the shells...' He fumbled about on another shelf until he found a box.

'Can I just say, you two don't look much like collectors,' he said as he handed over the ordnance.

'Do they have a look?' Tessa asked, smiling.

Doolan waved off her retort. 'It ain't so much a look as a feelin'. You don't *feel* like a collector.'

'What do I feel like then?'

'You feel like two people who're fixin' to bring a world of hurt on someone.'

'I'm guessing you've been in this line of work for a long time,' Tessa said, 'so your instincts are good. Let's just say there are some bad people trying to force a friend of mine to do something she doesn't want to do. I'm going to help her, and Danny is going to help me.'

Doolan seemed to consider this for a moment. Then the old shopkeeper nodded and pulled a small flat box from underneath a workbench and set it out on the table. 'Here's something that'll round out your collection nicely.'

He opened the box and Tessa grinned.

'A sawn-off shotgun?'

'Not quite. Say hello to the Super-Shorty Mossberg 500. It's a compact, stockless pump-action, chambered in twelve-gauge. To make it legal, the weapon is manufactured without a shoulder stock, so it's considered a smooth-bore handgun rather than a short-barrelled shotgun. But yeah, it's basically a sawn-off.'

Tessa laughed. 'I'll take it.'

'Hell, I'll throw in a KA-BAR knife for each of you as a gesture of goodwill.'

'I don't think there's going to be a lot of that in Cork before today is out,' Danny said, smiling.

'I'd probably best not know the details,' the old man said. 'You collectors can be a contrary bunch. Now, do you want these gift-wrapped?'

PART FOUR

47

They left Danny's Golf in their hotel car park and took Tessa's Capri, loading the boot with their newly acquired weapons cache.

An hour later, they were heading down a country lane towards Stokes's mansion, which looked daunting in the satellite picture the sarge had printed out for them. Maggie was on speakerphone. They'd dropped Pav back with her before leaving on their rescue mission.

'I've managed to get the plans of the house and grounds,' she said. 'I can talk you through it as you go.'

'Thanks, Maggie,' Tessa said.

'The place looks more like a compound than a mansion,' their friend told them. 'There are quite a few boltholes, so this isn't going to be a walk in the park.'

Tessa pulled up at a wooden sign and rolled down her window. The sign had been shaped from solid wood by someone who knew what they were doing, ornate lettering forming the words *Faoin Tuath*, which meant 'The Countryside' in the Irish tongue.

Tessa parked the car just beyond the gate, shut off the engine and got out. Then she hauled the bag of weapons from the boot and took out a gun belt Doolan had provided, fastening it loosely around her waist so as not to restrict movement. It had loops into which she put shells for the Mossberg, and holsters for both it and the Mark 25.

Danny did the same, loading shells for the pump-action into a leather tote, which he slung across his shoulder – he'd already loaded it with clips for his own handgun and the other P90. The KA-BAR he slipped through the back of the belt, letting the handle nestle into the small of his back.

They each had Bluetooth earpieces in, connected to their phones, which were both on conference-call mode with Maggie, back at the Hotel Isaacs.

Tessa put the bag, now empty, back into the Capri and, with the machine gun held at her side, looked at her accomplice. 'We ready?'

'Raring to go,' Danny said.

'I'm right with you,' Maggie agreed. 'So's Pavlov.'

'Let's do it then.'

Tessa and Danny jumped the fence and sprinted towards the house.

Going full tilt, the two friends covered the half mile between the road and the buildings in four minutes, coming to rest behind a patch of scrub within sight of the house. It was a grey day, and quite a few lights were on. Tessa could hear classical music playing somewhere inside and spied a couple of men through an upstairs window.

'The property is made up of a large, two-storey building which is the main house, and two blocks made up of single floors branch off from either side,' Maggie told them. 'I can't tell from the plans if these are storage rooms or not, but my best guess is that they're dormitories for the men I'm sure Stokes keeps on site. There are some smaller structures to the rear that are clearly sheds, and on a satellite shot I looked at, I could see bikes and quads parked out back too.'

'He has a selection of muscle cars parked in front of the main house,' Tessa said.

She could see a Trans-Am, a Maserati and a Porsche, as well as three Honda Civics, a Mitsubishi Lancer, a couple of Subaru Imprezas and one highly modified Volkswagen Golf from where she and Danny were crouched. 'Okay, thanks, Maggie. Let's do a recce and see what we can see.'

They made a circuit of the area, hoping they might catch a glimpse of Ellie through one of the windows, or maybe even hear someone mention her, but they weren't so lucky. There were security cameras mounted on the eaves of the house at three different points, but these were easily evaded. Danny had wondered if there might be dogs, but they saw none – there weren't even men patrolling the perimeter. In Tessa's experience, this meant that the resident preferred to keep the bulk of the security inside – which would make infiltration all the more difficult. Finally, they sat with their backs to what Tessa took to be a boiler room and waited.

Her heart was pounding, and she knew it wasn't from the run. She sat very still, trying to regulate her breathing, but suddenly she was hit by a wave of nausea, and leaned over and threw up what little food was in her stomach (she hadn't eaten since the pasta with Ellie the previous night).

Danny looked at her with concern. 'You okay, Tess?'

'I'm fine. Must have been something I ate.'

'That or you're afraid of what the body count will be,' Danny said gently.

'I don't want to kill anyone unless we absolutely have to,' Tessa said, lying on her back and staring at the sky.

'We won't,' Danny said. 'Not unless they leave us absolutely no choice.'

'Do I have your word on that?'

'Scout's honour.'

'I'm serious, Danny!'

'Tessa, you're my commanding officer. If you say we're going for a non-lethal intervention, then that's what we're doing.'

'Thank you. I know we're not doing this as Gardai, but... well, we still have to do it right. If we don't, we're no better than Stokes.'

'Agreed.'

It took a few minutes for the sick feeling to subside, but eventually it did, and she lay flat on her back and looked up at the sky, imagining himself a white speck in all that vastness. She let the huge expanse of the sky fill her vision, and then her mind. It was another trick she'd been taught, this time by an old sergeant she'd served under in Kandahar.

'Your brain ain't no use in a firefight, Tess,' the sarge had told her. 'In point of fact, it's the thing most likely to get you killed. Everything you need is there in your guts and your fingers and your heart – you've trained so much, the mechanics of it is programmed into you – it's second nature. You just gotta trust yourself and take those first few steps. Once you're up and movin', the rest will look after itself.'

Tessa closed her eyes and took three deep breaths, in through her mouth and out through her nose. She felt her heart rate slow, her thoughts dwindle to nothing, and her muscles relax.

'I don't think there's going to be a good time,' she said. 'So now is as good as any.'

'Roger that,' Danny said.

And they broke cover, ran to the closest door and Danny kicked it in.

SERGEANT WILLIE O'MAHONEY

He was in his office when he got the call to say that Cynthia O'Farrell was asking to see him.

'Yeah, send her up.'

His intention was to let her rant for a bit, take whatever abuse she intended to sling at him and then send her on her way.

Yes, he probably hadn't handled her daughter's case as well as he might have done, but then, he hadn't wandered too far off the reservation either. He'd treated her as he would any other kid who came to him with similar claims. He wasn't an expert like Tessa and her cronies; he was just an old-school copper trying to do his best in a lousy situation. There was nothing to be gained from beating himself up over it too much.

He just hoped Tessa and her crew would be able to bring the kid back in one piece.

Cynthia appeared at his door, peering in at him through the glass.

'Come on ahead,' he called to her, and she pushed her way in.

'What can I do for you, Mrs O'Farrell?'

'I don't want anything from you,' the woman said.

O'Mahoney could see she was at the end of her rope. She looked like she hadn't slept in days.

'You should go home, Mrs O'Farrell,' he said. 'There are some good people out looking for your daughter. I'll call you as soon as I hear anything.'

'I told you I'd hurt you if anything happened to my Ellie,' the woman said.

'And I don't blame you for the sentiment,' O'Mahoney said. 'If it was one of mine, I'd be the same way.'

'If it was one of yours, you never would have sent her to that awful unit.'

'I did what I thought best. I'm sorry if you disagree with my choices.'

'She's missing now because of those choices. She's in the hands of evil men.'

'We don't know where she is or under what conditions at the moment, Mrs O'Farrell.'

'I told you what I'd do,' she said, reaching into the large handbag she was carrying. 'I told you, to your face.'

Her hand came out of her bag carrying a revolver – a .38 Police Special.

'Mrs O'Farrell, it's an offence to bring an unlicensed firearm into a police station,' O'Mahoney said. 'I must ask you to give it to me for your own protection.'

'I'll give it to you alright,' Cynthia O'Farrell said and shot him twice in the chest, before putting the gun down on his desk and waiting calmly to be arrested.

48

The door to Stokes's stronghold slammed open, its frame splintered.

Tessa felt a cold calmness envelop her as that unnamed part of her stepped forward again and took control. She moved rapidly up the hallway, Danny coming behind, keeping her left and right flank safe. Tessa's mind was working rapidly. Several things were going on at the same time, and she ticked off each point as it occurred to her.

1. The door had given remarkably easily, which told her right away that Stokes didn't expect to be attacked in his own home. While there had been a few outside, there were no security cameras inside at all – at least none she could see so far. The front hallway was an obvious place to put a couple, yet there were none. Tessa hoped this lack of security would follow through the rest of the house, though she thought that unlikely. It seemed more reasonable to assume things would get

exponentially more challenging as they moved through the property.

2. To say that the mansion had little security ignored the fact that there was evidence – from the numbers of vehicles alone – of a large group of men at the location. Having gang members living on-site was probably as much about cementing bonds of solidarity and kinship as it was about maintaining a presence that would dissuade any local competition from mounting an assault. It was why militaries kept soldiers and their families in barracks on bases – why would anyone want to attack when they already knew a large number of armed opposition was embedded at the location? Tessa was in no doubt that any potential aggressors knew the mansion was heavily defended and kept clear as a result. So far, surprise was all they had going for them.

3. The floor was covered in a thick carpet so their steps made no sound as they moved, but the hallway was broad and high ceilinged, which meant that gunshots would bounce around the space like it was an echo chamber. If they wanted to find Ellie, keeping their presence dark was a priority, although Tessa had grave doubts they would be able to do so for very long. The fact they'd kicked the door in had probably already alerted someone to their presence.

The moment this thought crossed Tessa's mind she and Danny reached the hall's halfway point and a short young man with a crew cut burst from a door to their left. He was shirtless, clad only in grey boxer shorts.

'Hey, what the fuck are you doin' here?'

Tessa didn't speak. Instead she used the P90 as a club,

catching the youngster on the bridge of his nose and dropping him immediately before stepping over him.

Quick, clean and quiet, Tessa thought. *Let's hope we can keep it like that.*

'All okay?' Maggie's voice came through her earpiece.

'All good. Where does this corridor lead?'

'To the kitchen. My guess is it won't be empty, so prepare yourselves.'

'Roger that,' Danny said quietly behind Tessa.

There was a set of double doors at the end of the corridor, and she pushed them open carefully. Inside, as Maggie had indicated, was a kitchen that looked as if it had been plucked from the pages of a *Homes of the Rich and Famous* magazine – everywhere was polished surfaces, hand-painted tiles and top-of-the-line appliances. At the centre of it all was a square countertop that looked as if it had been made from sandstone and native wood. Four men were gathered around it eating sandwiches and drinking beer. Tessa recognised three of them right away as the gang members from the Nine of Diamonds.

And she knew that any hope of keeping things quiet was rapidly slipping away.

There was a moment when everyone froze – the three youngsters looked at them and they back at the youngsters (Tessa saw the skinny one had literally stopped chewing). And then – Tessa watched it happen as if in slow motion – the bodybuilder reached under his hoodie and took out a gun.

'Drop it.' Tessa heard her own voice – hard and clear – almost as if it was coming from someone else.

'No fuckin' way,' the musclebound youth said. 'There's a whole bunch of us and only two o' you.'

'The odds seem pretty even then,' Tessa heard Danny say, and knowing that the repercussions of the action were liable to be as messy as they were noisy, she shot the kid in the leg.

And mess and noise followed.

The P90 wasn't in itself a loud weapon – it was designed to be used as part of stealth missions – and it made a gentle coughing noise as the round was discharged. The wounded gangster staggered back, squeezing off a shot from his own gun, which happened to be a Colt Python. The bullet hit the wall four feet above Danny's shoulder, blowing a hole the size of a football in plaster that had been painted a muted shade of cream. The Python was *not* a subtle gun and made a sound like a cannon. As Tessa dived to the left and Danny to the right, she was subliminally aware that the three others had produced their own weapons.

There goes the quiet, she thought, but then she was rolling as a hail of bullets filled the air around her, tearing further holes in the wall and turning the front of a chrome-coloured refrigerator into so much scrap metal. Danny just had time to turn over an oaken table to create some cover – and they crouched behind it.

'Maggie, we're pinned down here,' Tessa shouted over the gunfire. 'What's our best exit?'

'There's a door in the top-right-hand corner of the room,' Maggie said. 'It leads to a utility room and from there to a reception area at the rear of the house.'

'If we don't do something fast, we won't be moving anywhere,' Danny said.

'Like what?' Tessa asked over the noise of the gunfire.

'I have an idea. I promise I won't kill any of them.'

'Be my guest.'

Danny took the Mossberg from Tessa's belt and checked its load, then waited until they heard the first 'click' of a hammer falling on an empty chamber, peered around the side of their hastily created shelter and shot the closest man – the skinny youngster – in the knee with the shotgun.

'Aw fuck, he shot me in goddam knee!'

The young man had fallen backwards and was wailing hysterically.

'Oh Jesus, Ted – how bad is it? Can you see it? I think me whole knee is gone!'

Tessa chanced a quick peep around the table. Blood was seeping from the wound, and the young men seemed stunned and numb. This had turned very real for them very fast.

'You bastard – you done disabled Wilson!' someone called at Danny. 'He's gonna fuckin' die! You went and killed him!'

'Jesus – don't say that!' Wilson wailed back.

'Take off your belt and wrap it around his thigh, a little above the knee,' Tessa called. 'Cinch it really tightly, or he'll bleed out.'

'Don't let me die,' Wilson begged, his tone bordering on real panic. 'You gotta help me!'

Tessa could hear steps pounding from above: reinforcements were headed their way. She peeped over the table again and, seeing the door Maggie had indicated, motioned to Danny, and they moved swiftly towards it.

'Oh Jesus, man, it hurts like hell,' Wilson was saying.

'Try to keep him talking,' Tessa shouted as they reached the door. 'It'll stop him from going into shock.'

'He's already in fuckin' shock!'

'All the more reason to keep him conscious. Now we're moving on, and if anyone follows, I'll take more than their leg. Are we clear?'

'Fuck you, bitch!'

'Answer me, or I'll just shoot you right here.'

'You won't get far anyway. They're comin'.'

'Tend to your friend.'

And then she was gone, following Danny into the bowels of the house.

A short hallway led from the utility room to what looked to be a lounge of some kind. There were framed pictures of sports teams on the walls, a full bar with bottles of liquor stacked on glass shelves behind it and a massive widescreen

TV that took up an entire wall. A pool table and three old-fashioned arcade-style video games completed the scene, and the furniture was all leather and patterned animal-hide. It was what Floyd, her former patrol partner, would have called a man cave. Tessa raised a hand, and they paused for a moment, listening for more sounds from above. Hearing none, she motioned they could move, and they passed through the space, stopping for a moment so she could press her ear to the door on the other side before feeling confident enough to open it.

'We're in the reception area,' she told Maggie. 'Where does the door lead?'

'The foyer,' her friend said. 'You can access the stairs to the next floor from there. I have to warn you though – there doesn't look to be much cover.'

They found themselves in a wide space that went from ground level right to the top of the house. It reminded Tessa of a hotel: the floor was covered in stone tiles, and there was a large table adorned with desert flowers and big, hardback books that seemed to be about local plant and animal life. A long and winding stairwell led upwards from the centre of the space, and she could see a landing that ran from right to left, many doors leading off it to what she assumed were bedrooms.

Tessa led the way up the stairs cautiously, but as she did so, men started to pour out of the door from the man cave. Danny didn't give the new arrivals time to lock sights on them – he opened fire, and he and Tessa took what was left of the stairs three at a time. Danny hadn't had the opportunity to aim, but Tessa heard the man in the front of the pack cry out, and she shot in the direction of the sound, feeling the gun purr in her hand as it did its work.

Her hope was to lay down a barrage that would stop the men from coming forward, giving them time to get to the top and find Stokes, whom she reckoned must be aware of their presence at this stage and taken refuge in a part of the house that would be difficult for them to get to.

Bullets thudded into the wood panelling around them, and then they were at the top of the stairs. Looking down, Tessa saw that the hallway below was full of men – she counted ten, and more were coming, but then they started shooting, and the two infiltrators were forced to duck below the wooden safety railing, which offered no real cover but somewhat hid their precise location.

Using her Sig, she took careful aim through the wooden posts and shot a man in the shoulder. He swore and fell back. Keeping her breathing slow and regular, ignoring the lead that seemed to fill the air all around her, she shot the two men on either side of the one who'd just fallen, taking each in the leg. They dropped, and as their fellows looked anxiously at their three fallen comrades, Danny took advantage of the lull and opened the first door he came to, coming face to face with a young blonde man sitting on a single bed.

'I'm not armed,' the youngster, who looked to be about twenty-five, said.

His hair was cut long, and he was wearing a T-shirt and sweatpants.

'We're looking for Ellie,' Danny said.

'She's not here,' Sweatpants responded.

'Stokes then.'

The man shook his head. 'You can't get out of here alive – you know that, don't you?'

'We'll see about that. Get up.'

Sweatpants did as he was ordered, and Danny pushed him out the door, following close behind just as the gangsters he'd managed to hold off came up the stairs from below.

'We'll shoot him in the head if you come any closer,' Tessa said. 'We're going to see Stokes, and then I'll let him go.'

'Keep back,' Sweatpants said. 'No one shoots until I give the word.'

What followed was a slow, painful, nerve-wracking dance. Tessa, Danny and their prisoner moved in slow, deliberate backward steps up the landing – Danny kept his Mark 25 pressed right into the man's temple and a KA-BAR at his throat. The group of armed men followed closely. Tessa maintained eye contact with a man at the front of the pack, who seemed to be enjoying himself immensely – as they moved, he was whistling between his teeth: Glen Campbell's 'Wichita Lineman'. It gave everything an even more surreal quality. She could see Danny from the corner of her eye – he too seemed utterly relaxed, as if he was out for an afternoon stroll. His lips were moving, and Tessa wondered if he was praying, but then she realised he was singing the lyrics to the song the gangster was whistling.

Every time Tessa and Danny took a step, the crowd of gun-wielding men mirrored the movement. Tessa found herself humming along with the melody of the old song, and knew that, if she survived, it would be stuck in her head for days. She could feel the tension in her shoulders and a knot in the pit of her stomach. She wanted to be sick again and made an effort to push the feeling deep down, where she could deal with it later.

'Which room is Stokes in?' Danny asked his captive.

'The one at the end with the stained-glass panel.'

'Keep coming nice and easy,' Danny told him. 'You're doing really well.'

'He'll kill both of you for this,' Sweatpants said.

Even though there was a gang of men only feet away, it was as if the conversation was a private thing between the three of them.

'You seem very confident about that,' Tessa said.

'I know the boss. He's a killer.'

'Well that's something we have in common then,' Tessa said, sounding far more confident and deadly than she felt.

They took another step. And then another, all of them moving in time to 'Wichita Lineman'. Then they were at a door which had a circular piece of coloured glass containing the image of an oak tree set at about eye level.

'This is it,' the youngster Danny was holding said.

'Open it,' Tessa barked.

'You fucking open it.'

Tessa was standing against the wall to the right of the door, and she reached over and turned the handle, pushing it open. 'Go ahead of us,' she said. 'Danny, let him go.'

His hands held above his head, Sweatpants called out, 'Boss, it's me, Baz. I'm coming in, okay?'

'Come right ahead,' a raspy voice said.

'Go on,' Tessa hissed at Baz. 'We'll be right behind you.'

They walked into what proved to be a long, decadently decorated room. Paintings of landscapes adorned the walls, and a large four-poster bed dominated the space. Stokes, dressed in a charcoal-coloured silk suit with a tailored white shirt was sitting in an armchair facing them, a Ruger SR9 in his hand.

Tessa took point, and Danny remained covering the crowd of men outside the door.

'You've got a set of balls on you, I'll give you that much,' Stokes rasped and shot Baz in the head.

49

Tessa was standing right behind Baz when Stokes shot him, and she felt the air move as the bullet went through the youngster's head and whizzed past a couple of centimetres to the right of her. Survival instincts kicked in and she took a step back, but as she did so, Stokes shot the young man, who was still somehow upright, a second time. As he fell, Tessa stepped around him, the Mark 25 in one hand and the Sig in the other, both levelled on Stokes, who in turn had his Ruger levelled on Tessa.

'You have a lot of guts coming to my house, little woman,' the lawyer said, his voice raspy and guttural.

'I'm here for Ellie,' Tessa responded. 'I'm taking her out of here.'

'Why would I let you do that?'

'Because I've played fair and asked nicely.'

Stokes raised an eyebrow. 'You've done what?'

'I could have killed a lot of your men, but I didn't. I'm not going to lie – one or two have holes in them – but they'll all live to fight another day. Other than the one you just killed, of course.'

'And what am I supposed to take from that?'

'Consider it a show of respect and repay me in kind. Let me take Ellie. She'll probably have already made you millions in the time you've had her here. Cut your losses. I think that's fair.'

Stokes shook his head and tutted. 'I don't consider that fair at all.'

From the corner of her eye, Tessa could see more and more men gathering on the landing outside. Sweat dribbled down the small of her back, and the guns seemed impossibly heavy in her hands. She had to fight to keep them steady.

'Boys, why don't you come in here and join us?' Stokes called.

Before any of them could move, Danny kicked the door closed. 'You and Tessa aren't finished talking yet,' he said pleasantly.

'I think we're very much finished.'

Stokes raised his voice so the men outside could hear him. 'I'm about six yards away from the door. I want you to shoot through it on my command.'

'If even one bullet comes through that door, I'll shoot you,' Tessa hissed.

'Not if I shoot you first.'

Tessa looked from the door to the man with the gun.

'I say we use the P90s to shoot them through the door and the walls,' Danny said very quietly. 'I know you don't want bloodshed, but we're severely outnumbered. I don't see any other way out.'

'We're not at that point yet,' Tessa said. 'If anyone has to die, it's going to be this sack of shit sitting in front of us.'

Stokes had heard every word, and Tessa thought she saw something shift in his confident demeanour.

'Before I give the order to shoot, can I ask why you believe Ellie is here?' the scarred man suddenly asked.

He still seemed quite relaxed, the gun held nonchalantly in his right hand, his legs crossed comfortably. But it seemed to

Tessa that he'd come to understand she was sincere. She didn't want to kill him, but if it meant the difference between saving Ellie and leaving her to his tender mercies, she would sacrifice his life without feeling much guilt over it.

'You took her,' Tessa said simply. 'We were in a hotel, and your men broke in and abducted her.'

Stokes shrugged. 'That was hours ago. A lot could have happened in that time.'

Tessa searched the lawyer's eyes. Was this a stalling tactic? Or was he telling her the truth? She gazed at him, and he held her stare.

'You don't have her, do you?' she asked at last, her voice little more than a whisper.

The man grinned, which wasn't a pleasant sight. 'No, I don't.'

Tessa felt herself sag, and it took everything in her to remain upright. 'Did she run away on you again?'

'Not quite.'

'So what happened?'

'She was taken.'

'You're trying to tell me that you abducted Ellie from me, only for someone else to abduct her from you?'

'That's about the shape of it, yes.'

'Do you know by who?'

'I certainly do. And I have a proposition for you.'

'What kind of proposition?'

'One that could profit us both.'

Tessa's knees were on fire from holding the same position for so long, and her arms had gone numb from keeping the guns extended. She felt light-headed and queasy from stress, and her head thumped from the intense concentration. She blinked sweat out of her eyes and heard herself say, 'What exactly are you suggesting?'

'I'll tell you where to find Ellie. You can go and get her, and

I give you my word I'll never bother her or her family again. All I want is the chip I put in her arm.'

'Why do you think I'd give it to you?'

'I think you, DI Tessa Burns, are a woman of your word. If you tell me you will, then I believe you. You've probably worked out at this stage that it contains the software for bitcoin mining her father removed from all my machines. The software in itself isn't illegal. There's no harm in your giving it to me.'

'Boss!' a voice called from outside. 'Do you want us to start shooting?'

'The natives are getting restless!' Danny said.

'Okay,' Tessa said to Stokes. 'You've got a deal.'

'What the hell, Tessa?' Danny said in horror.

50

'Ellie was supposed to be brought back to Faoin Tuath by my men when they took her from you, but neither she, nor they, ever came. It seems she was intercepted by a rival.'

They were sitting in the man cave. Stokes was sipping a glass of bourbon while Tessa and Danny had tea. The soldiers had all returned to their quarters.

'Mama Frida or the Cadogans?' Tessa asked.

'You're very well informed,' Stokes said, raising his glass in a gesture of respect. 'The Cadogans wouldn't concern themselves with something as trivial as a kidnapping. This was Mama Frida.'

'Have you received a ransom demand?' Tessa asked.

'No. If she has Ellie and the chip, Mama Frida has all she wants. The only issue is, Ellie doesn't know the chip is in her arm, or even what it is.'

'So your rival has the girl but not the software,' Tessa said.

'Precisely.'

'They'll want someone who can recreate the software for them then,' Tessa said, thinking aloud.

'They will.'

Tessa suddenly realised that Philip O'Farrell was supposed to be at Faoin Tuath. Yet she'd seen neither hide nor hair of him. 'Where's Ellie's father?'

Stokes opened his hands expansively.

'Alright then. Can you give me details of your rival's location – how many men, what level of resistance to expect, any tactical positions I should be aware of?'

'Mama Frida lives in the middle of Cork city,' Stokes said. 'She has one bodyguard, who is deadly. And she, herself, is absolutely lethal.'

'Can you just give me the address?' Tessa asked wearily.

'I'll text you the Eircode.'

'Thank you.'

ELLIE O'FARRELL

Ellie couldn't move.

Her entire body felt as if it was made of lead, and every breath was a struggle, her lungs burning and faltering each time she tried to inhale. That was what scared her most, that she would suffocate simply because the act of breathing had become too horrific to sustain.

Somewhere outside the bubble of her suffering, she could hear the simpering, baby-like voice of Mama Frida, urging her father on. She was only peripherally aware of the woman now, but she knew what the morbidly obese, perfumed gang leader wanted her dad to do.

She wanted the software that had the alphanumeric game on it.

That damned game seemed to be at the centre of everything.

They were in the studio apartment Frida had built over a gentlemen's club, The Snakebite Lounge. Ellie was fastened to a chair with cable ties, and the corpulent gangster was reclining on a chaise longue, watching her torment while her father worked on a laptop at a small table in the corner. The room looked like it had been taken from the palace of an Arab sheikh, the walls covered in drapes, a large hookah beside the chaise where the criminal matriarch sprawled.

Completely at odds with the decor, country and Irish music was playing over speakers affixed to the walls. Mama Frida seemed confused about the aesthetic she was trying to achieve.

Frida had spent a long time asking Ellie how she did what she did with the numbers. And Ellie was truthful – she told her she didn't know. Hadn't a clue in fact. When she saw what the game wanted done, she just somehow knew how to do it. It was sort of like magic, a special power she just... had.

Ellie told Frida, right from the beginning, that if she could teach someone else to do it, she would be happy to do so.

Frida also seemed to think Ellie might know something about the business her father and Stokes were involved with, but once again she truthfully admitted she could tell her nothing.

'That just won't do, sweetie,' Mama Frida had cooed. 'Everyone in town knows Stokes is making a bundle with your old man at HuTec. You're part of the arrangement your mean old daddy made. Don't tell me you ain't in on it.'

And so it went on for four hours. The rough stuff began as morning drifted into afternoon, when it became evident that psychological intimidation wasn't going to work. That was when Frida said, 'Laurence, would you bring me my medicine bag please?'

Her bodyguard – the man whom Pavlov had mauled when he'd encountered him in the hotel room the previous night (and Laurence had plasters affixed at various points to prove it) – returned to the room carrying what looked for all the world like a doctor's case.

'Now, sweetie, I should warn you that what I'm about to administer upon your person is going to make you very uncomfortable. But all your daddy has to do to end it is tell me what I want to know.'

Ellie looked up at her captor in fear and exhaustion.

'I'm working as fast as I can,' her father said, his voice wracked with guilt and grief.

'That may be so, but I have a feelin' you can go faster.'

Frida filled a syringe with a milky-looking fluid from a clear bottle. 'Do you know much about snakes, my sweet girl?'

'Only that I don't like them.'

'You're wrong, child. They're the most amazing creatures. They've been around, unchanged, since the time of the dinosaurs. They've made a home in every ecosystem on the planet, and in each one they're apex predators. I believe it's their success that makes people fear them so.'

'Or that they're gross?' Ellie suggested, desperately trying to keep her talking.

'If you really look at a snake, you'll see that it's actually very beautiful,' Frida simpered, hauling her bulk from the chaise.

'Come near me and I'll kill you!' Ellie warned, thrashing in her chair.

'No. You won't,' Frida said.

Suddenly Laurence was behind Ellie, holding her head still, preventing her from striking out with her teeth. He radiated a baking heat and smelled of rancid meat. Ellie's stomach heaved at the closeness of him.

'The tincture I'm injecting is a little something I engineered myself from the venom of the blue coral snake,' Frida continued, pressing the point of the needle into Ellie's neck. 'It's only a ten per cent solution – if I gave you much more than that, it would kill you in seconds. This is just enough to give you a little taste and to keep you honest.'

'You bitch!'

Frida smiled. 'I'd save your energy if I were you. It'll take a few moments for the toxin to kick in, so while we wait, let me tell you what it does. There's a very special ingredient in the blue coral snake's venom that works on the sodium transmitters in nerve endings. In very simple terms, it switches on all the sensory receptors in your body. You're going to go rigid as a board, sugar, and every cell in your entire system is going to dial up its receptiveness. I've watered it down enough so you won't pass out, and you'll retain the ability to speak, should you suddenly feel inspired to tell me anything. And, of course, you can scream.'

'You're not listening to me! I don't know anything!'

'We'll see, sugar. We'll see.'

'What difference does any of this make?' Ellie spat at her. 'Why do you care what Stokes is up to?'

'You prob'ly don't realise how much money you've been making,' Frida said, waddling back to her chaise and awkwardly sitting back down. 'You're the real prize, sugar. I can see why – you're pretty as a picture and smart as a butcher's dog. And you're mine now.'

'No, I'm not,' Ellie said, a strange tingling starting at the tips of her fingers.

'Oh, you are, child. I'm gonna make ol' Stokes an offer. I'll give you back to him after you make me ten million euro. And when you have, I'm gonna propose a deal: you can stay with him until you make him ten million, then we swap you back. It'll be like joint custody. By my reckonin', Stokes doesn't have the kind of imagination needed to dream up an epic plan. He's been playin' both sides of the field, tellin' me he was going to come in with me while also talkin' sweet to those Cadogan boys. If there's a new big boss in the south, it ain't gonna be no Communist revolutionaries from the six counties. It's gonna be me.'

'Why don't you talk to Stokes then? If my dad doesn't know, surely he's your best bet!'

'He's a hard nut to crack. Did you know it was me – well technically it was Laurence – who gave him his scars? What was it you used – sandpaper and a blowtorch, wasn't it? Laurence took most of the skin off one side of his face, and I shot him up full of something that made the experience even more intense, just so he got the most out of it. But he barely made a sound *during the whole thing. So it was most ungratifying. When it was done, I told him we were going to take a break, and then we'd come back and do the other half, and maybe after that we'd start working on some of his bits lower down. Sadly, he escaped during our brief recess, killed two of my men on his way out – I stopped keeping soldiers here after that. Laurence is enough to dissuade most intruders. But we do hold the memory fondly, don't we, Laurence?'*

The Faceless Man gave the smallest of nods.

'So, to conclude, your father is going to have to come through for me, or you're in for a very uncomfortable night. My, you don't look very well.'

Ellie had begun to tremble so violently she thought her bones would break against her restraints. She was certain she would pass out, but she didn't. Her vision dimmed, but she remained aware.

'It might help to scream, sugar,' Mama Frida said. 'Go on, child. Scream for ol' Frida.'

And Ellie vowed that, come what may, she would not.

51

They stopped in at the Hotel Isaacs and had a late lunch with Maggie.

'Should we call the commish and ask for backup?' the former family liaison officer asked.

'I don't want to involve Dawn in this,' Tessa said. 'She's got enough on her plate. And anyway, there's just this Mama Frida and one bodyguard. I think Danny and I can manage.'

'I've looked at the location,' Maggie said. 'You can access the place through the nightclub downstairs, but it's closed now, and you'd have to deal with an alarm system. There's one other entry point, from a fire escape that leads to a balcony. This door opens onto a short corridor leading to a studio apartment, basically one wide-open room with a small bathroom attached. There's nowhere for this Mama Frida to hide Ellie, but there's nowhere for you to hide either.'

'I'm not planning on hiding,' Tessa said. 'We're going in using that fire escape, and we'll deal with whatever resistance we encounter.'

'I like your subtlety,' Maggie said.

'There's no point in messing around,' Tessa said. 'We go in, take Ellie and get out. It's as simple as that.'

'Why do I suspect there's going to be nothing simple about it?' Danny asked dolefully.

The Snakebite Lounge was situated up an alleyway off Oliver Plunkett Street in Cork's centre. Mama Frida's apartment was above it, and street access was through a blue door with a buzzer right next to the nightclub's front entrance. Clearly that wasn't going to do.

Danny spied the steps of the fire escape and jumped into the air, catching the lower step and dragging the others down so he and Tessa could climb up to a steel safety door on the first floor.

It was made of some kind of reinforced metal and had a complicated-looking locking mechanism that was operated using a keypad. Had she the luxury of time, Tessa could have taken the electronics apart and rewired them with ease, but she was under pressure. Aware of the danger Ellie and her father were in, she decided to favour brute force over gentleness, pulled the Mossberg from its holster and blasted first the keypad (this was more out of annoyance than anything else) then the lock itself, giving it two shots. Danny gave the door a shove with his foot, and thankfully it swung open.

Inside was a narrow corridor, beyond which they could see what looked to be a bedroom. Standing in the hallway, looking at them passively, was a lean, bald man in a black suit. His face was covered in plasters, but beneath these Tessa could see he was the Faceless Man who'd broken into her hotel room. The same one who'd shot at Maggie before any of them had even reached Cork.

'No space for heroics,' Danny said quietly. 'He's not going to let us get past without drawing down.'

'I'm sorry to find you here, DI Burns,' the Faceless Man said. 'And I thought you were safely locked away, DS Murphy. I implore both of you to turn around and walk away now. If you don't, I will use lethal means to prevent you from going further.'

'Have it your own way,' Tessa said.

The Mossberg needed reloading, so Tessa made to draw the Mark 25, but before her hand reached it, the bald man exploded into a sprint, covering the distance between them in a second. He took the last metre in a leap and would have landed right on top of Tessa if Danny hadn't stepped in and caught him by the scruff of the neck, slamming him into the wall.

'Go!' the big detective gasped as the Faceless Man drove both fists into his face.

Tessa didn't wait. She ran up the corridor and into the room beyond.

52

My God, he's fast, Danny had time to think before the man caught him first in the eye with a jab then in the throat with a punch, and now he wasn't just half blind, he was also fighting for breath. He took a couple of steps back and tried to draw his handgun, but this time the Faceless Man, who still hadn't produced a weapon of any kind but had instead adopted a fighting stance in the hallway in front of him, bouncing fluidly on the balls of his feet, shot out a leg and hit Danny right in the wrist. The pain was immediate, shooting up his arm like an electric shock. The arm immediately went numb, and his fingers wouldn't work. He dropped his Glock and tried to swing the P90, which was hung around his neck on its strap, across to his left hand, but before he could do so, the man was on him again – he feigned to the right, but as Danny moved to counter, he lunged in to the left, and the big detective felt a sharp pain across his abdomen.

He's got a knife, Danny thought, and sure enough, the bodyguard now had a slim blade in his hand. Danny just had the chance to glance down at the jagged line that had been cut into his shirt, a red stain already spreading outwards from it, before the man slashed the blade upwards, and he felt his cheek sting. Desperate, he brought his left elbow (his right was still out of action) up as hard as he could, feeling it connect with the man's jaw.

It should have stunned him, but to Danny's horror, he just shook his head as if to ward off flies and spun into a roundhouse kick that caught him on the cheekbone, opening the knife wound even more (he felt it tear) and putting him flat on his back. He sensed rather than saw his opponent spring into another jump and instinctively rolled onto his side, flattening himself against the wall. It was lucky he did, because the man landed precisely where his chest would have been, the point of the knife embedded in the floor in the spot his right eye had just vacated.

Danny didn't waste any time. He scissored his legs, delivering a powerful kick to the back of the man's neck and knocking him forward. The man let go of the knife for a moment to steady himself, and Danny, seeing his opportunity, rolled over so he was literally on top of his attacker, pinning him with his weight and knocking him flat onto the floor, trapping the knife beneath them. Before he had a chance to squirm out of his grip, Danny grabbed Laurence's head and smashed his face into the ground: once, twice, three times.

He paused, waiting for the Faceless Man to move or fight back, but he was motionless beneath him. Allowing the head to drop to the ground, he got up painfully. To his relief, pins and needles were beginning to prickle their way up and down his right arm, which he took as a good sign.

He considered cuffing his fallen adversary, but decided he wasn't going to be getting up again any time soon. A quick examination told him that his stomach wound was superficial, and, picking up his Glock, Danny made his way carefully down the hallway to the room beyond.

53

When Tessa entered the apartment's main studio room, she found Ellie tied to a chair and soaked in sweat, her body rigid, her teeth clamped tight. A hugely obese woman with hair worn long about her shoulders and dyed jet black, her face thick with garishly applied make-up, was sitting on a low couch, a small handgun trained on the door.

Philip was working on a laptop in the corner, his fingers a blur over the keys, his face pale and tense.

'Well, well,' the corpulent woman said. 'You got past my Laurence. I didn't expect that.' And she squeezed off a shot at Tessa that went wide.

Tessa gave her a hard look and raised the Mark 25.

'Drop the pea-shooter now,' she warned.

Mama Frida, seemingly unable to believe she could be bested, raised the gun again, and Tessa put a bullet in her shoulder. The derringer Frida was holding thudded softly into the deep pile carpet. For a second, the obese woman seemed frozen in shock, but then realisation dawned, and she began to wail, making a noise like a frightened and angry child.

'Shut up,' Tessa said quietly.

Frida ignored her, or simply didn't have the capacity to comply.

'*I said shut up!*'

This worked, and the lipstick-coated mouth clamped shut, its lower lip trembling all the while. The sounds of the physical battle going on in the hallway were terrifying. Tessa tried not to think about Danny and the terrible danger he was in.

'What's wrong with her?' Tessa asked, motioning at Ellie.

'I gave her something to induce her to talk.'

'Give me the antidote. Now.'

'We bargain, sugar,' Mama Frida said, gripping her arm against the pain, blood seeping through her fingers into the cotton of the muumuu draping her massive frame. 'What you gonna give me if I tell you?'

Tessa trained the gun on her head. 'If you don't tell me what you've given her and where the antidote is, I'll put the next one between your eyes. That's the only bargain I'm making today.'

Mama Frida hadn't lived to be as old and successful as she was by being unable to recognise a genuine threat. 'In my bag. You'll find a wallet. A blue one.'

Keeping the gun trained on her, Tessa fumbled around in the leather satchel until she found what her prisoner was referring to. As she did, a battered and bloodied Danny stalked in.

'You okay?' she called over to him.

'Yeah, I'm good.'

Philip, who was still working at the laptop, called down, 'Will you hurry up and help my daughter?'

'You're in no position to give orders, Mr O'Farrell,' Tessa said. 'I sincerely hope you're now destroying whatever you've been working on.'

'I'll take a look,' Danny said and went over to Philip's workstation.

'There are six bottles in this wallet,' Tessa said. 'Which one do I use?'

'A small pink one,' Frida said. 'Fill one of the syringes.'

'What size syringe?'

'There's only two sizes in my bag. Use the smaller one. Fill it, sugar.'

Tessa fumbled with the pack, throwing anxious glances at Ellie. Finally, she realised she wasn't going to be able to load the syringe and hold the gun at the same time.

'I'm holstering this for a second,' she said to Frida. 'Make one stupid move and I'll hurt you badly.'

'I plan on staying right where I am,' Frida said, rolling her eyes against the pain.

Tessa worked as quickly as she could, checking to make sure the syringe was clear of any air bubbles, then moved to the girl, who remained stiff and contorted. 'Is there an ideal place to inject?'

'The neck works best. In the softer tissue near the collarbone.'

Tessa administered the dose, trying to stop her hands from shaking. As soon as the plunger was depressed, she stepped back, but there was no obvious change in Ellie.

'If you've lied to me...' she said, turning on Frida, but as she did so, something landed on her back and knocked her to the ground. She could hear ragged breathing, and then fingers were digging into her eyes. Blinded and in pain, her hand found the Mark 25, and she drew it, bringing it up to shoot over her shoulder at whoever was now upon her. Apparently aware of the danger, the person let go and fell back. Turning, Tessa gazed into what had once passed for the face of the Faceless Man.

54

His visage was a red mess, his nose broken and one eye swollen shut. The other was full of anger and hatred though, and it was focused on Tessa.

'Why, Laurence, you come back to me!' Frida said. 'This woman has hurt your Frida! I want you to hurt *her* – a lot!'

Tessa wasn't going to wait for the man to carry out the instruction. She raised the Mark 25 and shot him in the shoulder.

'*Laurence, kill her!*'

Tessa looked at Mama Frida as if she was insane – but then, to her horror, she saw the bodyguard stir, and in lurching, staggering movements he got to his knees.

Making a sound that was a cross between a growl and a wheeze, the injured man produced a slim knife from inside his jacket. He grabbed the handle of the chair Ellie was still tied to in an attempt to hoist himself up, but before he could do so, Danny, who'd crossed the room in three steps, brought the butt of his Glock down hard on the bodyguard's head, knocking him flat onto the ground. Laurence made a sort of mewling sound and rolled over.

'You get them, Laurence!' Frida called. 'Make them pay for what they've done!'

Tessa stepped on the bodyguard's knife hand, pinning it to the floor. The man made a thin, whining noise, but he released his grip, and Tessa kicked the blade away.

'You should stay down,' Tessa said to him. 'You're done – you just don't know it yet.'

The man wasn't to be dissuaded though and managed to hoist himself onto his elbows, his one good eye bright with determination and fury.

'For God's sake shoot him!' Philip called from his position at the laptop.

'Mr O'Farrell,' Tessa said through gritted teeth, 'if you don't shut up, I'll shoot *you*.' Then more gently to Laurence: 'Go on, lie down. It doesn't have to be like this.'

Something evil and predatory registered on Laurence's face as he spotted Frida's derringer lying just within range. He reached for it, and Tessa, sighing bitterly, kicked it away and hit the man with all the force she could muster with the butt of her P90. The bodyguard jerked once and lay still. For good measure, Tessa walked over and cuffed him to the leg of Mama Frida's couch.

There was a rustling movement, and Tessa turned to see, with a rush of relief, that Ellie had come around. She rushed over and used her KA-BAR to cut the girl's bonds. Danny helped her to sit forward while Tessa, her eyes filled with tears, massaged the girl's wrists and ankles. Philip O'Farrell, shaking all over, stood up and walked stiffly over to the chair but hung back, seemingly unsure how he should behave. Or if his presence was even wanted.

'What took you so long?' Ellie asked, laughing and crying at the same time.

'I'm sorry. I got here as fast as I could.'

'Traffic was terrible,' Danny offered, and both Ellie and Tessa laughed through their sobs.

Ellie slowly stood up, leaning on the two detectives. 'I feel as if I've just been run over by a truck.'

'Can you walk?' Tessa asked.

'I think so.'

'Let's get out of here then.'

'I'd like that. I've got something I need to do first though.'

And Ellie hobbled over to Mama Frida and drove her fist right into her torturer's face. 'How do you like that, sugar?' she spat before returning to Tessa and Danny.

'We should ring this in,' Danny said. 'Frida needs to be locked up, or she's going to be a danger to Ellie and her folks.'

'If we do, we'll be suspended from duty pending a *long* investigation,' Tessa said.

They were walking towards the door, Ellie held between them, when the sound of a shot from the derringer caused them to stop and turn.

Philip O'Farrell was standing in front of Mama Frida, holding the little gun. The criminal matriarch had a small bullet hole in her forehead.

'I think I've just saved you the trouble,' he said.

PART FIVE

55

They returned to the Hotel Isaacs to find the world in chaos.

Sergeant O'Mahoney was in intensive care in Cork University Hospital and Cynthia O'Farrell in custody pending an investigation. Dawn Wilson had come to Cork personally and suspended half the detective squad at Anglesea Street, and, along with a team from Internal Affairs, was interviewing each rigorously, examining their performance records closely and looking at the minute details of every single case to see where loose ends had been allowed to remain loose, and criminals therefore permitted to go free.

Ellie spent a night in hospital but was deemed fit to leave the ward the following morning. A junior doctor removed the chip using a local anaesthetic and gave it to Tessa in a clear plastic bottle.

The girl laughed when Tessa showed it to her. 'This is what all the fuss was about?'

'Yeah. I reckon it has a GPS tracker in it too, which is how they were able to follow us to the hotel and how they found you in that bar. The way I look at it, this was the doorway into the treasure trove, but your mind was the map to where the really valuable stuff was held. One was no good without the other.'

'What are you going to do with it now?'

'Maggie wants to take a look at it. After she's given it a once-over... we'll see.'

'Mama Frida is gone now,' Ellie said, 'so we don't need to be worried anymore.'

'I hope that's true,' Tessa said.

Ellie went home with her father that afternoon. The Burns Unit watched them drive away from the lobby of Cork University Hospital.

'That man needs to be arrested too,' Maggie said to Tessa. 'He's a danger to himself and the world around him.'

'I'm not sure he is,' Tessa said. 'He was naïve. He wanted to do the right thing, thought his discovery would benefit the causes he believed in and made the mistake of sharing it with an evil man.'

'Speaking of which,' Danny said, 'you made a deal with that evil man yourself. Are you going to come through for him?'

'I have every intention of bringing Stokes the chip,' Tessa said. 'I'm a woman of my word.'

Danny and Maggie looked at one another.

'She's got a plan, doesn't she?' Danny asked.

'I think we can count on that,' Maggie agreed.

Pavlov barked once in agreement.

The Faceless Man Mama Frida had employed as a bodyguard was in Cork University Hospital too, and Tessa went to see him after Ellie went home.

Handcuffed to a bed, his face bandaged and nose packed and splinted, most of the threat was gone from him. *Most* of it.

'Is your name really Laurence?' Tessa asked when he turned his good eye to look at her.

'No. It was a little joke of Frida's. Because of my facial reconstruction, I can't really smile. She liked to say that even if I was happy as Larry, you couldn't tell. Larry, Laurence. It was offensive, but then, so was she. But she paid well, and the work was light.'

'Until you encountered me and my team.'

'Yes. Each of you is quite dangerous, in your own way. Even the dog.'

'Were Stokes and Mama Frida working together from the start? The forensic accountants found money was going to her right from the beginning.'

'It was, but not quickly enough for her. She believed Stokes was being too cautious. It was his reticence that caused her to mark him before. It was supposed to be an object lesson, but it seems he didn't learn it well. She wanted more, and quicker, and she knew the child was the only way to achieve that. Stokes tried to mollify her, but she wasn't prepared to wait.'

'You killed Merrill, McGuinness and Wilde?'

'I did. Wilde wasn't my best work. But everyone has a bad day from time to time.'

'Were you the man Merrill saw in the water?'

'Yes. In another life, I was a member of naval special forces.'

'How did you snatch Ellie from under Stokes's nose?'

'It was simple. I bribed some of his soldiers. Stokes mistakenly believes he has all these young men and women under his control by force of charisma and will. He gives them guns and promises them the world, and every now and then he comes through for one of them, gets them a good job – which they usually lose pretty quickly – but it's enough to make the others think he'll do the same for them. When they stop being useful, he usually gives them some task where they'll either be killed or arrested, or if they're female, he pimps them out. It wasn't difficult to infiltrate his group, find out who was going to pick her up and bribe them to give her to me instead.'

'After which you killed them.'

The Faceless Man shrugged.

'How did you know we were coming to Cork in the first place?'

'Mama Frida has been paying off the higher ranks in Cork policing for years. One of the superintendents is close friends with someone in the minister's office. As soon as we heard you were en route, I was sent to prevent it.'

'Does your group have a vendetta against me, Laurence? Me and my people?'

'My group?'

'Your guild. The Unattested.'

'Detective Burns, we're all professionals. Nothing we do is personal. There is no vendetta. I will say that if we cross paths again, we'll ensure we have much greater numbers at our disposal. But you should see that as a compliment.'

'Do you know anything about my parents' murders?'

'Not in detail. I know your father was working on something that would have exposed corruption in some high-up people in Irish law enforcement.' The man made a harsh sound Tessa thought might be a laugh. 'Does that sound familiar?'

Tessa laughed dryly. 'Like father like daughter.'

'It would seem so. I also heard that he had the identity of a mole in my guild. Someone who was giving him information that might mean the end of our association. If there was such a person, your father died without giving up the name.'

'He was a soldier. A ranger. He was never going to give you what you wanted.'

'Some of my people believe *you* might know who this mole is.'

'If they ever existed, wouldn't they be dead by now?'

'Maybe. Maybe not.'

'I was a child. I had only the vaguest idea about what my dad was doing.'

'Just as with Ellie O'Farrell, information may be locked in your unconscious.'

'If any of you want to have a crack at trying to get that knowledge, I'm not hard to find, though so far, none of you have been very successful when we've encountered each other. Anyone wanting to make a run at me should take a good look at you first.'

'I didn't want to clash with you, DI Burns,' the Faceless Man said. 'You made it unavoidable.'

Tessa stood up. 'You know Mama Frida is dead.'

'I do.'

'It wasn't done by me or Danny.'

'I know. It doesn't matter. She was a foul person. I'll find other employment.'

'You'll be working in the prison laundry for the foreseeable future.'

'I'm confident I won't be incarcerated for long. I expect we'll see one another again.'

'I very much hope not,' Tessa said.

Tessa met Conor Stokes by the waterside in an abandoned part of Cork docks. It was early morning, and gulls pinwheeled and cried out above the river. In the distance, the sounds of traffic could be heard. Tessa had a travel mug of tea in her right hand, the plastic bottle containing the chip in the other.

'You have the software?'

'Right here.'

'I knew you'd be as good as your word.'

'What can I say? I'm painfully predictable.'

He held out his hand for it.

'How do I know you won't try to enslave some other gifted person to do your mining for you?'

'You don't. And that's none of your business.'

'Can I ask you something less... incriminating then?'

'You can ask.'

'Why did you tattoo Ellie? You could have put the chip in her without marking her like that.'

Stokes laughed.

'If I were to remove my shirt you'd see an identical tattoo in the same place on my arm. When I joined a youth gang in my early teens, I was given the mark to show my alliance. I wanted young Ellie to know she was mine, from that moment.'

'Didn't quite work out that way though, did it?'

Stokes shrugged.

'Did you ever think about how Ellie felt in all this?' Tessa said. 'That her father was actually trying to do right; he was just... just a weak man out of his depth?'

'Weak men don't fare well in this world,' Stokes said. 'Maybe he's learned that and will try to be stronger.'

Tessa sighed. 'You've been preying on the young men and women of this city for years, haven't you? Organising them into your own private army. Getting them to do your dirty work so you can give the appearance of having gone straight.'

'I was once just like them. Poor. Parentless. In and out of places like St Killian's. All those kids want is someone who seems to care, someone who's looking out for them, and they'll give that person anything. They may appear feral, but they're really just hurt toddlers underneath it all. Give them a hug and a lollipop and they're yours for life.'

'Or until they stop being of use to you. We found a kid floating in the river, shot in the back of the head, execution style. His prints were on the system;, he'd been in and out of juvie since he could walk. I showed a photo of him to Ellie, and while she's not certain, she thinks it was the youngster who helped her escape. Do you know anything about what happened to him? His name was Jason Kelly, I believe.'

Stokes shrugged. 'The name doesn't ring a bell.'

'With Mama Frida gone, you're top dog in this part of the world, aren't you?'

'I may invite some friends to expand down south. There is a vacuum now, and it has to be filled.'

'The Cadogans,' Tessa said.

'As I said before, you're very well informed.'

'I try to keep up. So you'd be the south-coast captain, with your hoodies and your socialist Republican arms dealers all marching to the beat of your drum, and a bottomless supply of cash coming from this algorithm and whatever poor genius you can find to operate it for you.'

'And the police all happily paid off,' Stokes said. 'I know your commissioner is trying to clean house, but I've started from ground zero before. Once you have one, others will follow. And I'll be able to afford to pay very handsomely for silence and some small acts of suppression and cooperation.'

'A fine plan,' Tessa said. 'And all resting on this little piece of plastic.'

She opened the bottle and took it out. It weighed virtually nothing.

'Such a small thing to have caused so much pain and suffering,' she said.

She put her travel mug on the ground, reached into her pocket and took out a small pack – the ones you get in hospitals and hotels – of bourbon cream biscuits, her favourites. She ripped the plastic with her teeth, took one out and had a bite.

'Sorry, I didn't have time for breakfast,' she said. 'Would you like one?'

'Thank you, no.'

'Suit yourself.'

A gull, scenting the biscuits on the wind, swooped down, coming in low.

'They're a real nuisance, aren't they?' Tessa commented.

In a rapid movement, she jammed the chip into the chocolate cream that was wedged between the two sides of the biscuit, half of which was still in her hand. Another gull swooped in, and Tessa tossed the morsel into the air, where the flying scavenger caught it on the wing, swallowing biscuit and chip in one gulp.

'You stupid fucking woman!' Stokes said, pulling a gun from inside his jacket and taking a shot at the herring gull, who screeched at him angrily and disappeared over the roof of the nearest derelict warehouse. 'We had a deal!'

'I won't be party to the enslavement of another person or give you the means to fund a criminal empire that would sentence this city to a reign of terror that would last for decades!' Tessa said. 'And if you think you can use the GPS tracker on the chip, I've got some bad news for you. My friend Maggie has removed it.'

'You fucking *bitch!*'

'You have no idea. I expect you believe you can intimidate Philip O'Farrell into writing another algorithm. Well, think again.'

She pulled up her T-shirt to reveal a small microphone taped to her abdomen. 'Old-school. Expect a call from the Organised Crime Unit. Out of respect for our deal, I'm giving you the chance to get the fuck out of Dodge before they come looking for you. I'd take that opportunity if I were you.'

Stokes scowled and levelled his gun at her. As he did, a shot rang out, and the concrete at his feet kicked up dust.

'That would be my friend DS Danny Murphy. He's on a rooftop over there' – she pointed to her left, across the river – 'with a rifle with a long-range scope. Put the gun away, or he'll put a bullet in you.'

The lawyer did as he was bid and put the gun back under his jacket.

'Now go,' Tessa said. 'Before I change my mind.'

Stokes turned and stalked up the pier in the direction of his car.

57

Dawn and Tessa sat beside Sergeant Willie O'Mahoney's bed.

The tough old cop had surprised the medical staff by coming around days before they expected he would, and he was healing well. One of Cynthia's bullets had lodged in his lungs, but the other had gone clean through, miraculously hitting very little as it did so.

'I've gone through your ranks like a knife through butter,' Dawn said. 'There's been three dismissals, one suspension and two of your lads will serve time. I couldn't help them.'

'Thank you, Commissioner. I should have done it myself. I thought I could lead by example, but some people, I know now, can't be taught.'

'I have some work I need to do with my own crew in Dublin,' Dawn went on. 'The poison has spread and needs to be weeded out right across the force. If you're interested, I could use a man with your expertise in police HQ.'

'I'm honoured you would consider me, but I'll respectfully decline,' O'Mahoney said. 'I like running an inner-city police station. And I want to keep a close eye on things, make sure there's no backsliding. I've always thought Cork could have the best police in the country, if we could all pull together.'

'There's no one I would trust to get that done more than you,' Dawn said.

'A little bird told me you wrote your statement on the circumstances of your shooting,' Tessa said. 'You've said it was an accident.'

'Sure it was. Cynthia found a gun and was bringing it in to me, to hand it in like. As any good citizen should.'

'And what, it accidentally went off?' Dawn asked.

'Just so,' O'Mahoney agreed.

'Twice,' Tessa said. 'While it was aimed at your chest.'

'Hell of a thing,' the sarge said. 'A freak accident. I hope Mrs O'Farrell is okay after her ordeal.'

'She's getting some help,' Dawn said. 'Dr Cleary has recommended someone for her.'

'That's good to hear,' the sarge said.

'You know, you screwed up a bit, but this is a hard penance,' Dawn said quietly. 'You could have died.'

'I allowed my fear and paranoia to cloud my judgement,' O'Mahoney said, 'and I put that wee girl in harm's way. I'm not surprised her mother shot me. Not surprised at all.'

'Shot you by accident,' Tessa corrected him.

'Well, yes,' O'Mahoney said, grinning. 'For the love of God, don't make me laugh! It hurts like a fucker.'

58

Tessa called Jim Sheils as she was on her way to say goodbye to the O'Farrells.

'Hey,' Jim said. 'How are things in Cork?'

'Good. We're finished here, I think.'

'Everything go as you'd hoped?'

'More or less. The good guys won.'

'I'm thrilled to hear it. So... will you be dropping by the sunny south-east any time soon?'

Tessa paused before saying, 'I'm needed back in Dublin, Jim.'

'Well you could always make a quick detour.'

'I don't think so. There's a lot of follow-up Dawn needs to do, and she's asked me to help her.'

'I will see you soon though, won't I?'

'I don't know. I don't think I can guarantee you will.'

'Oh.'

She could hear the coastguard breathing on the other end. She hated hurting him, but she knew this would hurt less than stringing him along. She wasn't ready. Not for what he wanted anyway. Tessa wished she was, but she knew herself well enough to know it would end in tears.

'Did I do something to upset you, Tessa?'

'No. You did nothing wrong. I'm... I'm just not built the same way you are. I live in a single room and keep my clothes in a suitcase. Being romantic makes me feel stupid, and I get embarrassed when people who aren't close to me know I'm in a relationship. You... you deserve better than that.'

'So do you,' Jim said quietly. 'You know, if you'd told me that, we could have worked through it together. I'd have understood.'

'That's funny,' Tessa said.

'Why?'

'Because I don't understand it myself.'

And she hung up.

59

The team were back in the O'Farrells' living room.

'Conor Stokes was found shot dead this morning,' Tessa told them. 'He was in his car in a lay-by near the airport.'

'Do you know who did it?' Philip asked.

'No. There was a note attached to the body. It was written in block capitals that said: *PEOPLE LIKE US LOOK AFTER EACH OTHER. YOU SHOULD HAVE KNOWN THAT.* CCTV recorded a woman leaving the scene, but the footage is too blurry to tell us much. We caught the car she was driving on a speed camera, but it had stolen plates. The local guys are looking into it, but I wouldn't hold out much hope.'

'So it's over,' Cynthia said.

'It is,' Tessa agreed.

'So long as you give up the whole bitcoin-mining thing,' Maggie said. 'And your company takes care about who they hire in future. I appreciate your wanting to give people a second chance, but I think there's probably a limit on that.'

'Agreed,' Philip said.

'You two have been given huge leeway,' Tessa said. 'You both committed serious crimes, and because of the circumstances of all of this – which were hugely stressful – and because we believe you're inherently good people, we've looked the other way. I want to stress that you have your daughter to thank for that. She deserves to grow up with both her parents, and she has, we believe, a very bright future ahead. Having her grow up in care wouldn't serve that future well.'

'Thank you, Detectives,' Cynthia said.

'You should consider thanking Sergeant O'Mahoney,' Danny said. 'He could have seen you go down for a long stretch for what you did.'

'I know. I... I thought I'd never see Philip or Ellie again. I was furious with him and didn't really care what happened to me.'

'Start caring,' Tessa said. 'You have a lot to live for. Honour that by getting your head sorted out.'

'I will.'

'You get one free pass,' Tessa said, looking from Cynthia to Philip and back again. 'If I hear either of you are involved in so much as a speeding offence, I'll come down here and throw the book at you myself. Am I being clear?'

Both parents nodded.

60

Ellie followed them out to the cars.

'I don't know how to thank you,' she said. 'You've all done so much for me.'

'Remember us when you're running Google or whatever you end up doing,' Danny said.

'I will. For sure.'

Danny hugged the girl, and Pavlov lapped her face, and Maggie, who'd worked with her less than the others, shook her hand. Then they both got into their vehicles.

Tessa smiled. 'You take care,' she said. 'You have my card. If you need me, for anything at all, all you have to do is call.'

'I think things are going to be okay,' Ellie said.

'Are you going to have the tattoo removed?'

Ellie grinned.

'I think I'm going to keep it. It's a reminder that no matter how dark things get, there's always hope. When Stokes made that man tattoo me, I couldn't see a way out. The situation looked so hopeless... but then that boy was there, and he helped me escape, and then I was able to call you and... it was all terrifying and at times it was awful, but Tessa, I'm here, and my folks are okay, and we don't need to be scared anymore.'

'Your parents both need help,' Tessa said. 'And you've been through some very scary stuff. You all need time to heal.'

'I know my dad isn't the toughest guy in the world, and I think my mam has always been anxious,' Ellie said. 'When Mama Frida had me, and I was scared and in pain, he was right there, and I knew I couldn't depend on him to save me. When I thought about someone doing that, I knew it was going to be you.'

'I wasn't ever going to leave you at the mercy of those people.'

'I know. I think my dad needs to learn to... to find his inner Jack Reacher. Or maybe his inner Tessa Burns.'

Tessa laughed at that. 'Or his inner Ellie O'Farrell.'

'I don't know about that.'

'I do. You're as tough as anyone I've ever met. Don't forget that. I reckon you can handle anything the world throws at you. And if you find you can't, you can always call me, or Danny or Maggie and Pav.'

Ellie put her arms around the detective. 'And you can always call me, if you need me.'

Tessa found herself tearing up at that. 'I promise you I will.'

They held each other for a time.

'I think you might be the best friend I've ever had,' Ellie said, her voice thick with tears.

'You're going to have an amazing life,' Tessa said, crying too. 'And you will have *lots* of great friends. I feel lucky that you number me among them.'

She stepped back and smiled at the girl.

'Goodbye, Tessa.'

'Goodbye, Ellie.'

Tessa got into her Capri and followed Danny, Maggie and Pav through the electric gates of the gated community.

Tessa Burns' life had been full of goodbyes. But saying goodbye to Ellie O'Farrell might have been the hardest.

A LETTER FROM S.A. DUNPHY

Dear reader,

I want to say a huge thank you for choosing to read *Her Lonely Soul*. If you did enjoy it and want to keep up to date with all my latest releases and other news, just sign up at the following link. Your email address will never be shared, and you can unsubscribe at any time.

www.bookouture.com/s.a.dunphy

I hope you loved *Her Lonely Soul*, and if you did, I'd be extremely grateful if you could write a review. I'd love to hear what you think, and it makes such a difference helping new readers to discover one of my books for the first time. I love hearing from my readers. I wouldn't be able to do what I do without you. If you'd like to, you can get in touch on social media or through my website. I'm pretty active on social media, and value each and every interaction with my readers. So thanks again, and I look forward to sharing more stories with you very soon.

Very best,

Shane (S.A. Dunphy)

KEEP IN TOUCH WITH S.A. DUNPHY

www.shanedunphyauthor.org

facebook.com/shanewritesbooks

x.com/dunphyshane1

instagram.com/shanewritesbooks

ACKNOWLEDGEMENTS AND AUTHOR'S COMMENTS

Writing the Tessa Burns series has been a labour of love for me.

It wasn't a series I'd planned to write; these stories weren't burning a hole in my consciousness trying to get out. However, once work on the series began, the process of writing was possibly one of the easiest I've ever experienced. I somehow *knew* these characters and felt a comfort with them I've probably never experienced before in my entire writing career – even when I was writing about myself and my own casework!

The Tessa Burns series was conceived in an attempt to combine both strands of my literary work: my child protection books and my crime fiction. One of the issues I'd faced with my crime novels was that a lot of readers who enjoyed my non-fiction, child-protection books didn't want to make the transition to my fictional works. Inspirational memoir readers are a loyal bunch and very dedicated to the genre.

With the Tessa Burns series, my publishers and I wanted to create something that would satisfy my crime audience and also hopefully offer something my non-fiction readers could appreciate. During a long Zoom call with my agent, the brilliant Ivan Mulcahy, and my editor, the talented (and tolerant) Susannah Hamilton, we chatted about how the team might be constructed, what kind of stories might work, how dark the series might be and how we could balance a procedural police series with the very real trappings of child-protection stories that had to have a ring of truth to them.

At the end of the call, Susannah asked me to go away and

write up an outline, breaking down each character and coming up with a rough plot outline for the first three books.

'And, Shane,' she said as we were signing off, 'if you can put a dog in the story somehow, that might be good. Readers like dogs.'

So Susannah Hamilton deserves all the credit for Pavlov, probably the biggest breakout character of the series!

I wrote the 'pitch': the overall concept, character sketches, the overall 'feel' of the series, plot outlines and titles, in a single morning. It all flowed that easily. When I sent the whole thing to Susannah, the only changes she made were to the names of the characters – she wanted a more Irish feel, and I was happy to comply.

And that was it: Bookouture signed on for the series, and I got to writing.

A new series, featuring a set of brand-new characters, with an untested concept involving the combining of two genres that don't usually sit well together made for a nerve-wracking launch. I was like an expectant father, worried to my core that something would go wrong and the happy day would turn into a tragedy.

I needn't have worried.

From the start, there was an outpouring of goodwill for Tessa and her team, and as I watched, the series crept up the Amazon charts, establishing itself within a few days as a serious contender in the police-procedural category as well as (to my surprise and, if I'm honest, delight) cosy-animal genre. I'm not sure there's much cosy about these books, but I'll take it!

And the reviews told me one very important thing. Untested concept or no, people were ready for these books. They *wanted* a badass team who were prepared to go to the mat for the kids they were setting out to protect. As one reader said to me in conversation at a book event: 'If you were a kid in trouble, Tessa, Danny, Maggie and Pav are exactly the team you'd want to have in your corner.'

When I heard that, I knew I'd done it. Because that is exactly what I'd hoped to achieve.

My characters had come alive for my readers.

When that happens, the magic, the alchemy of words on a page combined with the imagination of readers, has worked. And that's what every author is striving for.

Her Lonely Soul brings Tessa and her team to Cork, a city and county I've had the good fortune to spend a lot of time in. As in all the other titles in this series, every location mentioned is real. I've stopped in the lay-by in Dungarvan where Maggie and Pavlov see off Laurence, the Faceless Man early in the novel. I've been inside Anglesea Street station and have stood on the road outside, looking down at that Lidl sign.

I wish to stress that the Gardai who work in Cork are not the corrupt bunch I describe here, and I think it worth pointing out that Dawn is aware the rot has spread to Dublin too. In the world of these books, organised crime has infiltrated the institutions of society. But the world of these books is not the real world, just a somewhat heightened version of it.

For all that, the Cadogan gang, while not a real criminal collective, is based on a real group, as is Stokes's gang of young hoodies. Mama Frida is very close to a criminal matriarch I had the misfortune of dealing with some years ago when I was researching trafficking. So, heightened or not, all those details are completely accurate.

St Killian's isn't a real place but is closely based on several similar institutions I've had contact with during my own child-protection career. I'm not suggesting places like it aren't necessary; I simply feel they could be better resourced.

Bitcoin mining is a fascinating area, and I spoke to several people who'd engaged in it while writing this book. Thanks to hacker_blue and jethrotull.79 for giving me so much of your time. If you want to learn a bit more, I can highly recommend this site for further study and research: https://www.investope-dia.com/tech/how-does-bitcoin-mining-work

I've been contacted by several readers asking me if the idea of the Faceless Men and their guild, the Unattested, is rooted in reality in any way. The answer is a firm yes. If you'd like to explore the idea more, I suggest reading a book called *History's Assassins: Motives for Murder* by Don Mann and Jeff Emde. It's a fascinating (and chilling) read.

All the information Tessa and her team discuss with Dr Cleary about Ellie and her giftedness, not to mention her simi-larities to an individual like Kim Peek, are all completely accu-rate. There are, indeed, rare young people who can do all the things Ellie can do in this book. Such abilities can be a blessing and a curse. If you'd like to know more, I'd advise reading the highly enlightening *Living with Intensity: Understanding the Sensitivity, Excitability, and Emotional Development of Gifted Children, Adolescents, and Adults* by Daniels and Piechowski. It casts a light on areas of genius you might not ever have thought of, particularly the frustrations people with such capac-ities live with – how do you navigate a world where things you can do without even having to think about them are major chal-lenges for almost everyone else?

This book, and indeed the entire Tessa Burns series, wouldn't have been possible without the support and encour-agement of the entire team at Bookouture, but particularly the aforementioned Susannah Hamilton, who has had every reason to want to throttle me over the past couple of years but has always remained warm, kind and supportive in the face of the continued obstacles my slightly disorganised life has placed before her. Susannah, you are a true friend and a brilliant editor.

Ivan Mulcahy, my agent and dear, dear friend, is a pillar of strength, sage advice, and a fabulous person to share a few drinks and a laugh with. I love and appreciate him more than I can say.

Kristina and Jessica have had to put up with my late nights and disappearances into the office during my periods of intense writing. I cannot express how grateful I am for their continued love and support.

Richard, Marnie and Rhys – I love you all. Your support, kindness and belief in me continues to be a light in my life.

Tara, Jack and Conn are a constant source of joy to me. Thank you for being there through the good times and bad.

All the reviewers, readers, media presenters, podcasters, journalists and friends who spread the word about Tessa and the crew deserve a mention, as without them, these books wouldn't have been the success they turned out to be. Thank you from the bottom of my heart.

And finally to you, dear reader, thank you for returning again and again to follow me on these adventures. If you didn't want to embark on repeated journeys into my imagined worlds, and indeed my non-imagined ones, there would be little point in my doing what I do. These books are yours, as much as they are mine.

I look forward to sharing many more with you.

Until next time,

Shane (S.A.) Dunphy
Tramore, Co Waterford
29 February 2024

PUBLISHING TEAM

Turning a manuscript into a book requires the efforts of many people. The publishing team at Bookouture would like to acknowledge everyone who contributed to this publication.

Audio
Alba Proko
Sinead O'Connor
Melissa Tran

Commercial
Lauren Morrissette
Hannah Richmond
Imogen Allport

Contracts
Peta Nightingale

Cover design
Blacksheep

Data and analysis
Mark Alder
Mohamed Bussuri

Milton Keynes UK
Ingram Content Group UK Ltd.
UKHW030655130824
446895UK00004B/135